Window
on the
World

Widow on the World

PAMELA FUDGE

transita

Published by transita
3 Newtec Place, Magdalen Road,
Oxford OX4 1RE. United Kingdom.
Tel: (01865) 204393. Fax: (01865) 248780.
email: info@transita.co.uk
http://www.transita.co.uk

British Library Cataloguing in Publication Data
A catalogue record for this book is available from the British Library

Cover design by www.mousematdesign.com
Produced for transita by Deer Park Productions, Tavistock
Typeset by PDQ Typesetting, Newcastle-under-Lyme
Printed and bound by Bookmarque, Croydon

ABOUT THE AUTHOR

Pamela Fudge was brought up in Poole, Dorset. She wrote poetry, mainly for her family, when her three children were growing up, and then discovered a talent for short fiction, which has seen her stories published by most of the national magazines over a period of twenty years. *Widow on the World* is her third published novel.

Having been widowed, not once, but twice in recent years, Pamela is well qualified to comment on the adage that life goes on. She is also the first one to admit that it's not always as simple as it sounds.

Pamela was a home study tutor with *Writers News* for two years and a creative writing tutor for 11 years with many successes among her students.

Pamela still lives in Poole with two cats and a dog.

For more information about Pamela and her work visit: www.pamfudge.co.uk and www.transita.co.uk

ACKNOWLEDGEMENTS

Thanks to Transita for liking *Widow On The World* enough to publish it, and to my editor, Marina, for making editing seem so easy.

To the Romantic Novelists' Association for a very positive New Writers' Scheme report of some years ago. Without that initial encouragement I may well have felt inclined to give up on the joy of writing on more than one occasion. To the Society of Women Writers and Journalists and the Society of Authors, and the many lovely writers I have met at their regional lunches.

Thanks to my circle of writing friends for their support and encouragement (not only with the writing) especially Bruna, Pam W, Chris H, Nora, Lyndsay, Alan B and all my past students who became friends.

Especial gratitude to all the friends who have seen me through good times and bad – always there with the tissues or the bottle of wine (whichever was appropriate at the time) particularly Chris N, Jan, Karen, Robert M and Robert B. Not forgetting the admissions and midwifery teams at Bournemouth University who make working for a living such a pleasure.

A special mention for my dearest Auntie Gladys who read every single thing I had published. She didn't live to see

Widow On The World published but she had read the first draft. She was a great lady, my dearest friend, and will always have a place in my heart.

Most of all I would like to thank my children, Shane, Kelly and Scott, who have loved me, supported me, and grieved with me – not once, but twice – and provided me with the gorgeous grandchildren who were the real proof that life does indeed go on. They, along with their partners, Mike and Karen, together with my stepchildren and step-grandchildren have given me so many reasons to go on when the way forward hasn't been exactly clear-cut.

DEDICATION

In loving memory of Eddie and Frank.
The men in my life who were my life
through two great marriages.
This book is for you both
with all my love.

CHAPTER 1

I'D DREAMED OF MY HUSBAND MANY TIMES since his death – the difference was, this time I *knew* it was a dream. This time I knew there had been no mistake, knew that when I opened my eyes Rob wouldn't be sleeping by my side and that he wasn't ever coming back.

In those other dreams he was young again and vibrant. He had called to me, 'Denny, Denny.' It was his own sweet name for me, and I'd truly believed that if I reached out I could touch him and bring him back into my life again.

In this dream, he was the older, greyer, and more familiar forty-something version of the man I had loved for most of my life. He was still smiling as he walked steadily towards me, but in this dream I was fully aware that if I reached out there would be nothing there – and so I didn't even try.

In this dream, Rob stopped suddenly, just as I'd known he would. I could see that his tall frame was already fading, disappearing in front of my eyes. Almost passive in my acceptance, I watched an outline that was as familiar to me as my own steadily diminish.

Turning from me slowly, Rob took one last, long look back. I tried and failed to detect the teeniest hint of regret in the straight gaze, but was forced to accept the time for regrets was over – for both of us.

The grief that usually took hold as the dream faded was absent, the pain of parting no longer raw and new, but

1

tempered by an acceptance that had been a long time coming. I think I knew in my heart that Rob had come to say a last goodbye, and that he wouldn't be back.

One last tender smile, a hand raised in final farewell, and Rob was gone. I was left in no doubt, no doubt at all, that his purpose in coming had been to free me, to leave me in no doubt that he expected me to get on with a life that wouldn't include him.

Usually, after dreaming of Rob, my eyes would open with great reluctance to greet the dawning of yet another day I didn't want to face. Often I'd tried, without success, to go back and retrieve the remnants of the dream, but this time it was different. This time as I opened my eyes to the familiar room we had shared, ready to face a new day – a new life even – I had the beginning of a smile on my face and a heart open to the promise of new hopes and dreams. Whatever future was out there for me, I finally realised I was ready to face it.

'Denise. Denise, answer me. Are you there?'

The sudden shrill screech brought a dash of freezing water to my senses. It drowned my fledgling emotions, forcing the last remaining sweet tendrils of dream into oblivion – and some of my brand new optimism with it. I sat up, eyes wide, heart thumping.

This time someone was calling my name for real; the tone strident, urgent, and definitely female, was punctuated by the hefty and regular thud of my own brass door-knocker.

'Mum?'

It couldn't be. I turned my head to glance at the clock and gaped. My mother was *here*, at seven-thirty in the morning? Shaking my tousled head, I closed my eyes again, desperately hoping this was all part of the dream.

A hail of gravel clattering against the window brought me fully awake and tumbling out of bed. Stumbling and tripping over a thick tangle of a duvet that was half on the bed, half on the floor, I threw back a curtain and pushed the window wide.

'Well, there you are. I began to think I'd never rouse you. You always could sleep for England.'

I shuddered, closed my eyes, and then opened them again, but the vision remained solidly intact. Planted in the middle of the garden path, silhouetted against the blue of a Ceanothus shrub in full bloom, stood my mother. A taxi with the engine running waited at the gate.

I blinked again, concentrated as hard as I could, and felt my heart sink right down into the soft pile of the bedroom carpet. If the size of those suitcases was anything to go by, she was accompanied by just about all of her worldly goods.

*

'What do you *mean*, you've left home?'

Around me my own homely kitchen, with its array of solid pine units, offered absolute, everyday normality. In stark contrast I had this obviously deranged woman facing me across the table. It scared me a bit – no, actually quite a lot – because I had no doubt my mother had taken leave of her senses. Everything I'd ever read about Alzheimer's, nervous breakdowns, brainstorms, and anything of a similar nature,

3

flitted in and out of my head. It crossed my mind that she might be totally unhinged and therefore dangerous, though perhaps that was a bit imaginative, even for me.

Around us early morning sunshine filled the room with bright rays, and the sound of birdsong filtered through the open window. Cups and saucers, pretty floral-patterned china ones, were set out on the pinewood table that had been carefully chosen in happier times, by Rob and me, to complement the kitchen that had been fitted at great expense and was our pride and joy. The fragrance of freshly ground coffee was all around us, and everything seemed just as it should be. That all *wasn't* as it should be was becoming increasingly clear. I couldn't believe the world, as I knew it, was about to fall apart round my ears for the second time in twelve short months. Could life really be that unfair?

Lifting the untidy tumble of fair hair out of my eyes, I narrowed them and scrutinised my mother, looking for some clue. What on God's earth could have brought her here at the crack of dawn armed with a bombshell and a full set of matching luggage? I couldn't believe the way she'd dropped the demise of her marriage into the conversation – as casually as you pleased.

Watching as she calmly helped herself to a biscuit, even taking the time to pick the selection over to find a favourite, I wondered how I was supposed to handle this? Was it a joke? My parents had been married forever, with a marriage that was rock solid – or it certainly had been when I visited the pair of them less than a month ago.

I took a deep breath, 'You and Dad had an argument, right? Everyone has arguments. Rob and I had arguments. It's not such a big deal.'

My mother met my look with a straight one of her own, not responding immediately. I refused to give in or glance away, but studied her carefully. Close-up scrutiny confirmed that she looked much the same as she usually did. Odd, under these exceptional circumstances, surely?

Quite attractive for her age – well, pretty damn good for sixty-five years of age, actually – my mother, or Mrs Elaine Isobel Jefferson to give her full title, actually looked a sight better than I did. In my defence I have to say early morning never was my best time of day. Add to that the fact that my hair was badly in need of a good brush, not to mention the thorough wash that would also have benefited the towelling dressing-gown I wore, and there really was no competition.

My mother, in sharp contrast, appeared totally unruffled, her features remarkably unlined. She was also meticulously made-up for someone in the middle of a relationship crisis. Not even a hair of her carefully sculpted and stiffly lacquered head was out of place.

It struck me as hardly normal, that, finding time to fit a quick shampoo and set – and possibly even a chestnut rinse to disguise the creeping grey – in between cancelling out forty-odd years of marriage and packing a complete wardrobe of clothes. Good grief, she'd even taken the time to match her earrings and accessories to her navy knee-length skirt and jacket.

This whole crisis had to be about something and nothing, I just knew it. My mother was being breathtakingly off-hand about what appeared on the surface to be a spontaneous decision to change her whole life. You'd think she'd popped out on one of her all-too-frequent shopping trips, instead of turning her back on a marriage she had decided – apparently overnight *and* without a great deal of careful thought – was past its best.

She gave me another, even straighter look. She was good at those, had perfected her very own brand of glaring over so many years. I'd seen lesser men than my father, and better women than me, wilt under the blaze of that dark piecing gaze. She'd been known to reduce me to a quivering wreck with very little noticeable effort, and my growing older never seemed to lessen the effect her displeasure had on me.

I took a firm grip on my cup, and my courage, and matched her stare for stare. After all, she was in *my* house. Yes, she was actually, I realised grimly. I should keep reminding myself of that, because she had the unfortunate habit of making me feel like a child in primary school whenever it suited her to gain the upper hand.

'Your father and I do not have arguments. You heard me correctly the first time, Denise. I've left him.' With that she defiantly took a cigarette from the packet in front of her and lit up.

I felt my lips thin into a disapproving line. She knew full well how much I hated smoking in the house, hated it with a vengeance and always had. She'd probably lit the damn thing just to goad me, but I refrained from comment this time without too much difficulty. It seemed more important to get to the real reason behind her arriving on my doorstep with her extensive baggage in tow.

This clearly wasn't intended to be an overnight stay and I thought I should have something to say about that. Her plans were clearly destined to impact on any I might have, and on a fragile peace of mind that had been a long time coming and exceptionally hard to come by.

'Why?'

There, that was better, no comment, just a direct question, and a perfectly civil one, I'd have thought, under the circumstances. This was *my* house, I reminded myself again and a bit more firmly this time.

'Because we weren't going anywhere, dear,' she said with a condescending smile, and in the reasonable kind of tone she might use to a child of three.

'Going – ? You've only just come back from Gran Canaria.'

'Denise,' exasperation crept into the tolerant level of her voice and she flicked ash from her cigarette, very deliberately, into her saucer, 'I'm not talking holidays here, I'm talking relationships. I'm talking about marriage, mine in particular. We've hit a blank wall, your father and I.'

Lifting the cigarette to her lips she drew on it deeply, threw back her head, and blew a perfectly formed smoke ring into the air.

Well, she had me there. I didn't know what to do or what to say. I must have looked for all the world like a landed fish as I struggled, mouth opening and closing, with nothing coming out.

'You *must* have seen this coming,' she suggested, when I'd clearly given up on the struggle to find a suitable response.

Again that oh so reasonable tone, the insinuation that this wasn't the bolt from the blue that it so obviously was. That's when I started to get angry.

'Actually, no,' I glared at her with something very akin to real dislike surfacing inside of me. It was quite a scary feeling. The nearest I had come to such an emotion regarding this woman, at least in recent years, was a mild exasperation. Disliking your own mother was unthinkable, wasn't it? Well, it was to someone like me who loathed any kind of bad feeling and normally avoided unpleasant confrontational situations – but when I thought about my lovely, mild-mannered Dad, and what this would do to him, I suddenly became very, very angry.

My mother looked so smug, sitting there, relaxed and quite obviously waiting for me to take her side. Her side in what, exactly, I had no idea. She'd as good as admitted there had been no argument.

'I have to say that – no – after forty-odd years of marriage, I *wasn't* expecting your relationship to break up overnight. I never heard anything so bloody ridiculous, if you must know. This isn't the script from some soap opera, it's real life.' I was off then, on my feet and in full flow, hardly recognising myself in the shrill tone. 'You can't just wipe out all those years of loving marriage on a *whim*. Are you quite mad?'

'How *dare* you speak to me like that? I've thought about this many times, if you must know.' My mother came back at me immediately. Up on her own feet, hands flat on the table, she leaned toward me and matched me glare for glare. For all of her bravado, though, I could see that she was shocked by the ferocity of a verbal attack from a normally mild-mannered daughter – and not a little rattled, if I wasn't mistaken.

Satisfied, I sat down. 'Well, it's not something you've seen fit to share with me – or with Dad, either, I'm willing to bet. Did you even tell him you were going, or have you just walked out?'

Having the grace to flush slightly, she sank back onto her own chair, and for once her gaze refused to meet mine. 'Harry's away for a few days with his golf pals. I thought it was for the best to do it this way. He would only try to talk me round.'

Of course he would. The poor sod loved her. What did she expect of him? That he would help her pack, cheerfully send her on her way? She must know she was in the wrong, that there was absolutely no way she could justify her actions but, having said that, I knew my mother well enough to know she'd have a damn good try.

Determined to make the most of any advantage gained, I took a deep breath and stood up again. It made me feel more in control, somehow, despite the fluffy slippers and grubby dressing-gown.

'And so will I,' I stated baldly, 'because someone's obviously got to talk some bloody sense into you. It's hard enough for me to start over at forty-six, with my own home and a career. What on earth will you do? Where will you go? How do you plan to live with no income?' I almost added that jobs for sixty-five-year-old women, with no formal qualifications or training, were few and far between, but found I couldn't be that blunt – even as angry as I was.

My mother completely missed the point I was trying to make – but whether that was on purpose or by accident, it was hard to tell.

'So that's it.' She rose to her own feet – and in high heels she reached an impressive five feet nine inches without any effort – and looking down at me, she hissed, 'I never thought I'd see the day I wasn't welcome in my own daughter's house.' Hefting her giant handbag up onto her shoulder, she stalked to the door with the parting shot, 'Never let it be said that I'll stay where I'm not wanted.'

Rigid with fury, she marched into the hall, and even as I despised myself for doing it, I found myself running after her.

'Mum, Mum, wait,' I pleaded, 'I didn't mean it like that.'

Immediately I could have kicked myself. I should have waited, watched to see how she was going to manage to haul those huge suitcases back out through the door and down the path, this time without the assistance of a burly taxi driver. She must have had the same thought at the same time, because she spun round so fast the draught she caused almost knocked a china figurine from the hall table.

'How did you mean it, then?' she demanded, leaning towards me so that our faces were just inches apart. 'Throwing your mother out on the streets, that's charming that is. That's really nice. My own daughter ...'

The anger that had so recently deserted me, flew back in a rush that almost took my breath away – almost, but not quite. 'Now, just one minute, just *one* little minute.' I refused to give a centimetre this time, determinedly standing my ground. 'Correct me if I'm wrong, but *you* are the one who's so recklessly made yourself homeless, *and* without rhyme or reason, as far as I can see. You're the one dragging me into this – this fiasco, forcing me to take your side, into the bargain, because,' I put up my hand authoritatively as she went to interrupt me, 'that's the way Dad will see it. He'll think I'm encouraging you in this mad idea.'

'He wo – '

'*Will*,' I finished for her, with great emphasis, suddenly realising with clarity just how hurt my father was going to be by all this – and not least by my apparent involvement in it.

I groaned inwardly, wishing with all my heart that this could turn out to be a horrible dream I'd wake up from eventually. I should have seen it coming, of course, or something like it. Without wishing to sound self-pitying, I could honestly say one step forward and two steps back had become the recognised pattern of my life these past months. You'd think I would have grown used to it.

'You'd better unpack,' I said wearily, forced into a corner that was entirely of my own making.

I'd had a choice, right from the start, and I knew it. To invite my mother into my home or simply bundle her back into the taxi had been entirely my decision. The latter had only been an option, though, in the first moment or two of opening the front door. Allowing my forceful parent over the threshold had been a serious error of judgement on my part, and one I had a feeling I would be paying for, over and over again.

Getting on with my life, it appeared, was going to have to wait for another day.

*

Saturday wasn't the best day for shopping at Sainsbury's, especially the huge out-of-town outlet that attracted shoppers from far and wide with its vast choice and easy parking. I knew that, and I really don't know why I chose that particular day to do my main shop, apart from it giving me a valid reason to escape the cuckoo settling herself so comfortably into the nest of my home.

I wasn't sure, either, why I'd elected to shop there rather than at the smaller, more familiar, local branch of the Cheapsmart chain. Less choice there, of course, but less hassle, too, and there was the staff discount to consider. I was, after all, employed as the store's Human Resources Manager, a rather grand title to explain my role in a personnel department I ran with the aid of one assistant. However, it was too late to regret the decision to shop elsewhere for once and, as I reminded myself, it *was* widely agreed that a change was as good as a rest.

If the idea was to take my mind off what was happening at home, I have to say it worked like a dream. I'd forgotten it was a bank holiday weekend, and everyone would be stocking up as if for a siege. It was one long battle from finding a parking space, to selecting a trolley that would move even vaguely in a forward direction, before being forced into making decisions I wasn't ready to make about such crucial things as healthy eating versus comfort eating.

I'd used to love to shop at the store with Rob, but had resolutely avoided that particular shop since his death. The minute I pushed the trolley through the automatic doors, memories bombarded me swiftly from all sides.

I didn't even have to try to recall the way he'd insisted on tasting grapes or cherries from the fresh produce on display, laughing at my horrified insistence that it was shoplifting, or the way he'd sneak little treats into the trolley like a naughty child.

We'd discussed almost every purchase, sometimes at length, and though it was nowhere near the festive season, one memorable Christmas suddenly came into my mind. It had, hilariously, taken all of an hour to decide which box of crackers to purchase. Presentation and content were given monumental importance, and a decision had only been reached when we had begged for the intervention and advice of a member of staff.

I tried to smile at the memory, but in my still vulnerable state the lights in the superstore seemed too bright, the aisles too crowded, the choices too vast or too few. I had to fight to

13

retain my composure and to resist the overwhelming urge to abandon my trolley and make a dash for the door.

The air was filled with the sounds of children laughing or grizzling, mothers calling, husbands grumbling, and the tinny voice over the public address system above it all, continually advising shoppers of special offers available or ordering more staff to the busy tills.

Taking a determined grip of my fragile senses, I hovered round a seemingly unlimited choice of fresh fruit and vegetables. There was little comparison with Cheapsmart's far more limited selection, but I resisted the urge to go for something outlandish and probably inedible, and became determined to make a sensible selection.

Initially undecided, but suddenly mindful of my mother making herself far too comfortable in my home, I took immense satisfaction in picking out a fat green cabbage, when I knew perfectly well she preferred cauliflower.

I also gained spiteful pleasure in choosing big shiny red apples that would offer a real challenge to even a partial denture. Realising I was being childish didn't diminish my enjoyment one little bit. I supposed I should even thank her for giving me something to smile about.

'Denise.'

I jumped at the sound of my name, initially failing to recognise the vaguely familiar voice.

'I thought it was you. Don't usually see you here, especially on a Saturday morning. How are you?'

A vivacious dark-haired woman blocked my way. Her wide mouth was smiling, her eyes enquiring.

'Oh, Janice,' I laughed foolishly. Fancy forgetting my own sister-in-law, Rob's only sister, who had been a part of my life for as long as he had. 'You've grown your hair, I didn't recognise you for a moment.'

'Looks like I'm not the only one,' she indicated my own shoulder-length locks. 'Yours is the longest I've ever seen it. It suits you,' she added, grudgingly I thought, but perhaps I was being too sensitive.

I felt a sudden need to explain that the long hair was unintentional. Grown because of a reluctance on my part to go to the trouble of visiting a salon and being forced into making life-changing decisions I wasn't ready to make regarding styles and length. I fought the urge successfully, but touched my head a little self-consciously, and was suddenly very glad I had finally got round to washing my hair that morning. I supposed I had my mother to thank for that, at least.

'So, how have you been?' Janice showed no sign of moving, but looked me up and down carefully, as if checking it was only my hair that had changed.

I shrugged, 'Oh, you know.'

'Oh, I do,' she leaned over and touched my hand. 'I miss him, too, you know.'

I gripped the trolley harder, forced myself to acknowledge, 'I'm sure you do,' certain that she did miss Rob, in her own way, though they'd never been what I would call really close. It was something Rob had regretted but accepted, saying it was the 'way his family was'.

'I'm sorry I haven't been over recently, but I'm sure you're coping well. It's been over a year, after all, hasn't it? Time to move on and all that.' The sympathy was still there, but there was also a firm edge to her voice. 'I'm sure you don't need to be told that life goes on. Mine has. I can't tell you how busy I am these days, but I will pop in when I get a minute. If you ever feel lonely, you know you only have to ring.'

'That's nice of you, but I have my mother staying at the moment.' I never thought I'd be pleased to say such a thing, but at that moment I almost felt grateful that she was there.

'That's nice.' No mistaking the relief in her voice, and I wondered briefly how she would have dealt with a request from me for some of her time and her company.

Janice hadn't quite finished, still showing no sign of moving on, despite the impatient hands reaching round us for the produce we were blocking.

'Any news?' she asked finally, looking at me more closely than I liked.

I stared at her, 'What sort of news?' I was as puzzled as I must have sounded. I did nothing except go to work, come home, eat a solitary meal, watch TV and go to bed. In fact, on reflection, I supposed I should be thanking my mother for bringing some variety into my mundane life.

'Oh, you know,' Janice said brightly, head cocked on one side, 'just anything? How's your job? And Bobbi, how's she?'

'The job is fine, as it always has been, and so is Bobbi.' I smiled at the thought of my eighteen-year-old daughter. 'She's taken to university life and the nursing programme

16

like a duck to water. I'm really proud of the way she's been coping.'

I couldn't work out where all this sudden interest was coming from. After all, Janice could have picked up the phone any time during the past twelve months if she was that interested in my life.

'I hope you're getting out more now,' she said suddenly, adding as if she were an authority, 'it's what Rob would have wanted. He wouldn't expect you to turn into a hermit on his account. Well,' she changed the subject quickly, 'I must be getting on. Lots to do, you know. Here,' she snatched a bunch of flowers from her trolley and placed them in mine, 'have these, Denise. They'll cheer you up. We must make more effort to keep in touch,' and with that she sailed off across the store, the crowds in the aisles apparently clearing a pathway before her.

Only when I reached the check out some time later, did I finally realise what she'd been fishing for with her 'Any news?' and only then did I realise I was paying for the flowers she'd so kindly given me.

*

'Well, she's quite right,' my mother approved when I recounted the conversation with some indignation. 'You should be getting out more. No one would think any less of you for having a social life, or if you met someone else. Rob would …'

'How come everyone is suddenly an authority on what Rob would or wouldn't have wanted? I was the one married to him for twenty-odd years.'

17

'*Was*, dear, *was*,' she kindly accentuated. 'That's the whole point. Everything's changed now, and you're a single woman. You have needs – even I realise that. You're still a young woman.'

'Bloody hell.' I slammed my hands down hard on the table and crockery rattled against cutlery as I leapt to my feet. 'What is this? Is everyone dying for me to get a man in my life? I didn't *choose* to be single – not like you have apparently chosen to be single again. Rob's heart attack made that decision for me. Being here without him is not what I *wanted*.'

'Of course not, dear,' she soothed, looking surprised, 'but it's been over a year …'

'You sound like Janice. So it's been a year. Is that supposed to make me feel better? Well, it's been the longest, loneliest year of my life, if you must know. I want my life back the way it was, I want my future with Rob back. I want *him* back.'

My chair crashed to the tiled floor behind me as I backed away from the table, leaving my favourite lasagne untouched on the plate. Bursting into noisy sobs, I ran upstairs to the sanctuary of the bedroom I had shared with Rob every night of our marriage.

It was such a relief to cry, to stop trying to be brave for the first time in weeks. It still hurt so much to know that I would never see Rob again, and it felt as if that would never change, never become easier to bear. I'd been a fool to think, even briefly, that it would.

He'd been my whole life for so many years, and for all of the ups and downs of a long marriage. Like most people who lose a partner, I had never even imagined a time when he wouldn't be there, and then had suddenly found myself living with the unimaginable day after day.

It was too easy to say he was in a better place. Perhaps he was, but where did that leave me? Was it being totally selfish to want him back? I couldn't cope without him – I'd been a fool to think for a moment that I could. I didn't *want* to cope without him.

'Denise?' A tap, tap on the door and the sound of my mother's voice brought my head up. The 'I'm-trying-to-be-understanding' tone she'd adopted really jarred. 'Denise, can I come in?'

She wouldn't have turned up on the doorstep like that if Rob had still been around. He'd have had no compunction at all about turning her right around and straight back the way she had come. I knew it, and I had no doubt that she knew it, too. At that moment I really didn't feel as if I could ever forgive her for taking advantage of the situation I had found myself in, or for arriving just in time to ruin my first feeble attempt at coming to terms with it.

'Go away,' I said, quietly, 'just go away.'

*

I must have slept, because it was getting dark when I opened my eyes. The phone was ringing in the hall, and that must have been what had woken me. I lay quietly listening, making no attempt to get up to answer it.

Eventually, I heard my mother pick up the receiver and say my number. There was a murmured conversation, and I sincerely hoped the caller was my father. Perhaps he could talk some sense into her, because I doubted my own ability to do so.

I waited until the one-sided conversation had ceased and the receiver was replaced before going to stand silently at the top of the stairs. My mother was still in the hall, a bemused look on her face as she stared at the phone as if she'd never seen it before.

'Who was it?' I asked quietly, and watched her jump at the sound of my voice, before staring up at me.

'It was Bobbi. She's on her way home and says she has something to tell you.'

CHAPTER 2

'WHAT DO YOU MEAN?' I kept my voice calm and reasonable with great difficulty, 'How can you say you're leaving university and not going back? You haven't given yourself a chance – you've barely been there more than five minutes. I thought you liked it. You told me you'd made friends there.'

Bobbi stared at me in that insolent way that so many teenage girls have. So many other teenage girls that is, but not my daughter, not until that moment. I found I hardly recognised her.

'I've given it a go and I've decided nursing isn't for me, after all. Anyway, I don't want to be halfway up the country, I should be here – with you.'

I knew I should have been touched by the latter part of her explanation, but there was something about her words and her attitude that didn't quite gel. I had the strongest feeling there was more to this than met the eye.

'A few months of a course,' I pointed out, still reasonably I felt, 'is not "giving it a go." How can you make such a huge life-changing decision after such a short time?' I moved on to her second point, reminding her, 'It was *your* choice to go and train out of the area. If you wanted to live at home you could have accepted the place you were offered locally. Brankstone University has a very good name and I have to say that, especially financially, the option made more sense to me at the time. After all, I practically pass the campus on my way to work and could even have given you a lift in on study days.'

Bobbi glared at me from beneath fashionably plucked and thinly arched eyebrows. The look was remarkably similar to the one my mother had perfected over the years. A corner of my mind supposed I should have been grateful she at least had seen fit to make herself scarce on this occasion. My mother wasn't normally known for her tact.

'I might have known you wouldn't understand,' my daughter hissed, flicking back her long blonde hair and turning away.

What do I do? What do I do? I could feel myself floundering, because another moment would see her flouncing out of the door. I had to do something, say something, and quickly.

I reached out a hand, touched the slouching shoulder, and pleaded, 'Then please help me to understand, Bobbi. I'm not so ancient I've forgotten how difficult everything is when you're young. I promise to listen to what you have to say.'

She half turned, lips pouting under a slick of pale pink gloss. I couldn't help noticing that, despite the fact she was very obviously upset, no hint of a tear had been allowed to threaten the artistry of heavily kohled eyes or thickly mascaraed lashes. That was evidently another thing she had in common with my mother – even in the middle of a crisis appearances were, apparently, everything.

'You promise not to lecture?'

'I promise,' I replied immediately, with no idea how I was going to keep such a promise, given circumstances that were surely going to test every one of my negotiating skills.

I was never more grateful than I was at that moment for my years in personnel management. There was surely never going to be a better time to draw on all of that experience.

With a huge show of reluctance, Bobbi moved to pull out a chair, the legs scraping noisily against the tiled kitchen floor, and then she slumped down onto the wooden seat.

'I'll put the kettle on, shall I?' I suggested, a determined brightness to my tone that I was far from feeling.

A glance out of the window confirmed that the sun was fading fast, the threat of forecasted misty rain already darkening the normally bright room, though it was still only mid-afternoon. It felt like it had been a very, very long day.

I made Bobbi's tea in the mug with her name on it. Bought by Rob and I years before, it had somehow survived without so much as a chip. Avoiding both the 'best wife' mug and the 'number one Mum' one for myself, as neither seemed at all appropriate in the circumstances, I reached instead for a 'born to shop' one that would have been far more appropriate for my mother.

'Now, what's this all about, love?' I asked, setting the mugs onto dark blue coasters, and choosing a chair on the opposite side of the round table. A table that had seen so many family meals in the days we had still been a complete, if small, family unit.

For a moment I assumed those same poignant thoughts had come into Bobbi's head, as I watched her face crumble and her cocky composure disintegrate into heartbroken tears. The sentimental myth was dispelled the minute she spoke.

'I hate it there,' she sobbed, for once totally uncaring of the sooty tracks marring the perfectly made-up and very pretty face. 'The course is okay, I like nursing, but I just miss Jason all the time. I want to be with him – and he wants to be with me.'

I closed my eyes, blotting out the tragic face and remained seated with difficulty, but though I could feel my anger levels rising rapidly I kept a firm grip on my emotions.

I might have known. Christ, I might have bloody known that little shit was going to come back into my life to haunt me. It had all been too easy, too good to be true. To believe that Bobbi would be happy to move safely out of the area and stay out of his clutches had been too much to hope for, after all.

What the hell was going on around here? First my mother throwing God knows how many years of marriage out of the window without a second thought. Now my daughter throwing away the career she'd always wanted for an evil little waste-of-space like Jason Wigmore. What on earth was wrong with them both?

I wanted to laugh hysterically, I wanted to weep until there were no tears left to cry. I wanted someone else to shoulder the burden that was being heaped onto my fragile shoulders, or at least to share it, because – God help me – I didn't know what I was going to do.

'Mum, are you all right?'

For a brief moment Bobbi was being forced to feel concern for someone other than herself. She must have seen the colour drain from my face. I had felt it happen, myself, right after the heat of my anger had faded, leaving me cold, shaken and afraid of what I was being given to deal with.

'Hardly.' I reached for my mug with shaking fingers. I smiled, but I didn't know how, as I added, 'It seems to be one shock after another. First your grandmother and now you …'

'Yes, what *is* that all about?'

I could have said, I think it's about you both being totally selfish, disrupting plans and lives for no good reason that I can see. I could have said, if you are both so sure of what you want, then why the hell don't you go off and mess up your lives elsewhere and leave me to put the pieces of my life back together in some kind of peace?

Instead, I said, 'One thing at a time, eh? Tell me what's brought this on, when a few, fairly short months ago, you were quite happy to leave Jason behind. Nursing is what you always wanted, Bobbi, ever since you were a little child. Are you saying you want to throw those dreams away? You haven't even seen Jason – not since …'

Not since he slept with your best friend. The words hung in the air, I didn't need to utter them, we both knew they were there. She hadn't seen Jason since he let her down – big style – just when she'd needed him most, in those early difficult days when she was still trying to come to terms with the sudden death of the father she had totally adored.

'I have seen him.' Bobbi couldn't meet my gaze, but looked down, her long hair forming a bright curtain that shielded her face. 'He came looking for me. He's explained how difficult it was for him, seeing me so upset.'

Christ, my heart bleeds, I wanted to say. It was so difficult for *him* that he took the easy route and not only opted out all together when his young girlfriend needed him, but openly and immediately began a sexual relationship with her closest friend. He couldn't have been more cruel and uncaring if he'd tried.

'And Kerry?' My daughter seemed to have completely forgotten both about the involvement of her then best friend, and the way Jason had flaunted his conquest beneath her nose, carelessly breaking her heart when she was already devastated by the loss of her father.

Bobbi still refused to look up. 'Oh, her,' she said in a dismissive tone, 'that was a mistake. He wouldn't have looked at her twice, but she threw herself at him.'

I bit back the bitter retort that leapt unbidden to my tongue. Somehow, I had to be calm and strong. Somehow, I had to deal with this in a rational way. Ignore Jason, I advised myself, knowing even as difficult as that was, it was the sensible thing to do. Prioritise, that was the secret. Convince her to keep the career and the Jason problem might just sort itself out in time.

'It seems a shame, don't you think,' I began carefully, 'to throw away the career you always wanted? If you don't want to complete your training in Murrayfield, you still have the option of transferring to a place on the nursing course down here. We could find out about it, if you like.'

Her face actually brightened, and for the first time she really looked at me. 'Oh, do you think that I could do that?'

'I'm sure it's a distinct possibility.' I felt a glimmer of hope. 'I'll make some more tea, shall I?'

This was going better, better than I'd dared to hope once I'd learned that Jason had entered into the equation. Hell, Jason *was* the equation, but all wasn't lost, despite him and his bloody machinations. After a second cup of tea, I even relaxed enough to think about making a Sunday roast supper for my uninvited guests and was peeling potatoes when it all began to go horribly wrong again.

'How soon do you think it could be arranged?' Bobbi looked up from laying the table.

'Well, I don't think it will look good if you just drop out,' I mused, giving the matter careful thought, 'so you'd need to go back to Murrayfield initially, and start the ball rolling with a query letter to Brankstone uni to see if they'd consider you. They, in turn, would probably want to see a transcript of the training you've completed and ...'

Bobbi stopped what she was doing, straightening up and defiantly meeting my gaze across the kitchen, 'Oh, that's going to take ages. I can't possibly wait that long.'

I paused, too, gripping the knife tighter and letting the half-peeled potato slide back into the water. ' "That long",' I repeated, 'but in a few months you'll have completed your first year. That would probably be the ideal time to transfer.'

'But Jason's decorating his flat,' she stated flatly, 'He wants me to move in with him next week.'

*

Bank holiday weekends had been difficult since Rob's death, all those empty hours had always filled me with dread. Suddenly finding more reasons than usual – though admittedly different ones – to actually be glad to return to work on Tuesday morning was a little disconcerting to say the least.

Dealing with other people's problems, for once, seemed preferable to trying to deal with my own. Even so, my head was full of my possible options, easy or otherwise, for coping with the situation at home.

Favourite at that moment was driving straight past the staff car park and not stopping until I reached the Scottish border at the other end of the country. It wouldn't solve anything, but a holiday might be nice, and Scotland was as good a place as any. The distance from one end of the country to the other seemed particularly appealing at that precise moment, even if I knew and accepted that running away wasn't a real answer.

I'd always liked living on the south coast. I readily told anyone who would listen that we had the best of everything right here in Brankstone. With sandy beaches on the coast side that could easily compete with the best of the Spanish Costa's, it was flanked by large towns on either side with stores enough to meet the requirements of the most exacting of shopaholic tastes, *and* had beautiful lush countryside within easy reach all around. I didn't know who could ask for anything more except, in my case, the tranquil and trouble-free existence that seemed to be slipping further and further from my grasp.

I liked my job, too. A late starter in the career stakes, I'd worked long and hard to get where I was. Combining home and family with hours of study hadn't been easy, but I had been determined and Rob's support was everything I could have hoped for. I always said every qualification I gained belonged as much to him as to me, because I certainly couldn't have done any of it without him.

Achieving the position of personnel manager for the local branch of a relatively new and thriving supermarket chain was all I had ever hoped for. While the department was small – just myself and one assistant presently – it suited me very well, and I knew I had gained the respect of the head office with the fair but firm approach I had adopted.

I had a name for seeing things as they were, standing back and taking a detached view, when it would have been all too easy to become emotionally involved in most of the day-to-day staff problems that came before me and my 'team'.

All that training, all that reading, and yet it counted for nothing when faced with my own family problems. As I drove up and down the rows of cars, I felt a strong sense of disappointment. In my eyes, I had coped with so much lately, yet had failed to deal at all well with a couple of selfish people who refused point blank to see things from anyone's eyes but their own.

The weekend had been an unmitigated disaster. The arrival of my mother had been bad enough, but she was at least an adult and therefore responsible for her own actions. The subsequent arrival of my daughter was a different matter entirely. At eighteen years old, she might have been classed as an adult, but in my eyes she was little more than a child and was still my responsibility.

Whatever I tried to do or say to either of them hadn't helped in any way. Every discussion had developed into rows and recriminations all round, with everything going rapidly downhill, up to and including my own angry departure that morning, accompanied by the slamming of doors and the sharp and unrealistic advice to, 'Sort your bloody selves out before I get home, for Christ's sake.'

I wasn't feeling very proud of myself, as with grim determination I eased the silver Metro into a spot more suitable for a Mini. Wondering why there were never enough allocated staff parking places, I looked dubiously at the crack I was somehow going to have to squeeze through to exit the car.

However, there was a God, and also some benefits to an unintentional weight loss, I was pleased to notice, when I'd somehow slithered through the gap. Had I been my original, pre-widowhood size, I'd have been seriously considering an escape route through the sunroof, I guessed with a wry smile.

I took a quick glance round to see if anyone had noticed my undignified struggle to vacate the car, before I straightened up and smoothed the creases from a navy suit that was a tad looser on me these days than I would have liked.

Heading across the expanse of tarmac, I acknowledged the greetings of various other staff members as I went.

With my hair tied back in a style that bordered on the severe, the subtlest hint of make-up, together with my business-like attire and briefcase, I was well aware I looked every inch the professional woman of the modern day. Only I could possibly know it was all a front, a show for other people, and that my life was running out of control all over again – and this time I really didn't think I could pull it back together again.

Once at my desk, whatever my personal problems, I'd thought I was doing more than okay. By forcing myself to concentrate, I'd worked steadily and efficiently through the usual mound of paperwork without mishap and the morning had progressed unremarkably enough.

I was surprised when Josie walked into the large cupboard that passed as my office and placed a cup of strong tea in front of me without saying a word. The tea wasn't unusual, the fact that she was standing there with a troubled look on her face was. Something was obviously wrong.

Josie was not only my assistant and right-hand woman, but had become a very dear and supportive friend during the three or four years we had worked together – and that support had never been more appreciated than during the months since Rob's fatal heart attack.

She stood silently, unobtrusively, waiting for my attention and I finally looked up, to see clear concern in her steady grey gaze.

'What?' I asked, and then again. 'What?'

'The odd discrepancy in a petrol allowance is understandable,' she said wryly, 'though you haven't made those sort of mistakes for a while now. However, offering someone a substantial relocation sum on a house they don't even own is taking things a bit too far and I think Cheapsmart might just raise an objection to the sum involved.'

'Oh, God,' I groaned, leaning forward and burying my face into my palms. 'I didn't, did I? Please tell me you're joking.'

'I wish I was. You had that distracted look about you,' Jo elaborated, 'and I was concerned enough to check stuff I normally wouldn't have bothered with. Problem?' she asked, and added, 'Do you want to talk about it?'

Jo, above all people had been there for me in the early days of my bereavement. Jo was the first – apart from my own parents – to arrive with flowers and sympathy, followed by tasty casseroles and sound advice on managing my affairs. She'd recommended the counselling that had been so instrumental in my coming to terms with the great tragedy in my life, and it was she who had staunchly supported me as I found a way through the maze of my own overwhelming grief.

For a split second I considered denying that there was anything wrong, and then, capitulating, I said, 'Yes, please.'

Of all people, she would come closest to understanding. Presently in her early fifties, she'd struggled in her time with an ailing mother, now deceased, an alcoholic husband with a penchant for other women, now divorced, and she was still struggling valiantly to keep an errant son on the straight and narrow.

A bustling Harvester pub at midday might not have appeared, at first sight, the ideal place for an intimate conversation. From past experience we both knew better. Centrally placed, with the supermarket practically next door, an industrial park nearby and various offices within easy reach, it was the usual hive of activity when we entered.

With the bursts of raucous laughter, loud queries regarding the choice of drink and food, together with the general buzz as small talk and gossip was shared, there was little chance of anyone eavesdropping on a private conversation. In my experience, most folks were far too concerned with their own lives to have any interest in the stranger at the next table anyway.

I accepted the sparkling mineral water I had reluctantly ordered in preference to the large dry white wine that would have been my ideal choice. Jo and I both knew that alcohol wasn't the answer, much as it could appear to be a quick fix solution at the time. Not that I had anything against a good drink, if the time and place were right. I had been known to get smashed occasionally along with the best of them, but not in the lunch hour on a working day.

'I've ordered prawn salad sandwiches,' she told me with the confidence of someone who knew my probable choice well enough not to have to check. Taking the chair opposite, she checked that we were in a 'smoking' area before helping herself to a cigarette from a newly purchased packet. Lighting it, she sat back and asked, 'Well, what's it all about?'

I felt I had to ignore the question and come back with a comment of my own. 'I thought you'd given up smoking.' I tried not to sound accusing, because I knew from when Rob gave up, years before, how hard it was to quit.

She managed a wry smile, before offering the excuse, 'Petie.'

I immediately felt dreadful and said so. 'Oh, Jo, here I am ready to unburden myself to you, and I haven't even thought you might have problems of your own.'

Peter, or Petie as she always called him, was her son, an only child who had caused her grief practically since the day he was born. Yet her patience with him was never-ending. She always insisted that if she could stick with him, one day he would turn his life around. I wished I had her faith, but with Petie's track record I had to say it seemed increasingly unlikely.

'What's he done this time?' I carefully kept any hint of criticism from my voice. It wasn't my place, and he wasn't my son. However I could offer a sympathetic ear and was more than happy to do so.

'Drink-driving.'

I stifled a groan. In recent months the one thing in Peter's favour was that he had, at last, landed himself a half-decent job and even found a place to live, flat-sharing with some mates. The bad news, in the light of this latest development, was that the job involved driving – and if he had his licence taken away ...

'I know,' she looked at me and shrugged. 'You don't have to say it. I've asked myself a thousand time what it is with him. He always takes two steps forward, and follows it by taking four steps back. I have no more idea why than you have.'

'What will you do?'

'What can I do?' she came back, her tone resigned. 'He's my son, and I love him dearly, but it's time he took responsibility for his own actions. I'm trying very hard to let him do just that.'

I wanted to applaud, to say – and about time, too – but I knew how hard it was for Jo to let go. I just reached out and silently patted her hand.

Jo stared into space for a minute, perhaps seeing a future for Petie that she really didn't want to see, and then she mentally shook herself. I could almost see her doing it, before she turned her attention to me.

'I've told you mine – now tell me yours,' she ordered, and then peered at me. 'It's not something similar I hope.'

'What, a drink-driving charge hanging over me with a non-existent social life like mine?' I joked feebly. 'Chance would be a fine thing.'

The sandwiches arrived, so we tucked in and chewed companionably for a few minutes and then, into a thoughtful silence I dropped my news.

'My mother moved in with me over the weekend – apparently her marriage to my father is over – just like that. Bobbi's decided to quit her nursing programme and move in with Jason, so she's also at home, temporarily, too.'

It took quite a lot to shock Jo, given her background and experience of family problems, but her mouth dropped open and then she muttered, 'Jesus Christ, you poor bloody thing.'

Her unique brand of sympathy brought ready tears to eyes that were only too ready to cry. I blinked them rapidly away, smiled wryly and said, 'I knew you'd understand.'

'What have you tried to make them see sense?'

'Oh, you name it.' I ticked them off on the fingers of one hand, 'Reasonable discussion, group and one to one. Screaming matches where everyone has a go at everyone else. Nothing's come anywhere near working so I'm open to any suggestions.'

Jo grinned back at me, 'Move in with me and leave them to get on with it?'

'Don't tempt me,' I pleaded.

'What a weekend,' she commented, 'for both of us.'

'Oh, yeah, and one more thing that I almost forgot.' I took another bite of sandwich and added with my mouth full, 'My sister-in-law obviously thinks I should have a man in my life by now.'

Jo's face cracked into a big beaming smile before she told me, 'Well, I never thought I'd say this about her, but that appears to be one thing Janice and I do agree about.'

'Oh, you.' We both stood up and I gave her a playful push. 'All I've got to say to that is – you first.'

*

Talking to Jo had actually helped more than I would have guessed, as is often the way when you share a problem. I even thought I might take a leaf out of her book, step back

36

and let my mother and daughter take responsibility for their own actions. So what if they threw their futures away? That was the whole point, wasn't it? It *was* their futures – and their prerogative to throw them away.

Who knows, I thought, crawling home through the rush hour traffic and trying hard to look on the bright side, they may both have come to their senses in my absence, or at least be prepared to talk reasonably.

Second thoughts told me that was probably expecting too much. I did think, however, that with two women living, uninvited, in my house with nothing better to do, a home-cooked meal ready and waiting on the table wasn't too much to ask for.

A nice tasty humble pie, courtesy of the pair of them, would have been very welcome indeed, but was highly unlikely. I'd happily settle for simple food and a touch of contrition, I decided, and as that surely wasn't too much to ask for I allowed myself the luxury of a little anticipation.

I realised I'd been a little premature in my hopes when I arrived home and found it was too much to ask to even be able to pull into my own driveway. The battered relic of a car blocked my path. I didn't recognise it, but I had a horrible suspicion I knew who it belonged to. A two hundred yard walk from the nearest kerbside parking space did nothing to improve my mood.

'That awful boy is here,' were my mother's words of greeting.

'So I see,' I said grimly, pushing my briefcase into the understairs cupboard and hanging my suit jacket on the hat stand in the hall.

The kitchen was cold and dark. So much for the meal I had foolishly thought might be a possibility. I set to, making my displeasure felt with the banging of saucepans and crashing of cutlery, very much aware of my mother hovering ineffectually in the background.

'What are you going to do about him?' she asked, peering over my shoulder and watching me peel potatoes as if she'd never seen it done before.

'I don't know,' I replied shortly, 'or even what I'm going to do about you,' I added under my breath.

'What's that, dear?'

I sighed. 'Nothing – nothing at all.'

The clump, clump of heavy feet coming down the stairs brought my head up, and I turned as the kitchen door opened. Bobbi stood there, smiling diffidently, and behind her stood the young man I considered to be every mother's nightmare – and particularly mine.

'Hello, Mum. Good day?'

I didn't have to ask what they'd been doing upstairs. Bobbi's normally immaculate make-up was non-existent, her beautiful long hair messy and tangled. There was a graze on her chin that had obviously been caused by an unshaven face and enthusiastic kissing, and to top that, a very large love-bite on her neck. Jason's defiant and very visible stamp of ownership, I guessed.

He appeared beside her, an apparently careless arm draped around her shoulders. I knew it had been placed there for my benefit. The thought of that little creep all over my lovely daughter almost made me want to throw up. I dearly wanted to wipe the knowing smirk from Jason's face, but I'd read all the books and 'agony aunt' advice available. Without fail, they all warned that alienating the object of your child's affection, or forcing a choice between parent or passion, almost certainly meant the parent losing out.

With a huge effort, and focusing my attention on savagely digging eyes from the potato I was holding, I offered, 'Perhaps you'd like to stay and eat with us, Jason? You can tell me all about the decorating you've been doing. Turning out as you'd hoped, is it? I hope you've consulted Bobbi over the choice of colour scheme, since she's apparently going to be sharing the accommodation.'

Christ, I was proud of myself. Not a hint of criticism or disapproval had been allowed to enter my tone. My mother was staring at me open-mouthed. I'd obviously taken leave of my senses as far as she was concerned. I knew from bitter experience that she would have handled things very differently in her day.

She had actually started to comment, with a, 'Well ... ' totally ignoring my frowning look, when Bobbi, with a quick glance in Jason's direction, said, 'Actually, Mum, we – Jason and me – wanted to talk to you about that. Didn't we, Jase?'

'Yeah.' He managed to shoulder himself away from the door-frame that had been supporting him, and he stood there, the insolent little smile still firmly in place.

I had the strongest feeling I wasn't going to like what was coming, and as I normally did in times of crisis, I began to take notice of all kinds of inconsequential things. Like the way Jason's gelled strands of hair fell right into his eyes, and the fact that he looked far younger than his twenty-one years – despite the carefully cultivated designer stubble which did little either to improve his appearance or to hide a crop of adolescent spots.

I also noticed his top was from the French Connection label – the item sporting a logo that could have caused offence in some quarters if read quickly enough – and that his jeans carried a Levi label. Both were brands even I recognised as relatively expensive, yet Jason could afford to wear them despite his never having worked a full day in gainful employment in his life to my knowledge.

When Jason didn't elaborate, Bobbi rushed in, words tripping over themselves in a way that told me, quite clearly, she was expecting my immediate disapproval and rejection of whatever was planned.

'It's not Jason's fault, really it isn't,' she gabbled, trying and failing to meet my eyes. 'He's done a lovely job of the decorating, but the six month rental period is up and the landlord has refused to renew it. It's very difficult at this time of year to find anywhere – with the holidaymakers, you know …'

'Tha's right,' Jason joined in once Bobbi had laid the groundwork, 'but we still want to live together …'

'Because we really love each other, don't we, Jase?'

'Yeah, 'course,' he muttered, lifting his head and letting his insolent gaze meet mine, as he offered the suggestion, 'So-o-o-o, as you've got plenty of room, and could do with the company, we thought we'd live here with you.'

CHAPTER 3

J ASON HAD BEEN EVICTED FROM HIS FLAT, OF COURSE. Even my mother could work that one out, and she was outraged. 'They can't just do that,' she hissed, when the very uneasy meal was eaten and cleared away.

Sausage and mash wasn't my favourite meal at the best of times, but I'd had trouble forcing so much as a morsel past my lips. My mother and Bobbi managed to make a bit of a brave attempt to appreciate my efforts, but only Jason completely cleared his plate with great gusto and every appearance of enjoyment.

'It looks very much as if they have,' I murmured, mindful of the pair lolling on the settee in the next room, though the TV was blaring and they'd be unlikely to hear.

It had been very much fait accompli, with Jason's bags already ensconced in my daughter's frilly and virginal bedroom and his sparse toiletries and Fahrenheit aftershave on the bathroom shelf, before I'd ever been consulted – never mind asked for my permission or approval for the new living arrangements.

'Well, what are you going to do about it?'

I straightened from loading crockery into the dishwasher and took a deep breath before turning to face her.

'About what, exactly?' I enquired acidly, the helpless fury I'd been feeling for days finally beginning to get the better of me. 'Oh, you mean about the fact that my house appears to be turning into a hotel, with every Tom, Dick and Harry

42

moving in.' I stopped then and interrupted myself, my tone dripping with sarcasm, 'Oops, no, let me correct that because my father, Harry, appears to be the only person who *hasn't* moved in complete with bags and baggage. Everyone else is busily making themselves at home without so much as a by-your-leave.'

My mother managed to look deeply affronted, even her coiffeured and lacquered hair appeared to bristle with self-righteous indignation, 'If you mean me ... ' she began.

'I mean,' I fumed, no longer even trying to keep my voice down, 'all bloody three of you. Don't you think ... ' my voice rose another decibel or two, 'that I've had enough to deal with these past months? Don't you think ... ?'

The door opened and Bobbi hurried in, closing it firmly behind her and glancing worriedly towards the sitting room. 'Shhh,' she muttered, 'Jason will think you don't want him here.'

'You obviously don't want *me* here,' my mother pursed her lips in a way that showed deep vertical lines around them that weren't normally nearly so apparent.

'Or even me,' Bobbi pouted, 'your own daughter. Daddy would ... '

'That's *enough*,' I made sure I made myself heard above their protests. 'I don't even want your Dad – Rob to you, Mother – brought into this, because I think both of you – and him,' I jerked my head in Jason's general direction, 'know exactly what he would have said – and – ' I held up a hand to stop further objections, 'I don't think – not for one minute – that any of you would be here now if *he* was.'

Bobbi burst into noisy tears, and my mother and I squared up for an exchange that I had a feeling was going to get very heated and rather nasty. In the background, I was vaguely aware of the television still blaring and the sound of a phone ringing that might, or might not, have been part of a programme. Before a word could be spoken – though several were poised on the tip of my tongue – the door opened and Jason's unshaven face appeared, surveying the scene before him through the thick strands of lavishly gelled hair for a long moment.

'I answered the phone,' he advised finally, 'seein' as no one else seemed bothered. It's her old man,' he went on, jerking his head in my mother's general direction, 'wanting to know if we knew where she was. I've told him she's left him to move in here. Was that right?' He looked from one stunned face to another, before nodding and saying, 'Yeah, I thought it was. He wants to speak to someone. Sounded a bit upset.'

With one more insolent, smirking glance round a room that had suddenly gone so silent you could have heard the proverbial pin drop, Jason began to withdraw the head that was pretty much all we'd seen of him. The door began to close, and then opened again to allow him to peer back in, 'You can let us know wha's happenin' about us movin' in, darlin',' this casual remark was directed at Bobbi, 'when you've sorted yourselves out.'

With that the door was closed firmly, but not before the black cordless telephone receiver was placed carefully on the kitchen unit closest to the door. We all stared at it, but no one moved to pick it up. I noticed vaguely that a gravy spill was almost touching it, and then gave my complete attention to the fact that all the worktops needed wiping down and the dishwasher hadn't yet been set in motion. Anything was better than thinking about the poor, unsuspecting man on the other end of the phone who hadn't a bloody clue what was going on.

I went to the cupboard under the sink for the J-cloths and Mr Muscle kitchen spray, and told my mother quietly to, 'Speak to him, then.'

She looked at the phone as if it were an explosive device, making no move to touch it until, finally, Bobbi picked it up and pushed it firmly into her hand.

'Why don't you take it upstairs, Granny?' she said, in an almost kindly fashion.

When my mother finally did as she was bid, Bobbi added powder to the dishwasher and pressed the buttons to programme it, before putting the kettle on, all in silence.

*

I found myself relating the whole thing to Jo, next day, needing her sympathy, her understanding and, most of all, her commonsense view of it all.

'With my mother out of the way,' I told her, 'I was just screwing myself up to address the problem of Bobbi and Jason, when the bloody doorbell went and into all this terrible atmosphere came Adam. Can you believe it?'

Jo took a huge drag on her cigarette, then coughed a bit and blew the smoke out of the window. She wasn't yet used to the smoke hitting her lungs again, but was obviously making a concerted effort to regain her former expertise and with it her enjoyment of the deadly weed. I knew I should have stopped her, there were enough reminders that the building was strictly non-smoking, but I just didn't have the heart nor, to be honest, the inclination.

'Adam Mitchell?'

I nodded, and she continued, 'Poor sod, fancy walking into all that angst. He must have enough of it in his own life with that wife of his. How is he – and her, of course?'

I'd known Adam for as long as I'd known Rob. They were mates, had been at school together, but became as close as brothers over the ensuing years. Jo knew all this, and she'd met Adam a few times at parties and family gatherings.

I'd had hopes in the past that perhaps, eventually, she and Adam might end up together, though Rob had always scoffed at the notion, reminding me of Adam's taste for glamorous younger women. Even I had to admit that, though Jo was many things, glamorous wasn't one of them and neither was age on her side as far as Adam was concerned. With her rounded figure, soft greying curls and a fondness for hand-knitted sweaters and pleated skirts, comfortable was more the word that sprang to mind when you thought of Jo.

Jo was that bit older than Adam, too, of course, maybe by as much as eight years, but she'd have been so good for him. I was sure he'd have seen how great she was if he could only have got it into his head that appearance was pretty immaterial, and that what was under the surface was much more important. Unfortunately, any ideas I'd had in that direction were always destined to come to nothing anyway, because as Jo so rightly said, there'd always been that wife of his. Though how the marriage had lasted as long as it had was a mystery to me.

Jo laughed and echoed my unspoken sentiments almost exactly when she said, 'Christ, I've known some rocky relationships, but theirs has been hanging by a thread all the time I've known you.'

'Well, not any more, Jo, and it's not funny. She's finally left him – for good this time, I think.'

Jo's hand crept to her lips, the crimson nails that were her one touch of glamour a splash of colour against a sweet, but pale face that cried out for a dab of subtle make-up.

'My God, she must be mad. After all the complaining she's done about the long hours Adam works, the bitching about lack of money for life's little necessities, like designer labels and cleaners, and now, when he finally has something tangible to show for all the hard work, she buggers off. *Why?* Is there someone else?'

I felt myself shrug, 'No idea. Adam thinks not, but then he always did believe everything she told him. I felt really sorry for him. He's been such a mate to me since Rob died, though I have to say I haven't actually seen Lisbet since the funeral.'

Jo shook her head, and her mouth twisted in clear disbelief. I knew how she felt, I'd been shocked to the core, myself, from the moment Adam dropped his own particular bombshell. As I told Jo over the mid-morning cups of instant coffee and the illicit cigarette, it had almost made me forget the previous two or three I'd had dropped on me. Somehow, despite Jo's very accurate description of Adam's marriage 'hanging by a thread', it was obvious that neither of us had been expecting it to actually fall apart, and if we were shocked, how on earth must Adam be feeling?

'It seems to be one thing after the other at the moment.'

Laughing, Jo said, 'I'm surprised he didn't want to move in, too.'

I groaned loudly. 'My God, Jo, don't even go there. Can you imagine it? I'll be offering asylum seekers tents in the back garden by next week. Did I ever complain that I was feeling lonely? Just tell me to shut the what's it up if I ever do again. D'you suppose this could just be Rob's way of keeping me busy?'

'Well, if it is,' she grinned, drained the last of her coffee, stubbed her cigarette out in the saucer and, standing up, said, 'I'd better have a word and tell him he's gone way over the top this time. Oh, and Denise?' I looked up at her and she grinned, 'You really shouldn't let me smoke in here, you know it's forbidden and could get us both the sack.'

'Oh, you.' I flapped my hands at her, and found myself saying, 'Many more problems dumped on my doorstep and I'll be taking it up myself.'

We went back to work, but I found it difficult to concentrate knowing that nothing had been resolved yet regarding my increasing number of house guests. In a way, Adam's unscheduled visit had, at least, given me some breathing space, because it had been late by the time he'd left and bed was the only real option.

In any case, I was reluctant to get into a big discussion without some long hard thinking about exactly what choices were open to me, apart from the obvious one of turning the whole lot of them out onto the street, or the more cowardly method of simply waiting to see what happened in case it all sorted itself out.

The hope that my father's irate phone call might have sent my mother scuttling back home was dashed, when she returned to the kitchen red-eyed, but defiantly determined to continue with the ridiculous charade of insisting that the years of her married life were over.

The vain expectation that Jason might at least have the courtesy to make himself a bed on the couch was also dashed, when I went wearily upstairs to bed to find the door to Bobbi's room firmly closed on the pair of them. I was then forced to listen to the very obvious proof that my daughter was an adult, with an active and obviously very fulfilling sex life to prove it.

*

Despite the nature of my job, I tend to avoid confrontation in my personal life. Live and let live has always been my motto. As far as I was concerned, people behaved in certain ways for their own private reasons and, whether they appear to be right or wrong to the outsider, at the end of the day it's up to them.

Live and let live is fine, up to a point, but when it encroaches on your own personal space, and there's no obvious end to the arrangement in sight, I do think some discussion is advisable. When I arrived home day after day from a full day's work to be greeted by the same scenario I quickly recognised that, in my case, it was also unavoidable.

There was never so much as a snack meal ready and waiting for me. Added to that my normally neat house was beginning to look as if it really had been taken over by refugees. The television was usually playing to itself when I came in, and the washing machine seemed to be continually dealing with what looked suspiciously like full and never-ending loads of Jason's filthy clothes.

Ever the polite hostess, as had been instilled in me by my mother, I grimly prepared meals, vacuumed, tidied and said nothing until, after a particularly bad day, I decided enough was enough and, finally, totally lost it.

Standing in the hall, among discarded shoes and a greasy tool box, with every nerve jangling, and, for all I knew, steam coming out of my ears, I screamed like a banshee that they should 'get their bloody arses down those bloody stairs before I came looking for them with a bloody gun.'

I'd have laughed out loud if I hadn't been so furiously angry. Talk about a way with words, I thought. The English qualifications I'd gained over the years clearly weren't worth the paper they were printed on.

My mother was first to appear, blinking over the top of the banister as if surprised to see me standing in my own house, in my own hallway.

'Oh,' she said, 'Is it that time already?'

Ignoring the question, as she had ignored my screaming demands, I said, in a barely audible tone, 'Would you come down here, please? And make sure those two,' I jabbed a furious finger in the direction of Bobbi's closed bedroom door, 'get down here, too.'

'Um,' she seemed lost for words for a second, followed the direction of my pointing finger with a reluctant gaze, and then said, 'I think they're busy.'

The anger came back with a whoosh that almost lifted me right off my feet.

'Bobbi, Jason, downstairs – *now*.'

It was a tone I hadn't used to Bobbi since she was at school. I hadn't needed to, she usually recognised the signs of my wrath long before I got this angry. She would know she ignored my demand at her peril, and that was just as well, because the way I felt at that moment I was quite capable of throwing all three of my 'house guests' out onto the street and damn the consequences.

Back ram-rod stiff, I turned on my heel and stalked into the kitchen. The sight of abandoned plates of partially-eaten snack food, dirty mugs, and worktops littered with empty crisp packets, bread wrappers and crumbs only served to fuel my anger.

By God, I decided, surveying the mess, something is about to change round here or I'll know the reason why.

My mother trailed into the room behind me, looking band-box fresh compared to my wilting end-of-the-office-day creased and jaded appearance. From one hand dangled a slim romantic novelette, from the other a lace handkerchief that looked ready to be brought into service should this discussion threaten to get at all uncomfortable.

'I thought about starting a meal,' she began, 'but I didn't know what to do ... ' her voice tailed off, and her gaze dropped, as I stared at her in patent disbelief and then meaningfully at the fully-stocked fridge-freezer.

She knew, and I knew, that, besides a talent for shopping till she dropped, the one other thing my mother was spectacularly good at was running a home and feeding a family.

Before she could offer more excuses, Bobbi appeared in the room looking sheepish and Jason came behind looking defiant. They were both in a state of disarray, with clothes creased and untucked, buttons undone and faces flushed. Not hard to see what their energies were being concentrated on, and I found myself trying and failing to recall if Rob and I had ever been as rampantly sexual.

'This has got to stop,' I said, as clearly and calmly as I could manage.

'What?' Three voices in various querulous tones asked the same question in unison.

'Do I have to spell it out?' I looked around me, willing them all to try and see this from my point of view, and then smiled bitterly. 'Yes, I see that I do.'

'Oh, God, not a bloody lecture,' Jason muttered, barely audibly, but loud enough to get my blood boiling again.

I spun around. 'You,' I said, 'shut your insolent mouth before I put you out onto the street, bag and baggage, complete with the never-ending bloody washing that's going round in my bloody machine day after day using my bloody soap powder and my bloody electricity.'

He went to speak, even went so far as to open his mouth, and then obviously thought better of it and clamped his lips together sullenly.

'Mum, you …' Bobbi began, and then she shut up, too, and backed away from the savage look I sent her way.

'Right, sit down – all of you,' I ordered in the tone of voice that gave them no choice at all.

I intended to remain standing myself, since I was looking for any advantage I could gain. They shuffled to the table, dragged out chairs with varying levels of noise and showing varying levels of disgust. The body language when they were finally seated showed clearly they were really in no mood to listen. My determination, however, was such that I was prepared to keep them – by force, if necessary – captive in my kitchen, until at least a few basic house rules were hammered out. Enough, I had finally decided, was enough.

'This is my house.' I began by stating the obvious. A timely reminder, which I thought should set me at an advantage.

There were odd under-the-breath mutterings, to which I replied, 'I wasn't asking you to agree, merely stating a fact.' I stared at each of them in turn and not one of them could meet my straight gaze. To Bobbi, I added, 'I do know this is still your home, but it remains *my* house, and you have all come here uninvited for your various reasons.'

There was a bit of uncomfortable shuffling, but no one disagreed.

'Now,' God, I was finding this a chore already, and had to force myself to view the mess around me as a reminder that this was not going to be even vaguely workable unless I took a firm stand. 'What I want – No. Actually, what I *expect*, from each of you,' I fixed Jason with a hard stare, 'and this includes you. In fact, it especially means you, since you're not even family – as far as I'm aware – yet.'

'Mum, I – ' Bobbi began indignantly. As ever she was always prepared to fight Jason's corner, though he didn't need or deserve it.

'Bobbi, shut up,' I kept my tone mild, but with that authoritative edge that brooked no argument.

'Is this going to take long, dear?'

My mother was subjected to a look that would have stripped paint, and she, too, fell silent.

'I'll start again,' I informed them, 'and I wouldn't interrupt, if I were you. *Any* of you.'

I forced myself to think of the way they had each taken advantage of my vulnerability, and if I was looking for fuel for my anger it certainly worked.

'You are all here uninvited and for reasons I don't even pretend to agree with or understand. You are taking advantage – in fact it wouldn't be an exaggeration to say you are completely taking the piss.'

Three pairs of wide eyes stared at me and I knew I finally had their complete attention.

'Now,' I continued, 'I don't intend to throw anybody out …' three people exhaled, 'yet,' they held their breaths so that the silence was absolute as they waited for me to go on, 'but I expect you to abide by my house rules and, by God, I don't expect ever – *ever* – to come home to this …' I swept an outstretched arm round the littered and cluttered kitchen, 'again.'

The silence continued as three pairs of furtive eyes took in the very obvious reason for my displeasure.

'I could be very reasonable and say I'll give you a week to get your act together, but ...' I put up a hand before anyone could speak, 'I don't feel like being reasonable. I'll give you until tomorrow, but the effort starts now and it starts here. I'll be upstairs having a bath – and that had better be bloody clean – and when I come back down I expect to be able to eat a meal that someone else has prepared, in a kitchen that someone else has cleaned. Following that I expect to be able to watch a programme, of my choice, in a neat and tidy lounge.' My gaze swung to Jason, and I added especially for him, 'Fail to pull your weight at your peril, young man. I'm in no mood to be tested by the likes of you.'

With head high I walked out of the kitchen, mindful of the stunned silence I had left behind. My back was rigid as I climbed the stairs, but I found that by the time I reached the top my legs were shaking so much that I had to grasp the banister or I would have fallen.

Talk about call my bluff, I acknowledged. I had never laid down the law like that. Well, realistically, I had never needed to before. If I had any doubts about the rights and wrongs of me taking the stand that I had, they were dispelled the minute I realised I was going to have to take a cloth and a bottle of Flash liquid cleaner, not to mention a degree of elbow grease, to a ring of grey scum that circled the bath, before I could happily get into it.

*

'This is better, isn't it?'

I smiled, without feeling the least bit like smiling. I was well aware that I may have won the battle, or at least the initial skirmish, but I was still far from winning the war.

I hoped I looked firm and in control. Surely, no one would guess, at least not from looking at me, that the majority of my time in the bath had been spent quietly sobbing into a blue flannel of Rob's that I hadn't yet had the heart or the inclination to dispose of.

There was a subdued air round the table, but the kitchen looked more as it should, and the meal in front of us, though just a simple Spanish omelette, was hot and nutritious.

'I don't think I was being unreasonable, do you?' I looked round the table at each person in turn. 'After all, at this moment I *am* the only employed person in the house. That being the case, it hardly seems fair, *does it?*' I used heavy emphasis and another straight look at each culprit. 'That I should also be the only one to be cooking and cleaning.'

'Well,' my mother began dubiously, 'as we're guests …'

'*Uninvited* guests,' I pointed out, keeping my tone hard. 'There is a subtle difference.'

'Don't keep saying that,' Bobbi pleaded, adding unwisely, 'I'd have thought you'd be gl – '

'Glad of the company?' I finished for her. 'Yes, you said that before. In the normal way, I would be glad of the company, Lord knows I would, but not like this. My future was taken away, I had no choice in the matter, but you all seem intent on throwing yours away like so much garbage.'

There was a babble of protest, which I carefully ignored, calmly pouring myself a glass of water from the jug in the centre of the table and taking a long cool sip.

'You'll hear me out first,' I told them, taking strength from a picture of Rob that smiled across the room at me from the kitchen windowsill. It was one of the later photos, taken not long before he died, and one in which he sported the short greying beard that I had come to love, 'and then you can have your say,' I continued, 'I'd be very interested to hear about your future plans anyway. From all of you.'

Surprisingly, it was Jason who asked, 'So, what do you have in mind for us? You *do* have something in mind, don't you?'

Was I imagining it, or was there the teeniest hint of respect creeping into his tone? Then he lolled back in his chair, spoiling the illusion by adding, in his more normal insolent tone, 'Only I was wondering if you could hurry it up a bit. Me and Bobbi have got plans for this evening.'

I bit my tongue and refrained from asking, with a degree of sarcasm, if they included a trip to the pub or the cinema funded by the DSS.

'You'll just have to humour me for a bit,' I told him, in a fairly agreeable tone, 'since you're a "guest" in my house.'

'We will do our bit, Mum, from now on,' Bobbi promised, and looking to my mother for support, she asked, 'Won't we, Gran?'

'Mmm? Oh, of course, dear,' my mother quickly agreed.

'I intend to see that you do,' I used my best, business-like tone, adding, 'by providing you with a rota that ensures you each do your fair share of the chores and cooking.' There were varying murmurs showing various levels of dissent, but I cut across it all to say, 'This is not open to discussion. You all either pull your weight or you find alternative accommodation. It's as simple as that. Your choice.'

*

'Bloody hell,' Jo said, 'I reckon I should have tried that with Petie. Did they agree?'

'I didn't ask,' I smiled grimly over the lunchtime sandwich in our usual corner of the Harvester. 'I just went off and wrote it up and I've left them with it this morning.'

'I can hardly wait for you to come in tomorrow.'

It was clear from her tone that she had her doubts about the success of a scheme that depended on co-operation from the parties involved. I had no hesitation in admitting to some serious misgivings of my own. If this didn't work, I had no idea what my next move would be, but that was something I wasn't prepared to admit to.

'Any more from Adam?' Jo asked then. 'Madam changed her mind and come back to the family mansion? I'm not just being nosey, I do like Adam, and hearing about other people's problems makes me feel better about my own. Sometimes it's nice to know you're not the only one – selfish as that may seem.'

I couldn't prevent a smile, 'A four-bed semi-detached in Lower Brankstone is hardly Buckingham Palace,' I pointed out, 'and, no, Lisbet hasn't returned.'

'And you know this, because..?'

'Adam phoned last night.'

'And..?'

'I said I'd meet him for a drink tonight,' I confessed reluctantly, rushing to add, 'Well, we couldn't talk any sense with everything that was going on in my house, and it wouldn't feel right for me to go to his …'

Jo's face lit up, 'You're going on a date,' she said, not even trying to hide her glee.

'I am *not*,' I almost choked on my sparkling mineral water, horrified she should suggest such a thing, even though part of me knew full well she was just teasing me. 'It's nothing of the kind. I'm just offering an old friend the kind of support he was good enough to offer me when I needed it. It's just a drink.'

Jo stared at me, and then laughed shortly, 'My God, Denise, I was only joking, but what's that saying? "Methinks the lady doth protest too much".'

I tried to laugh off my obvious over-reaction. 'Well, if it's what you're thinking, other people will think the same thing.'

Jo shrugged, 'So what if they do? You're a free agent. You can do what you like. It's been over a year since Rob died, and you *are* entitled to have a life outside of work, home and family, you know. No one would think any worse of you if it was a date.'

I knew she was right, but the idea made me feel thoroughly uncomfortable. I wasn't ready to go on anything remotely like a date. The only reason I had agreed to meet up was because it was Adam, who had no interest in me in that way, as I had none in him and never had.

Now, Jo's comments had raised serious doubts about the wisdom of what had previously seemed a perfectly innocent outing.

'I shan't go.' I ignored the dismay on her face. She was a fine one to talk, anyway. Jo had given men a wide birth ever since I could remember. 'I'll ring him as soon as I get back to the office and tell him it's no longer convenient. I'll get him round to supper, once things have settled down at home. Yes,' I was almost talking to myself at that point, 'that's a much better idea. No one could possibly read anything into that.'

'Oh, but ...'

'I might even ask you to come along too. The more the merrier.' I was getting into my stride by then, full of self-righteous indignation. 'I refuse to let the gossips have a field day at my expense.' I stood up and reached for my handbag. 'Have you finished that sandwich, only I've got a phone call to make and there's no time like the present.'

CHAPTER 4

THE MORE I THOUGHT ABOUT IT, the less sensible meeting Adam on my own seemed. It would probably invite not only comment, but also speculation, for us to be seen sitting cosily in a pub together. The fact that even Jo saw an innocent drink as a 'date' said it all really, in spite of the fact I had never, not even in my wildest dreams, seen Adam in the role of anything other than a good friend. If people started talking about us it could change our entire relationship – and not for the better, if my instincts were to be trusted.

In a state of panic, I started trying to reach Adam to change our arrangements the very minute I arrived back in my office, but whoever came up with the saying that begins, 'the best laid plans ... ' was definitely talking about me, no doubt about that. I was still trying when I left to go home. I was continually clicked into the answer-phone at his home, and his mobile seemed to be permanently switched off.

I knew I could leave a message, but each time something made me think better of it. What if Lisbet was back? I wouldn't want her to think there was something going on between us and leave again because of it – because it seemed anyone could get hold of the wrong end of the stick if Jo's 'joke' was anything to go by.

It also seemed a bit unkind to cancel our meeting without some kind of explanation and what could I say? That something had come up. It seemed a bit cruel to give the impression – in an answer-phone message, at that – that Adam was at the bottom of my list of priorities, given the blow his self-esteem had obviously recently been dealt.

How I got through my afternoon appointments, I don't know. It was difficult to show any real interest in recruitment drives and marketing ploys, let alone mediate fairly in a petty squabble that had blown up between staff in the meat department, when I had more pressing things on my mind.

I did think about just telling Adam the truth, but I went all hot at the thought of explaining that people might get the wrong idea about this meeting. He might think that *I* thought it was a date. He might think anything. If I could only speak to him, personally, I would come up with something more acceptable than that. I was good at thinking on my feet and dealing with awkward situations, after all.

I'd ring him from home, I decided. After all, there'd surely be plenty of reasons to cancel waiting for me there, if the past few nights were anything to go by. For once I was almost comforted by the thought of the apparently never-ending family aggravation. It would be much easier to let Adam down gently if I had someone, or something else to blame.

When I got there the first thing I noticed was that I could pull into my own driveway. Okay, so Jason's battered red Escort was half parked on the lawn – and how Rob would have fumed about that – but you couldn't have everything in life, even I knew that.

The second thing was the smell of something hot and delicious which met me as I stepped inside the front door.

My mother had been busy, obviously – and she wasn't the only one. The hallway had clearly been vacuumed and was cleared of clutter, a peek into the lounge told me a similar story. I felt my spirits lift and realised it really didn't take all that much to make me happy, after all.

'That smells del …' I was saying, as I pushed open the kitchen door, and was immediately rendered speechless. Nothing could have prepared me for the sight that met my eyes.

Not my mother standing over the hob, stirring something in a pan with one hand, while reaching to tilt the lid of another to prevent the contents boiling over. Not even Bobbi standing there.

'*Jason.*'

'Oh, hi, Mrs Moffat,' he greeted me more cheerfully than I could ever remember. 'Good day down the mine?'

'What..?' I took in the picture of him enveloped in one of Rob's jokey barbecue aprons. It was the one with the underwear on the front that made the chef look as if he were wearing bra and suspender belt and little else. In spite of myself, I felt my mouth twitch.

'Just spag bol.'

My mystified expression brought forth more detail.

'Spaghetti Bolognese. My own recipe, made from scratch. Well,' he amended with an unexpected dash of honesty, 'Originally it was my Mum's – before she buggered off – but I've added a pinch of this and that to improve the taste over time. It used to be quite a favourite in our house, especially with my brothers. I'm not keen on those ready-made jars of sauce, are you?'

'Um, no.'

I was beginning to recover my powers of speech by this time and so, it seemed, had Jason. I thought he might have spoken to me more in the past few minutes than in all the time I'd known him.

'Well, you did the rota,' he continued chattily, 'but left me out of the cooking duties, which didn't seem quite fair to the others. Can you give them a shout now and tell them that it's ready? Not bad for timing was it?'

When we sat down to eat, I think the rest of us were all pleasantly surprised. Jason's first attempt at a family meal, at least in my house, was delicious and I didn't hesitate to say so, always believing in praise where it's due.

I'd have been impressed had he resorted to using a jar of the sauce he so obviously despised, but to think he'd gone to the time and trouble of making it himself from scratch was almost unbelievable. I was surprised, and pleased, by Jason's attitude as much as by his cooking. I didn't mind admitting as much to Adam, later that same evening.

Yes, well, I *know* I said I was going to cancel meeting him for a drink, but with one thing and another I completely forgot about trying again to make that phone call until it was much too late to reasonably cancel – and, anyway, Bobbi wouldn't hear of it.

'Mum, you can't possibly let Uncle Adam down.' She was obviously shocked that I would want to. 'He's going through a tough time and needs your support. I know you've had a long day,' (that had been my feeble attempt at an excuse, when I realised I'd have to tell my house guests what 'appointment' I'd forgotten to cancel), 'but it's only a drink for heaven's sake, it will do you good to get out of the house for something other than work, too.'

'Are you sure it's a good idea?' My mother chipped in, obviously determined to voice her concerns. 'What will people *say*, dear?'

For perhaps the first time in my entire life I was actually *grateful* to Elaine for trotting out her stock phrase, though I did take a moment to wonder what she thought these same 'people' might be saying about her own present situation. Did she think she was above being gossiped about? I was as taken aback as she was by Bobbi's sudden and violent reaction.

'Oh, for God's sake, Granny,' she fumed, a look of complete disgust on her pretty face. 'Mum's entitled to a life, you know, and this is Uncle Adam we're talking about. He was Dad's best friend and he's known Mum for ever, too. I can't believe you, or anybody else, would see any harm in two old friends meeting for a drink.'

'I'm only saying ... ' my mother protested.

'Well, *don't*.' I'd never seen Bobbi so up-in-arms, and not only on my behalf, too, but also Adam's, it quickly became apparent. 'Please, don't do this to him, Mum. He looked really upset when he popped in the other night, and he was so great with us when Dad died.'

My mind was suddenly made up, and I was more than a little ashamed that it had taken my eighteen-year-old daughter to remind me of something I should never have forgotten.

What other people thought about us meeting for a drink was their problem. I should never have let the possibility of idle gossip prevent me from offering a friend my support or my company, and I felt terrible that I very nearly had. After all, I wouldn't have hesitated if Adam had been a female friend like Jo, would I?

'You're right, but I'm going to be very late.' I stood up and looked round at the messy kitchen.

'Leave all this to us,' Bobbi definitely had her bossy-head on, 'We'll clear up. *Won't* we?' Even Jason acquiesced under her hard glare. 'You go and have a quick shower. Oh, and Mum ... ' I paused in the doorway, 'wear something nice.'

It *was* almost like getting ready for a date. I had so used to enjoy getting ready to go out with Rob and, I realised on reflection, that I'd missed it. I also noticed that I was a bit out of practice. I'd used to have all my preparations down to a fine art, but it had been so long since I'd been anywhere socially, or bothered very much with my hair or make-up that I'd almost forgotten how. I couldn't prevent a frisson of excitement, as I stared at my flushed face in the mirror: it was followed swiftly by a touch of apprehension that I immediately dismissed. It was only Adam I was meeting, after all.

'Shall I put your hair up?' Bobbi popped her head round the bedroom door as I fiddled with foundation and searched for a subtle eye shadow.

I smiled at her gratefully. 'Oh, would you, love? I hadn't realised just how much my hair has grown, and I never do anything with it except tie it back, and that's a bit ...'

'Boring,' she finished for me.

'Severe, I was going to say,' I contradicted with a smile, appreciating this new, improved atmosphere between us, 'I thought I'd wear my black trousers and ...'

'Borrow one of my tops,' Bobbi offered quickly, obviously having decided the contents of my wardrobe were boring, too.

'They're a bit ...' I didn't need to finish, and we both looked at the black, cropped top she was wearing with her hipster jeans. I didn't need telling I didn't have the figure, nor was I anywhere near young enough to do either garment justice.

'Not all of them,' she insisted, 'I've got a lovely blue one that will suit you. I find it a bit, you know ...'

'Boring,' I finished helpfully. 'Go on then. Let me have a look.'

By the time she came back with the top dangling from a hanger, I had my best trousers on and was viewing them with dismay. What had fitted my previously comfortable size fourteen figure was now hanging from a smaller waist and bottom most unbecomingly.

'You've lost weight.' Bobbi stated the obvious, and passing me the top she said, 'Put this on. I won't be a minute.'

*

'And that,' I found myself telling Adam, 'is how I come to be here dressed from head to foot in my eighteen-year-old daughter's clothes. If you don't want to be seen in the company of mutton-dressed-as-lamb, I shall quite understand.'

Adam smiled his slow, familiar, and slightly lop-sided smile and my heart lifted. I felt it was worth feeling a touch foolish just to see it. He hadn't had much to smile about lately, when all was said and done.

'You don't look much older yourself, Dee. In fact, you're looking absolutely wonderful. Tell Bobbi she obviously has great taste these days.'

I laughed at his remarks easily. We were such old friends and I wondered why on earth I had allowed myself to get into such a state about meeting him away from the house. In fact, I found I was enjoying myself hugely, and with the aid of a large glass of Chardonnay was relaxing more by the minute. Bobbi had insisted that she and Jason would not only drop me off, but pick me up later, too.

'Don't be silly, Mum. Jase won't mind, will you Jay?'

He shook his head obediently – probably as much taken by surprise by this suddenly and unexpectedly assertive Bobbi as I was myself. It was good to see that she did still have a mind of her own sometimes.

'After all,' she went on, 'there's not much point going for a drink if you're not going to drink, is there?'

'I suppose a glass of wine or two won't hurt,' I agreed, resolutely ignoring my mother's look of strong disapproval. 'I should have let Adam pick me up, after all, but I was trying to be independent when he offered.'

I have to say, I'd felt a million dollars when I found I could fit into Bobbi's size ten black boot-cut trousers. I was sure I hadn't been that size since – oh, probably, since I'd married Rob, and slipped into a comfortable relationship and the motherhood that followed eventually, with ease. The trousers were a tad snug, but I was more than prepared to breathe in all night to feel as good as I did in them.

'Oh, no, Mum, you can't wear those shoes with those trousers.' Bobbi, viewing the outfit, had stared at my serviceable court shoes in horror, and then burst out laughing. 'The fashion police will have you arrested. I'll fetch my black boots.'

Bowing to her superior knowledge and grateful for her generosity I accepted the loan of what I knew were a brand new pair of ankle boots. Again, they were a touch tight, but they gave me a bit of height and refused to let me slouch as I might have done in my well-worn shoes.

Finally, it seemed, I was ready and feeling pretty good. The sleeveless top was in a beautiful royal blue. It was also a shade that I seemed to recall was much favoured by the female cast of the hit *Dallas* TV programme in its eighties heyday, and besides being one of my favourite colours was one that had always suited me.

The top was one more item that was snugger than I would have liked. Though round-necked and therefore not low-cut, it accentuated my breasts in a way I wasn't quite comfortable with. However, I didn't want to offend Bobbi by refusing to wear it when she'd been so generous, and it looked perfect under my own black jacket. I'd just have to remember to keep the jacket on, that was all.

Jason was flipping the passenger seat forward to allow me access to the back seat when I went outside, but he did a double take as he straightened and caught sight of me.

'Mrs M, you look a right babe.'

I shouldn't have been so flattered by the ridiculous comment, and especially coming from someone like Jason, but I flushed to the roots of my hair. I had to get a real grip on myself or I'd have gone all girlie and giggly, and just how pathetic would that have been?

Well, Bobbi had worked hard and the result was that I was out, all dressed up like a dog's dinner, and enjoying myself in spite of everything. I looked at Adam again, smiled and took a sip of my drink. It might not be a date, it might only be Adam, but I was out socialising for the first time in a very long time and it felt really good. In fact, it felt so good I had to remind myself – quite sharply – of the reason we were there.

'I'm so sorry,' I said quickly, 'about the other night. I know you wanted to talk, but you could see how it was and I can't see it getting any better in the foreseeable future. Privacy in my house these days is in pretty short supply, I can tell you.'

'Want to tell me about it?' Adam offered but, in fairness to him, I shook my head and resisted the urge to unburden myself and get his viewpoint.

It wasn't hard when I reminded myself that I at least could bend Jo's ear while, apparently, Adam had no one to confide in. He'd also listened to me quite enough times over the past year or so.

'We're not here to talk about me.' I leaned forward encouragingly. 'Now, what's happened? Has Lisbet really gone for good?'

Adam's brown eyes were dark with pain as he nodded, and I grieved for him. Lisbet was such a bitch. How much worse must it be to have someone you loved choose to leave you, than even to lose them through death? At least I'd had the comfort of knowing Rob would never have left me voluntarily. It was a thought that had often kept me going through my darkest hours. I had no idea what was going to get Adam through his.

'Did she give a reason?' I asked gently.

'Oh, yes, she finally confessed to falling for tall, dark, handsome and muscle-bound – not to mention a good bit younger than me, and her, come to that. I think she's known him a lot longer than she's letting on, though she says they met only recently at the gym,' he added bitterly by way of explanation, 'and his name's Rich, apparently.'

Probably by name and nature, I thought caustically, if I knew anything about Lisbet. She'd hardly leave Adam, just as his property maintenance business was taking off in a big way, for someone who wasn't able to keep her in the style to which she had rapidly become accustomed.

'I'm so sorry,' I told him, and reached out to touch his hand. If we'd been standing I'd have given him a big hug. I knew – who better? – just how lonely he must be feeling, and how welcome human contact was when you felt like that.

'I know you are,' he managed the glimmer of a smile, 'and I know that you, of all people, understand. You and I also know that this was a long time coming, too, don't we?'

I have to say I was taken aback. While I'd had my own views on Lisbet and her behaviour with the opposite sex, I'd always had the feeling that Adam was either completely in the dark about the extent of it, or that he simply accepted it as the way she was and chose to ignore it.

He saw my look and interpreted it pretty accurately. 'You thought I didn't know or that I didn't care, is that it?'

I didn't really know what to say, and took a quick gulp of my drink to hide my confusion.

'I know I've been a fool. I suppose I thought she had a bit of growing up to do and would settle down one day.'

People always made huge allowances for pretty, fluffy little blondes, I thought, and wondered why that was. Even Rob had seen no harm in her, insisting it was just her way.

Well, her way had caused rows in no end of our friends' marriages. I couldn't remember one occasion or get together when she hadn't made a beeline for someone else's husband. It had seemed to amuse her to pout and tease until the poor guy didn't know which way up he was, and his wife was ready to blow a gasket.

'Another drink?'

I reached for my bag – or should I say Bobbi's – and said quickly, 'My turn.'

'I offered first,' Adam pointed out, 'and you're doing me the favour of listening to my woes.'

'As if you haven't spent months listening to mine,' I scoffed, standing up. 'Please, Adam, let me.'

'Next time,' and with that he was off to the bar with our glasses.

Sitting down again, I watched him go, and sighed. He was such a lovely man, and Lisbet needed her silly blonde head testing.

Sitting back, for the first time I viewed my surroundings. Apart from my regular lunchtime trips to the local Harvester with Jo, I hadn't been into a pub for a long time and this was one that wasn't familiar to me. Having said that the place had the look of almost every other pub I *had* been into in the dim and distant past.

Mahogany bar and furniture, dark – fake – beams criss-crossing the ceiling and deep-toned floral carpet on the floor. Even the customers never seemed to change much from pub to pub and with the passing years. Only the theme pubs seemed to attract the trendy youngsters, but this one, like many others, relied much more on its delicious cuisine to attract a regular clientele, offering a varied menu on a daily basis, both lunchtimes and evenings.

Despite a hefty helping of Jason's 'spag bol' my mouth watered at the tempting array of dishes on offer and I toyed idly with the idea of treating my house guests to a Sunday lunch that none of us had to cook. I realised I must be mellowing towards them and hoped the feeling, and the improved behaviour that was probably the cause of it, was going to last.

On the far side of the room I caught sight of what I thought was a vaguely familiar face. However, I must have been wrong, since the woman pointedly ignored my tentative wave, turning all her attention to her food and her companion. Oh, well, it was an easy mistake to make. She was one of those nondescript types, thin, mousey-haired and dressed from head to toe in beige, who tend to look a little bit like everyone you've ever known, but can never quite place.

'Thanks, Adam.' I took a sip of the refilled glass of wine, and felt myself relax even more. I heard myself say, 'I was just thinking I might bring the family here for Sunday lunch. Why don't you join us?'

The minute the words were out, I regretted them. What on earth was I thinking? Tonight was supposed to be a one off. Adam knew where I lived if he wanted to talk again, or he could phone me, for heaven's sake. Another thing, *I* might have to put up with my house guests but that didn't mean I had to inflict them onto all and sundry.

'I'd love to.'

'Pardon?' My jumbled thoughts came crashing to a halt, and I stared at Adam.

'I said, "I'd love to",' he repeated. 'Cooking for one is no fun at all, as you must know only too well.'

He obviously wasn't aware that family lunches weren't always a better option – especially if most of the recent ones in my house were anything to go by.

'My mother will give you the third degree,' I warned.

'I doubt it,' Adam commented dryly, 'since she's just done a Lisbet to your Dad.'

Oh, my God. He was right. Even more embarrassing. Oh, well, it was said and done now, too late to retract the invitation. At least there would be a whole bunch of them, so there'd be none of that nonsense about it being misconstrued as a date.

*

The one thing the evening had done for me, I reflected later – when I was safely home and tucked up in bed for the night – was to highlight my complete lack of a social life. Another thing it had done, was to show me I was actually *ready* to get out and about again, though I hadn't even thought about such a possibility in all the long months since Rob's death. Too busy concentrating on getting through each day, I guessed, and then I realised with amazement that the days had actually been getting easier, almost without me being aware of it. I supposed I did have my troublesome family to thank for something then. Who'd have thought it?

I had really enjoyed the evening, though it hadn't been arranged for my benefit. Adam was good company, even when he was feeling as down as he had obviously been that evening – and with very good reason, I reminded myself. Of course, it had also helped that I felt totally safe with him, and not threatened by him in any way. There was a lot to be said for platonic friendship, even if some folk refused to believe such a thing existed.

The thought of going out socially with someone I didn't know scared the life out of me, I discovered when I idly explored the idea. Then I laughed dryly. Chance would be a fine thing. When all was said and done, guys had hardly been beating a track to my door, had they?

So much for being pounced on by men, married and single, when it was discovered you were widowed. The only attention from the male species I'd experienced in recent months had been a wink from the milkman – who might well have had something in his eye – and a guy who had held the door open for me at the bank, and had either let it slip from his fingers a bit too soon or had touched my bottom. I preferred to believe it was the former, but I certainly didn't hang around to see if it was the latter and he was going to try and follow it up.

I wasn't looking for a man. It was too soon and I had enough problems in my life, but I really missed being half of a couple, and the security that gave you. I missed having someone of my own, someone who knew me, inside and out – someone who cared just for me.

Then I heard Bobbi and Jason come up to bed. Forced to listen to the graphic sounds of their more than adequate sex life, I found there was something else I was beginning to miss, too.

CHAPTER 5

WITH MY MIND ON OTHER THINGS, I'd completely forgotten to mention the Sunday lunch arrangement to Bobbi and Jason, when they joined Adam and I for a final drink before bringing me home the night before.

First thing next morning, before I left for work, I went looking for Bobbi who was actually up at a reasonable hour for once. Predictably, she was with Jason watching television. However, since they'd obviously made a reasonable attempt at some housework first, I had no real cause for complaint.

'Oh, dear,' she said, looking guiltily at Jason, 'Sunday's a bit difficult. We really wanted to spend the day together – just the two of us.'

Spend the day together? *Spend the day together?* My tone was rising dangerously, even if it was only inside of my own head. They did nothing *but* spend all day *every* day together. Then I saw the little sly look that passed between them and was left in absolutely no doubt about *how* they intended to spend the day.

Part of me was outraged by their brazen attitude, another much bigger part of me was as jealous as hell, I realised with a start. I suddenly recalled days, so long ago I had almost forgotten them, when I had been just as eager for love, days when all that mattered was enjoying one another's company, and exploring one another's bodies. I'd almost forgotten – but, oh, yes, especially the exploring and enjoying of one another's bodies and responses.

I turned away quickly, suddenly all too aware of the tide of hot colour that scorched my face, and the heat that flooded my body at the long-forgotten memories. I probably wouldn't want to be Bobbi's age again, with all those hormones raging out of control, and the animal urges that practically dictated overt sexual behaviour, but God, how I missed having someone to love. Having someone to love, not just in a physical sense, in every sense.

'Don't worry about it,' I threw the comment over my shoulder, a touch of acid in my tone, and went looking for my mother.

She was lying on the bed in my pretty blue guest bedroom, reading one of the trashy romantic novels she enjoyed so much, wearing a gaudy floral caftan I'd never seen before, and a green facepack was slapped on thickly and keeping her expression rigid.

'Sunday? Well, I did half promise to have lunch with your father on Sunday,' Elaine's tone was reluctant, her lips barely moving, 'to "talk things over", as he so quaintly put it. Though, I don't know what there is to talk about and, anyway, I'd much rather have lunch as a family.'

I was outraged, and asked icily, 'So, suddenly, Dad's not family any more?'

Caught on the hop, she blustered a bit and frowned so hard that, I noted with satisfaction, the facepack weakened and cracked liked a poorly plastered ceiling. 'Now, that's not what I meant, at all, and you know it. I would just rather …'

'Your invitation has just been withdrawn,' I said, very definitely. 'You have a prior engagement. I expect you to keep it – and so does Dad,' I added under my breath.

I was glad to go into work and wasted no time throwing myself onto Jo's tender mercy.

'Families – never there when you need them,' I complained bitterly, and pleaded, 'but you could come with me, Jo. Go on, or else it's going to look like I invited him out to a pre-arranged lunch under false pretences.'

Jo roared with laughter, 'No, it won't. This is Adam we're talking about. Adam Mitchell, who has known your whole family forever. I promise you he will accept any explanation you offer at face value.'

'But I'd really *like* you to come.'

'As if you don't see enough of me all week at work,' Jo's tone was dry. 'You'll be asking me to move in with the rest of them next.'

'Having you there would be preferable to that selfish bunch,' I assured her darkly. 'Believe me.'

'Anyway,' she shrugged, 'I can't help you this Sunday. Petie's promised to come round, and I have to be there for him.' She held up her hand before I could speak. 'I know what you're going to say, and that it's all true, but I still like to see that he eats a square meal now and again. He's so thin, I'd swear I've seen more fat on a chip.'

'Bring him with you.' I couldn't believe what I was saying, but I *was* desperate, and desperate measures were called for. 'No, really,' I continued quickly, seeing the dubious expression on her face, 'I'd really like to see Petie again.' I *almost* meant it.

*

Saturday morning dawned, the weather fine and warm, and it found me up early and aiming to do something that had been foreign to me for quite some considerable time – shopping for clothes on my own account.

The last time I'd indulged in any serious retail therapy, it had been on Bobbi's behalf. The most I'd had to do was to position myself outside changing rooms as the admiring audience, murmur appropriate words of approval, and provide the majority of the necessary cash for her going-away-to-university wardrobe.

Having spent the previous evening viewing the contents of my own closet, it was hardly surprising after the raid on Bobbi's much more adventurous range of wearing apparel, that I'd found everything in it sadly lacking in anything approaching fit and style. Why I was looking for an excuse, when I really didn't need one I didn't know. After all, no one was telling me I should justify my actions. I still made a point of reminding myself it wasn't on to keep borrowing Bobbi's stuff, that just one evening out had proved a few additions to my wardrobe were a necessity rather than an extravagance

It would also be nice to wear something of my own that flattered my new slimmer shape. I truthfully hadn't noticed how my clothes were hanging on me, and having no one to notice for me hadn't helped. Anyway, I allowed, in a sudden burst of honesty, if I didn't admit how great I'd felt dressed in Bobbi's clothes, I would have been deceiving myself.

It was a shame Bobbi was apparently going to be 'busy' on that day, too. I felt sad when I recalled our many family shopping-expeditions of the past. Rob – unlike the majority of men, if my colleagues' regular moans were anything to go by – had adored shopping, and could always be persuaded to come along to carry bags and treat us to lunch.

When my mother also declined to join me in the sort of outing she normally adored, I was very surprised. I wondered if she was still intent on punishing me for taking a stand over the Sunday lunch business, or if she was, in fact, showing her disapproval of this first small step back to rediscovering the person I'd used to be in my pre-widowhood days. I didn't know why I felt it might be the latter, it was just an impression I'd gained, even though she'd been the very one – for months now – urging me to 'pull myself together' and 'get on with my life'.

I not only found it difficult to understand this cut-off-your-nose-to-spite-your-face attitude, but discovered I also had a real crisis on my hands. It was obviously a case of venturing to the shops alone or not going at all.

'I can't do it,' I spoke aloud to my reflection, my heart quailing at the thought of tackling the multi-storey carpark in town, not to mention the crowded Arnedale Centre, without some friendly support. 'I can't.'

'Yes, you can.'

I physically jumped. It was as if Rob had really spoken. I could hear his voice as clear as day and, of course, he was right. Hadn't I managed all the other things I'd achieved over recent months, just by doing them? Hadn't I learned that the first time for everything was always the worst?

However, going into town was the one thing I had been carefully avoiding, apart from that one time with Bobbi. I'd still been so numb with grief then, anyway, that I'd walked round in a complete daze.

I was lucky, I suppose, that working for a supermarket chain had made food shopping easy and, especially in the early days of my bereavement, there'd always been someone willing to collect a few items to save me the bother. Somehow I'd either managed to find pretty much all I needed at the local shops, or I went without, but there were other things I'd had to do out of necessity, and I was sure I could do this.

'Jase and I can drop you off, if you'd like.'

Bobbi's offer indicated she was probably having a fit of conscience. I hoped it wasn't that she could see how terrified I was. Reminding myself she shouldn't be here at all, but away studying at university, gave me the strength to say airily, 'Oh, no, I'll be fine. I only asked in case you fancied it.'

'It's just that Jase hates shopping,' she offered, by way of explanation.

Somehow I doubted that. Shopping for anyone other than himself was probably nearer the mark. Clothes like his weren't picked up at the local flea market, even I knew that, but shopping in company might mean him having to put a hand in his pocket for someone else's benefit. Such acts of generosity were obviously foreign to his nature – as was borne out by the fact he'd never yet thought to reimburse me in any way for his bed and board.

That thought made me resolve to bring up the subject of *all* my presently non-paying guests contributing something to the family budget. It hardly seemed fair to expect me to keep the whole bunch of them, yet it was something that had obviously not occurred to even one of them.

Right, I squared my shoulders, shopping first, and then I'd certainly be more than capable of dealing with a few other pressing issues.

'I'll be fine,' I told Bobbi airily, and picking up my handbag I walked out of the door on legs that were decidedly shaky, but doing exactly what they were supposed to do, none the less.

The drive into town calmed me down quite a lot. After all, I was used to driving in traffic from my daily journeys into work and back. It took me an age to find a parking space, but at least I'd had plenty of practice with the regular struggle to find a spot in the staff car park, and finally drove into an awkward corner without hesitation.

Leaving the car was another matter, and my nerves were back in a rush. Adrenaline propelled me into the shopping mall and, once there, I didn't stop until I reached the approximate centre of the place. Had I stopped sooner, I might have found myself giving in to the urge to get the hell out of there before I'd managed to buy a thing.

I stared round in a daze. It had all changed. Everything appeared so much bigger, yet so crowded. The garments in the windows seemed far too glamorous and certainly far too young for the likes of me. I just didn't know where to start looking for anything more suitable.

Panic and fear almost overwhelmed me. I could hear the rapid beat of my own heart drumming in my ears. Boom, boom, boom, boom. I had to literally force myself to stand still, because I knew if I so much as moved a muscle I would have taken to my heels and run – and kept running until I was safely locked inside my car.

Having come so far I really didn't want to take what would have been an enormous step back, and not the one I definitely wished to take forward. Forward could lead to the new future I had so recently begun to see was possible for me.

I stood my ground and gradually, very gradually, the panic began to subside. I went from feeling so hot that I could feel myself perspiring, to so cold that I was literally shivering – and then eventually I became quite calm. In fact, I was so calm it was hard not to think I might have imagined the whole thing.

I began to focus on the shoppers milling around me, to take notice of the snatches of conversation. To look at what people were wearing, perhaps with a view to discovering fresh ideas for the new me.

'Oh, this jacket, Mags? It was a real bargain. I found it in the Next sale and …'

'Can't beat M and S for their undies, but I like BHS for …'

'Cost me a fortune in John Lewis, but worth every penny …'

I let the voices flow and ebb around me, and began to look around me for the shops I'd heard mentioned. It was all coming back to me now. After all, these shops had been almost as familiar to me as my own home just a few short months ago. For today, all I had to do was to concentrate on one thing at a time, perhaps getting just one outfit. There would be other shopping trips, I was sure of that now.

*

Less than three hours later I returned to the car, puffed up with inordinate pride, and laden down with colourful carrier bags, emblazoned with the names of some of the better-known shops.

I'd even managed to treat myself to a pot of tea and a sandwich at the coffee shop in one of the department stores, and struck up a conversation with a total stranger whose table I'd shared, into the bargain. The plump fifty-something lady, seeing my numerous bags containing what was obviously clothing, helpfully recommended the name of a boutique I hadn't tried.

'Oh, you must call in on Leigh next time you're in town,' she urged. 'She has some lovely things, rather more sophisticated than the skimpy things the kids love so much,' she added tactfully, 'and you have the figure to do her garments justice – unlike me.' She patted her ample hips ruefully and took another bite of her doughnut.

'Pricey?' I queried, appreciating her helpful and friendly nature.

'No more than some of the better shops,' came her answer, 'and what you get is excellent quality, in styles you won't see every other person wearing when you go out.'

'That's really kind of you.'

I carefully made a note of the name and whereabouts of this apparent gem of a place and, collecting up my purchases, I made my goodbyes. Though I doubted that we had a similar taste in clothing, judging by the comfortable pinafore dress she was wearing, I was still grateful for her interest and I knew that out of courtesy I would pay the place a visit.

Loading the bags into the car I felt really proud of myself. I *could* do this. I had proved it. The only one stopping me before had been *me*, and I was quite sure that next time it would be easier. I could become the sort of confident, independent woman I had often admired, but never aspired to be in the past because I'd always had Rob. In my elated, yet strangely vulnerable state, simply thinking about him brought the suspicion of a tear to my lashes, and I blinked furiously, suddenly cross with myself.

I had to think positively, it was the only way. I'd had my years with Rob, and no one could take them away, no matter what. I mustn't wish for what might have been, because no one knew better than me how pointless that was. Rob was gone, but I was still here, and I still had a life to live. It was obviously going to be different, but that didn't mean it wasn't going to be good. I was just beginning to realise that fact.

Life was what you made it, wasn't that what everybody said? I knew that Rob, of all people, would applaud what I had achieved that day, and appreciate the effort it had taken.

Heartened by that thought, I reversed the Metro out of the minuscule corner space that hadn't grown any bigger while I'd been gone, and with a new confidence drove out of the car park.

I was almost home and beginning to feel inordinately pleased with myself. Singing along with the radio, I was already anticipating a warm welcome at home and a hot cup of tea, when it happened.

I'd noticed the jeep-type vehicle following behind was rather close, but had been trying to ignore it, as you do, by concentrating on my own driving. Well aware that not all road users demonstrate good manners or often even any kind of consideration for their fellow travellers, I had no intention of increasing my speed because some moron was running late for something and was obviously trying to intimidate me.

I eventually braked, and then stopped, when the traffic lights in front of me suddenly changed to amber and then red. To my horror the jeep kept going, veering up onto the pavement on my left at the last moment and clipping my wing mirror as it drew level.

Glaring at me through the open window was not the aggressive, testosterone-laden male I'd been expecting, but a quite ordinary-looking dark-haired girl, probably no older than her mid-twenties.

After snarling a string of expletives I barely understood, never mind recognised, she shrieked, 'Bloody old grannies like you shouldn't be driving. Dawdling along at twenty miles an hour, cluttering up the roads, you're not safe to be let out.'

All I could do was stare at her in fascinated horror, and before I could say a word in my own defence – even if I could have got one out – she swept round me, the jeep's engine squealing in protest, bumped down over the kerb and out onto the road in front of me.

I fully expected her to jump the lights and keep going, but she hadn't finished yet, as quickly became apparent. Revving the engine to an ear-splitting roar, she drove forward a yard or two and then reversed back towards me. I closed my eyes and waited for the crash, but when I opened them again she was driving forward with an obvious view to repeating the exercise, perhaps with disastrous results the next time.

I did the only thing I could think of, and pressed down on the car horn – *hard*. All I could think of was drawing someone's – anyone's – attention to what was going on. I was suddenly aware that I needed witnesses. That I had become a victim of the road-rage I'd heard so much about.

The girl must have realised, at the same time as I did, that people were turning to stare, and that the occupants of cars waiting on the opposite side of the road must have seen what was happening. Thank goodness, the lights changed at that moment and she took off with a squeal that probably took all of six months' worth of tread from the jeep's tyres.

Everyone around simply continued going on about their business, now that the incident had passed. The cars at the lights moved off, and those behind me tooted respectfully to draw my attention the fact the lights were now green. I couldn't quite believe it. It was as if the whole episode had never happened and obediently I resumed my journey, too.

I hadn't gone very far when I realised I was shaking too much to drive safely and began looking for somewhere to pull over. I was, perhaps, five or ten minutes from home, but I didn't feel capable of coping even with that short a distance.

I felt sure Rob was with me when I spotted a large gap in the line of pull-in parking bays outside the row of local shops. Spaces there were practically unheard of, as I knew only too well, especially one large enough to drive into without manoeuvring.

'Thanks, Rob,' I whispered, and with a sigh of relief I turned the engine off and leaning forward, I rested my forehead on the steering wheel.

A tap on the passenger-side window almost made me jump out of my skin, and for an awful moment I thought the driver of the jeep had come back to attack me physically. Half expecting to be dragged from the car, I peeped up nervously and found a grey-haired lady peering through the glass with a worried expression on her face.

'Are you all right?' she mouthed, and looking relieved when I nodded, she indicated the shop directly behind her and said, 'Why don't you come in for a cup of tea? You look very shaken.'

I could hardly hear her, but her evident concern made me want to cry. The most frightening thing about the whole episode was that no one seemed to care. I thought about those onlookers who would probably have let the jeep driver do as she would, without any one of them getting involved or even turning much more than a hair.

I nodded gratefully, even managing a half-hearted smile, and climbing stiffly from the car, made my way round to where she was standing. A faded sign over the shop front proclaimed that this was Peg's Place and I wondered if the lady was Peg.

'Come along, my dear,' she touched my arm gently, 'let's get you inside. A cup of hot, sweet tea is what you need.'

I went with her willingly, and into a café I had seen many times on my travels, but had never before been inside. Why would I want to visit a place like that, after all, when I lived nearby?

I found myself looking round with interest as she led me inside, realising the narrow frontage with its one plate-glass window and single door was deceiving. Inside there was plenty of room for tables able to accommodate up to four people on either side, set against the yellow-painted walls, and a wide pathway through the middle leading to the counter set at the back and to one side.

By the time she had set a steaming mug of the strongest tea I had ever seen in front of me, tears were running in a steady stream down my face. I felt extremely foolish and was only relieved that, being late in the day, there were very few customers to view my distress.

'Thank you so much, you're very kind. How much do I owe you?'

'Oh, no, dear,' she shook her head emphatically, 'I wouldn't dream of taking any money.' Sitting down on the opposite side of the table, she asked kindly, 'Would you like to talk about it?'

Well, everything came tumbling out in a torrent of anguish that went back months, to before and including Rob's sudden death, the struggle to behave normally afterwards, the more recent problem of house guests I didn't need or want and, finally, the frightening road-rage incident.

'Oh, you poor dear.'

Her kindly tone only made me cry harder. I thought I was never going to stop.

'I thought I was doing so well today,' I gulped, mopping my eyes with the paper serviette she proffered, 'and now I just wish I had stayed at home.'

'You can't let folk like that get the better of you,' she advised sagely, 'or before you know it we'll all be prisoners in our own homes. I've been mugged, you know.' Seeing my surprised look, she nodded. 'Oh, yes, had a week's takings stolen and suffered two black eyes in the struggle to hold onto the money – but I'm still here, aren't I? My only compromise to modern lawlessness was to empty the till more frequently, and agree to my son banking the takings for me. Otherwise I go on in just the same way as I always have.'

Peggy, for that was indeed her name, kept talking. It was all about anything and nothing, but as she talked my tears dried as suddenly as they'd begun to flow.

'Thank you so much,' I said, reaching out to touch a hand that was, quite unexpectedly, wrinkled with age.

Finding myself looking into her face – really looking for the first time – I realised she was much older than I had first thought, probably well into her late sixties or even very early seventies. A good age to be still running her own business, I thought, especially one as energetic as this evidently thriving café.

'We have to help each other,' was all she said, dismissing my thanks as unnecessary, 'or what are we here for.'

The few remaining customers had long since gone, it being well past closing time, and before I left I helped Peggy to clear the tables, though she insisted, 'There's no need, dear, I can manage.'

'I thought you said we should all help each other,' I came back at her with a wry smile, and she laughed.

'I'd like to come back,' I told her, 'but as a paying customer next time.'

'You'll always be welcome,' her tone was firm, 'and now you get off home and sort out those visitors of yours.'

'I will, and th ...' I bit back the thanks she refused to accept, and said instead, 'I'll see you soon.'

*

'Where on earth have you been?' Bobbi pounced on me the minute I stepped inside of the front door, her pretty face showing real concern.

'Let me put my bags down,' I pleaded, 'and I'll tell you what happened.'

I have to say even Jason, who appeared to care about very little – including my daughter, it seemed sometimes – was suitably horrified.

'You should have phoned me,' he began aggressively, 'I'd have ...' and then he realised, 'You don't have a mobile, do you? For Gawd's sake, Mrs M, you must be the only person in the whole of the western world without a mobile phone.'

'I can't afford one,' I muttered crossly, adding under my breath, 'unlike you, of course.'

I knew nothing about the blasted things, except they appeared to be extremely expensive, and a complete and utter nuisance, going off everywhere, and often at the most inconvenient times. I had never had the least desire to own one.

Jason always seemed to have the very latest model, if Bobbi's enthusiastic comments in the past were anything to go by, while she appeared quite happy with a bog-standard pay-as-you go. How he afforded such a luxury item and the price of the calls on top was a mystery to me.

That reminded me of my resolve to discuss the cost of living, but I allowed it to be shelved temporarily while we all sat down to enjoy an excellent chicken korma produced by my mother in her own inimitable style, with an impressive array of accompanying dishes.

'What did you buy, Mum?' Bobbi asked when she'd cleared her plate of a second generous helping.

I noticed that Jason – who was already on his third huge plateful – managed to look at least a little bit interested, but my mother feigned total disinterest. I pressed my lips together and gave her a look, which she totally ignored. Now, what on earth *was* her problem?

None of them could know I had brought them each back a present. The items were bought in a fit of generosity, because I was feeling so good, not only about my own personal purchases, but the successful shopping expedition in general. I had even included Jason because I wasn't quite hard-hearted enough to leave him out and, yes, I did realise I needed my brains tested but that still didn't spoil my enjoyment in choosing something for each of them that I'd felt they would like.

Purposely, in an attempt to make her feel guilty, I produced my mother's gift first. I could see immediately that she was quite taken aback, and that made me feel that I had scored a well-deserved point.

What was it Rob had always used to say? Oh, yes, 'You can't fight ignorance with ignorance.' Well, we'd see if he was right.

It was a pretty blouse in her favourite blue, not hideously expensive, but tasteful, for all that. She couldn't hide her pleasure, in spite of herself.

'Oh, Denise, how lovely, that is kind of you. Thank you.'

'That's okay, you're very welcome,' I assured her, and funnily enough, I found I meant it. It didn't stop me adding, though, 'There was a pretty skirt that might have gone well with it, but I wasn't sure if it was exactly what you would like.'

You should have come with me, was what I meant. My mother knew it, and she had the grace to look a touch ashamed as she offered, 'I *will* come with you next time.'

Futile to tell her it was *this* time I had so badly needed her company.

I'd bought Bobbi a red cropped-top, nothing more than a scrap of material that was only half-way decent. It was just the type of thing I most disliked, so I was sure she would love it – and she did.

'Oh, Mum,' she squealed, holding it up against herself and whirling around the kitchen. 'I've seen this in Top Shop, and it was really expensive. You shouldn't have … What am I saying? You should, you should, and I love it.'

She hugged and kissed me exuberantly, and for a moment we were just as we had used to be, before someone else influenced her life and thinking.

That thought brought me back to Jason. He was sitting at the table, still, watching the proceedings with a little smile. I had to say he looked as if he was enjoying Bobbi's pleasure and that, in turn, made me glad I hadn't left him out, after all.

When I put the bag in front of him he looked totally taken aback. 'For me?' he asked, making no attempt to open the bag, so that Bobbi reached over impatiently to do it for him.

A Ralph Lauren shirt, with the little logo on the breast to prove it, was folded neatly inside. In a rather smart navy-blue, and I'd been assured by the shop assistant that it would go down very well with someone of Jason's age.

He lifted it from the bag with such a peculiar expression on his face, that I immediately said, 'You don't have to keep it if you don't like it, Jason. The shop will exchange it. I checked, and I have the receipt.'

'For me?' he said again.

He looked so totally bewildered I was certain I'd made a dreadful choice, though I thought it was a touch ungrateful of him to show it so clearly. Couldn't he have slipped it quietly back to the shop without me knowing, or even worn it once and then thrown it away?

It was only when Bobbi stopped her twirling for long enough to say, 'You love those, don't you, Jase? Fancy Mum knowing just what you'd like, when she doesn't even know you that well,' that I looked at him closely and realised he was so taken by surprise that he didn't know what to do, or what to say.

He eventually managed a quiet, 'Thank you,' but no more than that, so I was surprised when, later in the evening he sought me out and, almost shyly, handed me a mobile phone.

Even I could see it wasn't the most up-to-date model, not dinky or in an eye-catching colour, just plain grey and almost a smaller version of my own cordless land-line phone.

'It's not new, and it's only pretty basic,' he was almost apologetic, 'but it does work, and as it's a pay-as-you-go you just need a sim card, from any mobile phone shop, and £10 voucher to start you off. I've even got a spare charger I can let you have.'

'Oh, no, really ... ' how could I say I didn't want the damn thing without offending him.

I was still carefully formulating the words, when he continued, 'You should have been able to ring the fuzz – police,' he explained, seeing my puzzled look, 'today. With one of these you only need to press 999, just like any other phone. Even if you never use it for anything else, it'll be there if you need it.'

Well, seeing as he put it like that. I supposed it wouldn't take up much room in my bag. Before I could say so, or express my thanks, Jason had started to speak again, it was quite amazing for someone who had barely seemed to know how to string two words together in all the time I'd know him.

'I know I might seem a bit of a tearaway to you,' he grinned, as if it couldn't have mattered less what I thought, 'but I've never gone around frightening old ladies and I don't agree with those who do – man or woman. Anyway,' he took advantage of my stunned silence, 'it's only an old phone and I'd do the same for my Mum, if she was still around.'

CHAPTER 6

'CHEEKY LITTLE BEGGAR,' Jo laughed her head off when I related the whole tale – complete with Jason's devastating comments – the following lunchtime when we met for the pre-arranged Sunday lunch at the Slug and Radish.

'It's not funny,' I said sternly, but couldn't prevent the slight curl that lifted the corners of my mouth, 'being classed as a little old lady when you're only in your mid-forties does nothing for a fragile ego, I can tell you.'

'What happened to his mum?' she wondered, and I shrugged.

'I never heard Bobbi say much about Jason's family, apart from the fact there was a lot of them. I wonder why he doesn't live at home?'

'No room,' Jo suggested, and then went on, 'or could it be the fact he doesn't pay his way at your house indicates similar problems to those I had with Petie?'

She looked over her shoulder, as if she expected him to arrive at any moment, and I risked a fearful glance myself. I was kind of hoping he wouldn't turn up, but knew I could hardly complain if he did. I couldn't expect Jo to give up the time with her son that was rare these days, just so I wouldn't have to be alone with Adam which, in turn, might give judgemental folk the opportunity to pick up the wrong end of the stick.

'What are you going to do about your lodgers?' she asked, more out of curiosity than nosiness, I could tell. 'You can't just let them behave like squatters. You know that they're all taking advantage of your present vulnerability, don't you?'

'Mmm,' I nodded ruefully. I did know, and part of me was very angry about that and eager to seek a confrontation. Another part of me, the more cowardly part that had always left such things to Rob, was just hoping against hope that everything was going to sort itself out without me doing a thing. That's what I told Jo.

'You know it's not going to happen, though, don't you? Have you spoken to your Dad about this situation with your Mum?' I shook my head, and offered the excuse, 'Well, it's only been a few days really.'

'Weeks,' she reminded me. 'Have you been in touch with the university about Bobbi?'

This time I was pleased to be able to nod. 'They said she'll have to make a decision soon or lose her place on the course, though they were really sympathetic. I used her dad's death as the excuse, said she was still having problems coming to terms with it. I thought they'd be more sympathetic, than if I said it was boyfriend problems. Do you think that's terrible?'

This time it was Jo shaking her head. 'I think Rob would want you to use anything, and everything, it might take, to give Bobbi time to see sense and reconsider the advisability of her present actions,' she said.

I was cross at the feeble tears that welled in my eyes, but told her honestly, as I blinked them away, 'I find it so difficult to cope with the crap that life keeps throwing at me, Jo. I don't want to sound self-pitying – I know everyone has their share of problems – but losing Rob has been so hard, I really don't need all this other shit as well.'

'Why don't you tell them that?' she suggested, but before I could respond, Adam and Petie arrived simultaneously and took the conversation in a different direction.

The change in Petie was astonishing. In the past he'd always reminded me of Jason – in all the worst ways. Perhaps the fact he was wearing glasses made the difference, I thought, watching him shake hands with Adam, and then go off to the bar with him. The specs made him look studious, calmer, but they didn't explain the absence of the slouch I had come associate with him, or the lack of an insolence that had always been part of his manner towards anyone older than himself.

'So what are you doing these days, Petie?' I queried, as he returned to the table, placing a glass of wine in front of his mother, a coke for himself next to it, and then sat in the chair next to her and across the table from me.

'Driving a breakdown truck.' There was a hint of pride in his tone, I thought, and he elaborated readily, 'I either get the vehicle going, or I tow it in to the garage for repair.'

'Oh, right. It must suit you, you always did like cars.'

No sooner were the words spoken than I could have bitten my tongue off. Petie had a record as long as your arm, and every offence was to do with cars. From stealing petrol, wheels and car stereos, through to joy-riding, and simple speeding, Petie had been to court for them all. The latest, the drink-driving charge, was just one more thing to add to an already formidable list. Talk about putting the boot in, I could feel my face reddening, and was horrified at the thought of upsetting Jo.

'Oh, I'm ...' I began.

'Don't be,' Petie saw my discomfiture, and in a most un-Petie way went out of his way to show my embarrassment was misplaced. 'I did the crimes and served my time, in a manner of speaking, by doing community service, mostly.'

Adam had arrived back by this time, and he put in, 'And did you learn anything?'

'Not as quickly as I should have done,' he admitted ruefully, 'or I wouldn't have one more act of stupidity hanging over me. I don't think Mum really believes I'll ever learn.'

Jo protested with commendable speed, but I'd seen her despair when her son had been summoned to court for the umpteenth time for driving with no tax, insurance or MOT certificate. She'd always sworn Petie looked on them as optional extras.

'I don't blame you,' his tone was surprisingly gentle, and for the very first time I could see the very real affection he had for his mother. 'I know I've let you down a thousand times. I can't promise I won't do any of it again, but this time I really intend to try. She's great, isn't she?' the question was aimed at me, and I agreed without hesitation.

Being there was what parents were for, and I knew that. There had been times in the past when I'd needed my own and they had never intentionally failed me. Part of the reason I couldn't be too hard on my mother, I supposed, was that I knew she'd always *tried* to do what was best in any given situation – though maybe sometimes not quite hard enough. Whatever Bobbi decided to do with her future, whether I agreed with her decisions or not, I knew I *would* be there for her. It made me think back to what Jason had said and wonder whether his mum had died or just left, and whether that had anything to do with his behaviour.

'What happened to the family lunch?' Adam asked, quirking an eyebrow in my direction.

I didn't know what to say. I could hardly say the youngsters preferred to spend the day in bed, could I? My face began to burn at the very thought.

I was just *so* relieved when Jo leapt to my rescue with a flippant, 'It still is a family lunch – just a different family. You don't mind, do you?'

'Lord, no. It's always nice to see you, Jo – and a pleasure to meet your son. He seems like a nice lad.'

The hopes I'd fostered, and Rob had scoffed at, that Jo and Adam might one day get together as a couple were totally misplaced. Watching them I could see that it wouldn't work between them on a romantic level, and finally understand why that was so, even without the added complication of a biggish age difference.

Friendly and at ease as they always were, there was definitely no spark between them. Shame really, I thought, because they'd have been so good for each other.

If I never met anyone else I knew it wouldn't really bother me, because with Rob I'd had the love and strength in my life that came with a good, strong marriage. Those two had never known real love or loyalty in a relationship, and I felt so sad for them both that it was so.

Still, it was early days for Adam, he wasn't even divorced yet, but once he'd accepted it was over with Lisbet, he'd soon meet someone else. There was plenty of time. Well, there was for Jo, too, I conceded, but she'd been on her own so long now that the idea of her finding someone – or even wanting to – appeared ever more remote.

'What?' I suddenly realised three faces were looking at me expectantly, and said again, 'What? I was miles away.'

'Yes, how *are* your visitors?' Adam grinned, obviously assuming that's where my thoughts lay, and then more soberly, he asked, 'and how's your dad coping without your mum?'

'I'm ashamed to say, I don't really know,' I admitted, 'I'm probably trying too hard not to get involved. By forcing my mother to take the call each time he phones, I keep hoping he'll manage to persuade her to go back.'

'And is it working?' Jo asked, knowing full well it wasn't.

I shook my head. 'I know. You don't have to tell me. I'm playing my usual game of hoping if I ignore everything that's going wrong, it'll eventually all put itself right. Rob always said I was good at that, but I have to say it's sometimes worked – and there's no harm in hoping, surely?'

Petie spoke up, then, which surprised me. 'I expect that's what Mum did with me to start with, but then she forced me to take responsibility for my own actions, pushed me out into the real world, and showed me I was on my own.'

I knew some of it, but it was good to hear an account of what happened from Petie's point of view. 'How did it make you feel?' I asked, 'especially about your mum?'

He laughed, and freely admitted, 'Oh, I certainly didn't thank her at the time. She was my mum, she owed me, or that's what I thought, but you know what?'

I shook my head, willing him to go on.

'That was when I started to respect her. As long as she let me use her, I was quite happy to go on doing it.' He shrugged then, before continuing, 'Probably because I'd seen my dad and my nan doing the same for years. Poor Mum,' he said ruefully, and gave her a hug.

I wanted that hug, but I wanted it from Bobbi. However, I was beginning to see I wasn't going to get anything like it for myself, unless I started earning it – and I knew it wasn't going to be easy.

I looked at Adam, hoping from the thoughtful expression on his face that he was beginning to realise that he had let Lisbet walk all over him, too. It didn't take Einstein to work out she'd had very little respect for Adam, precisely because he gave and gave without asking anything from her in return. He could never believe he deserved the love of such a pretty little thing – and there was no denying Lisbet was very pretty – and consequently he hadn't managed to either keep her love *or* gain her respect.

He deserved better and I wondered why he'd never realised it. Especially when you considered the number of other, equally lovely, girlfriends he'd had in the past. He was a very good-looking guy, with his own dark hair and rather nice white teeth, with a few years to go till he hit the big five-o.

I suddenly recalled the party Lisbet had thrown for his fortieth – and the way she had gone out of her way to humiliate him during the entire course of the evening. She'd always had a penchant for anything in trousers – the younger the better, and especially if they belonged to someone else – as had been proved over and over that night.

Sitting there with us, in the busy pub – when he thought no one was watching – he had this lost expression on his face – as if he couldn't quite grasp the way his life had fallen apart. It was a look that had an uncomfortable familiarity about it, because I knew it was the self-same way I had looked for weeks – no, months – after Rob had died. For all I knew, I still did sometimes.

'Thanks, Petie,' I smiled at him, surprising myself with the growing liking for a young man I had never had the time of day for previously. I realised with a start that now he wasn't that sullen, lank-haired individual I had become used to seeing slouch into the office, permanently on the scrounge, he wasn't that bad looking, either.

The slight tan he had gained from somewhere might have helped to clear up his acne, and also lightened his hair a shade, but it wouldn't have changed his whole demeanour.

That had to be down to him – and the mother who had finally forced him to stand on his own two feet.

'Roast beef all round, is it?' Adam rose to his feet

'Not for me,' I insisted, 'I'm having pork, and *I'm* paying, since I invited you all here.'

There was a flurry of protestations, the most surprising from Petie, but I was having none of it. I wasn't broke yet – despite the freeloading guests who seemed determined to eat me out of house and home – and I didn't often get the chance to treat my friends.

'I'll be deeply offended if you don't let me do this,' I fixed each of them in turn with a steely glare, 'but I'm quite happy for you to return the favour in the future.'

'Even me,' Petie queried with a grin.

'Oh, especially you,' I laughed. 'Being seen with you will upgrade my street cred no end.'

Adam walked to the bar with me, and before we parted to order the food and drinks at the designated areas, he warned, 'Careful – that lad fancies you, you know.'

I have to say he didn't sound too happy about it, but I thought it was hilarious. 'Don't be ridiculous,' I tittered, 'he's just a kid, and I'm an old lady – as I've been told already twice this week.'

'Hardly.'

He looked me up and down in a most un-Adam-like way. It made me feel suddenly self-conscious, and I wasn't sure if I liked it. It was one thing to be worrying a little bit about what people might think, that was only natural, but it was quite another thing to let folk start putting it into my head that I wasn't safe with a single one of the male population. I felt quite cross with Adam, and that wasn't like me at all.

'Don't be ridiculous,' I snapped, and stalked away to order our meals, leaving him to make his own way to the bar. He was confusing me with the likes of Lisbet, I reckoned, and he'd better learn, pretty damn quick, that we weren't all man-mad.

*

'I thought I'd make lasagne or something for Jason and me,' Bobbi greeted me the minute I arrived home, after what had turned out to be a most enjoyable – and extremely lengthy – lunch. 'I don't suppose … ' she began a shade pathetically.

Recognising a request for help might be coming, I jumped in first, 'Ooh, don't make any for me, then. I'm absolutely stuffed. I think I'll go and catch a film on TV and let my lunch go down. You carry on, though,' I invited, 'you know where everything is.'

'Oh, do you think Granny..?' Bobbi's tone was still hopeful.

'Probably won't be back for ages,' I said airily, trying not to get too hopeful about the fact that she obviously wasn't back already. Did it mean that she and Dad were talking, then – really talking? I thought it seemed like a good sign.

I tried to hide my irritation when I walked into the lounge to find Jason sprawled along the length of a sofa meant to seat four, with the pages of *my* Sunday papers scattered on every available surface and on the floor, too. The annoying buzz, buzz of Formula One cars careering round a track was emanating from a TV turned up to full volume.

'I think,' I hinted levelly, 'that Bobbi might need a hand in the kitchen.' I'd like to have suggested it might also be a good idea for Jason to remove his gelled head from my best cushions, but I kept that thought to myself – with an effort, eager to preserve the recent better feeling between us.

'Oh, she can manage.'

He didn't even remove his gaze from the small screen for a minute, and I felt my temper raise a notch, despite the mellowing effect of two glasses of Chardonnay.

'I actually think she might appreciate your help *and* your company,' my tone remained satisfyingly even, 'and,' I continued, 'there's a television in the kitchen.'

'The picture's too small.'

Christ, had I actually thought I'd seen a change in this lad? Had I honestly thought that treating him like a human being – a member of the family – was going to make a difference? Well, I supposed you had to live and learn. It was obviously time for me to make a stand.

'Well, I'm afraid it has to be the small screen or nothing, Jason,' my tone became flint-like – or at least, I thought so. 'For *once* I would like to watch my own television in my own lounge. I don't actually think that's too much to ask, do you?'

I finally had his attention, watched him wrestle with the desperate desire to argue, think better of it, and finally fling his trendily Timberland-shod feet to the floor with a hefty sigh. He threw me a look that would have blistered paint and took a step toward the door.

'Were you going to leave the papers all over the place like that?' I queried sweetly, a feeling of power sweeping over me in a tide of self-satisfaction at having got my own way so far. 'Only my mother might like the chance to follow the news – with the pages put back together in some semblance of order.'

I had pushed my luck, even I was sensible enough to recognise that, but having started I wasn't about to give an inch. I looked at the mess of newspaper pages, I looked at Jason, and prepared myself for an argument or at the very least for some mild abuse.

'As if it matters what order the pages are in,' he muttered, but to my immense relief he gathered them all up and began shuffling them back together as he made his way to the kitchen.

I could hear him complaining bitterly to Bobbi before he shut the kitchen door with more force than was strictly necessary, and then the sound of Formula One at full volume filtered its way through to me.

I didn't care, for the first time in a long time I had my beautiful chintzy lounge all to myself. I sat back to enjoy the film version of *Forever Amber*, one of my all-time favourite books, with a huge sigh of contentment and a great deal of satisfaction.

*

I must have fallen asleep for some time, and when I opened my eyes to find my father leaning over me, I thought I was dreaming.

'Dad?' I said, and then realising it actually was him, I threw out my arms and cried, 'Dad.'

I was on my feet in a minute and hugging him as if my life depended on it. My father was here, the one person in my life who remained constant. A little thinner, perhaps, but otherwise looking much the same as he usually did.

'I didn't mean to wake you,' he murmured, holding me tightly, 'You looked so peaceful, lying there. You won't have had much peace, of late, if what your mother tells me is true.'

I drew back, looked into his dear face, and asked, 'Have you sorted it out with her? Is she going home with you?'

My hopes soared at the thought of having one problem solved with no more effort required from me. They took a rapid nose-dive as my father shook his head. The look in his eyes broke my heart.

' 'Fraid not, love. Your mother is adamant that she needs time – to find herself – whatever that means.'

My mother's trouble was, I diagnosed privately and with real bitterness, she had too much time on her hands and spent too much of it watching the likes of Jerry Springer and Trisha on TV. She should try getting a life – a real life – and making herself useful. Getting a job in a charity shop would be a really good idea for someone who had never worked a full day in her whole life.

I was furiously angry. I felt that we should be sticking together and insisting that whatever she wanted to do was entirely up to her, but she should be prepared to do it in her own space and with her own money. I tried to say so, in a roundabout way.

'So, you've taken back the credit cards and cheque book, then, have you?'

My father looked shocked, 'Oh, I couldn't do that, love. I'm sure she'll come to her senses, given a little time. We'll just have to be patient.'

Patience was a commodity I was fast running out of. What on earth was it with these women, so spoiled and pampered that they didn't know what side their bread was buttered? What was it with these men, kind and thoroughly decent, who allowed themselves to be treated like doormats?

Perhaps the Jasons of this world had the right notion. 'Treat 'em mean and keep 'em keen,' certainly seemed to work for some. Perhaps Adam and Dad should take a leaf out of his book.

Instead of ranting, I turned to humour. 'Perhaps I could come and live back home with you, then,' I suggested, only half joking, 'and leave this lot to get on with it.'

Dad touched my face sympathetically, 'Getting you down, having a houseful, is it?'

I managed a smile, but part of me seriously felt like crying. 'You could say that. You'd think I'd be glad of the company, wouldn't you?'

'And what are you two up to?'

My mother's head appeared round the door, and watching my father's face light up just at the sight of her, I felt angry all over again. Didn't she know how lucky she was to have the love of such a good man? Didn't she realise he wouldn't live for ever? That one day she might not have the luxury of choosing to leave him, because one day he simply

111

wouldn't be there to leave? My mother had obviously learned nothing from Rob's sudden death.

'Talking about you, what else,' I retorted irritably.

'Oh, please don't be cross with me,' her tone was silly and almost childish, as she came across the room. Her comments were aimed at both my father and me, but all of her attention was on him. She knew how to wind him around her little finger – she always had. 'I just need a little time to …'

'Find yourself,' I finished for her, with much more than a trace of sarcasm in my tone. 'Whatever *that* means.'

'Don't be facetious, dear.' She gave me a look that would have shrivelled a lesser person. 'Your father understands, don't you, dear?'

I think that was when I made up my mind to take a stand. Never one to play games, myself, I couldn't understand this trait in other people. Why not be straight about what you felt and what you wanted? At least give the other person in your relationship a chance to understand what was going on in your head, and a choice regarding their own wishes.

Well, I was going to sleep on this – and then tackle the matter head on. I'd been behaving as if I *had* to put up with these selfish people who not only invaded my space, but dictated their own terms and made decisions without so much as a by-your-leave. Well, things were about to change.

CHAPTER 7

'NOT GOING TO WORK? What do you mean, you're not going to work?'

My mother stared at me in amazement. As well she might, I admitted to myself. It was almost unheard of for me to take a day off sick, never mind for me to take a day off for no apparent reason.

Well, it was done. I'd phoned Jo and the store manager to make my excuses and, as far as I was concerned, there was no going back. As distasteful as confrontation was to me, even I could see that the present state of affairs couldn't be allowed to drift on indefinitely.

There were several issues here, and they all needed to be addressed individually. This would need the involvement of all those concerned – and that included me.

Before I could even begin to explain any of this to my mother, the door opened and Bobbi wandered into the kitchen. She was rubbing her eyes sleepily, until she saw me.

'Oh, you're home.'

'Yes,' I agreed levelly, 'I'm home. It *is* my house and I am quite entitled to be here.'

'But, what about work? You *never* take time off work.'

'That's what I said,' my mother chipped in, and they looked at each other, nodding, and then they both stared at me.

God, I was really that predictable, wasn't I? I suddenly recalled from some time – way back – Rob saying I didn't have a spontaneous bone in my body. Had he been trying, in his thoughtful way, to tell me I was boring? Had he been right?

'I'm not going to work today,' I forced myself to concentrate on the matter in hand with difficulty, 'because there are one or two things that need to be discussed.'

There was an instant change in their demeanour. My mother and my daughter became equally defensive and began to talk over each other, neither of them making any real sense, from the bits I could make out. I just put up my hand, palm towards them – with authority, I felt – and to my surprise they both fell silent.

'Not here, and not now,' I asserted. 'I'm calling a meeting, in an hour, I want you both – and Jason – dressed appropriately, and ready to sit and discuss this present situation in something approaching an orderly manner.'

'But, Jason …' Bobbi began.

I could stab a guess at the rest. Jason didn't get up that early, or something similar that boiled down to Jason not liking to be told what to do. Well, that was tough. He could like it or he could lump it.

'I'm not asking,' I interrupted my daughter, 'I'm telling, and I expect you all to be there or suffer the consequences – and there will *be* consequences.'

Scenting trouble, they shuffled off, looking at each other again and then over their shoulders at me as they went.

In the hour I had given myself, I prepared a rarely used dining-room as if for a boardroom meeting. I didn't want us cosily seated round the kitchen table. This meeting was official and that was the way I wanted to conduct it.

I set out pads and pens on the freshly polished surface of my formally extended mahogany table, and paused in the doorway to take a satisfied look back, before going to dig out proper cups and saucers and make real coffee. I was even dressed as if for a meeting in a new navy skirt suit, purchased on my recent foray into town. Confidence might begin from inside, but knowing you looked the part on the outside, too, could bolster it up no end, as I knew only too well.

Eventually the delegates began to arrive, with punctuality I admitted to finding surprising, but pleasing nonetheless. They slunk into the room, one by one, and I poured coffee, offered biscuits, and indicated seats. For the first time in what felt like a very long time, I began to feel fully in control.

'What's it all about?' Bobbi asked, and I heard Jason add, 'Alfie,' under his breath, and snigger childishly at his own witticism.

A look was enough to quell his exuberance and remind him that this was serious. I was done with playing games, and the sooner they all understood that the better.

'It's about,' I began, using Bobbi's question as an opening, for want of finding a better one, 'the three of you living here …'

'But you already went into this, dear,' my mother pointed out kindly, 'and we all agreed to pull our weight – which even you must admit we have been doing – so …'

It was the 'even you' that I found infuriating. Elaine said it as if I were the hardest taskmaster, the most unreasonable of people, and that gave me the shot of steel I needed to deal with these family members as if they were strangers.

'So ...' I glared at her, 'doing *your share* of the housework and cooking does not even begin to deal with the several issues that are going on around here. I am going to ask each of you some straight questions – and I expect some straight answers.'

Jason sniggered again, and I turned on him in a flash. 'If that's the best we can expect from you, you can go and pack your bloody bags *right* now.'

There was a swift intake of breath from Elaine and Bobbi, and even Jason looked thoroughly taken aback.

'You can't ...' Bobbi began.

'I *can*,' I retorted, 'and I will, unless you all start taking me seriously. Now, more coffee, anyone, before we get down to business?'

I filled their cups without waiting for their assent and then, for a moment, I remained standing, just to show I was in command.

Turning to my mother, I began, 'Perhaps we could start with you.'

Elaine looked startled to say the least, and visibly paled under the carefully applied foundation. She was dressed as if she, too, were really attending a board meeting, smart in a silver grey trouser suit I had never seen before.

'Start with me, dear?' she quavered, 'In what way, start with me?'

'Start with you,' I began to explain as if she were a backward child, 'as in, what are your future plans? Where do you intend to live – and how?'

She looked horrified. 'What? Discuss my personal details in front of..?' she looked around the table and then back at me.

'They'll be talking about theirs in front of you,' I pointed out, 'and it does seem to me as if you are all in pretty much the same boat, in terms of lack of income, lack of direction, and lack of accommodation – because you must all realise you can't stay here indefinitely.'

The last remark was followed by a stunned silence and, finally, I knew I had all of their attention.

*

'What happened?' Jo was agog as we shared our usual lunchtime sandwich in the Harvester.

'Predictably, it all ended up as pretty much a shambles. There was a lot of shouting. Accusations that I was selfish, and a poor excuse for a mother – and a daughter – were levelled at me. I had all that room, so what possible reason could I have for practically throwing them all out onto the street.'

It was a relief to share the spiteful and, I felt, totally untrue remarks that had been levelled at me, with someone else. I badly needed someone to agree with *me*, and Jo of all people would surely see my side.

Jo choked on her prawn mayonnaise sandwich. 'What did you say?' she rasped, red in the face with coughing.

'I told them I was moving into something smaller because I couldn't afford the upkeep.'

Her eyes were streaming by this time, 'Is it true?' she managed in between gulping for air.

'What?' I asked.

'Well, both, really,' Jo mopped her eyes and her complexion began to return to a more normal colour. 'You can tell me to mind my own business, of course, but I thought Rob left you well provided for.'

'He did,' I began, ' the house is paid for, of course, and there was insurance money, but I'm not rich, Jo. I still have to work, and I really don't see why I should do so in order to keep three individuals who are making choices – about their lives admittedly, but which will also have an impact on mine – without the means to back them up.'

'So are you really going to move? I thought you had no intention of giving up the house you and Rob shared.'

'That's how I *did* feel,' I admitted, 'but times change and you have to move with them. Living in that house isn't going to bring Rob back and, to be honest, the thought of living in a little house just big enough for me begins to sound more and more appealing.'

Jo laughed out loud and applauded. In spite of the lunchtime chatter around us, people turned momentarily to stare, and neither of us really cared at all. It was an exhilarating feeling.

'Well done, Denise,' she was almost cheering. 'Welcome to the real world, where everyone looks out for number one.

We should all be taking responsibility for our own actions and no one else's.'

'You don't think that's really selfish?' I sounded anxious and I knew it.

Having spent most of my childhood trying to please my parents, and my adult life taking care of a husband and child, it really was foreign to my nature to adopt this very different approach. I was seeking a reassurance that was swiftly forthcoming.

'You?' Jo derided, 'You don't have a selfish bone in your body. Don't you dare let them try to convince you otherwise. Anyway, back to this meeting. What, if anything, was the outcome?'

'I let them escape,' I admitted ruefully, 'but only on the understanding that they came back to the next meeting with their future plans drawn up and ready for discussion.'

'So that's good, then, isn't it?' There was a query in Jo's tone, and she was looking at me intently.

'Well, it is,' I allowed slowly, 'but I promised to produce something of my own.'

'And?'

'And it's made me realise I haven't actually got any future plans. I haven't had a single one since Rob died, apart from getting through each day as best I can.'

Jo's tone was so gentle, it almost made me cry, as she asked, 'Then, don't you think it's about time you started thinking about making some?'

She was right, of course. Jo usually was. I couldn't just drift along for ever. I was still relatively young. I still had a future. If Rob's death had taught me anything, it was that life was not only precious, but fleeting, and definitely not to be taken for granted.

Did I still have hopes, dreams not realised? I supposed I used to have, before I got caught up with cosy domesticity – but that was all a very long time ago. Did I have any that were still relevant today? Because, if not, Jo had made me realise, I had better come up with some.

*

In the days following the road-rage incident I found myself, more often than not, popping into Peggy's café for a cup of tea and a chat on my way home. No one at home ever noticed if I was ten minutes or a quarter of an hour later home at night.

I found the visits slotted quite happily between the hustle and bustle of a busy working day, and the increasingly tense atmosphere between the residents at home.

It was obviously harder than my 'guests' had initially thought for them to come up with genuine reasons for their continuing existence in my house, because they kept putting off the follow-up meeting. The board and lodging issue hadn't been discussed at all at the original one, to my shame, but I did think I'd given them enough to mull over for the moment. I was quite prepared to bide my time.

Peg's Place was as plain and simple as its name and it became my haven of peace. Ever bright and cheerful with its floral-patterned tablecloths, the yellow laminated menus on display offered good, value-for-money, no-nonsense meals. There were pin-boards on display for the use of regular clientele and these were awash with business cards advertising various companies, tradesmen and local taxi firms.

The walls were dotted with a surprising number of celebrity photos, all nicely framed, and even personally signed in the majority of cases, by those who had come inside to take advantage of Peggy's hospitality. Two large frames given pride of place were completely filled with pictures of cast members, both past and present, of popular television soap operas. I was impressed because it could only be Peg's reputation for good, if simple food, that had brought those people in.

In the short time I'd been using the café I had come to know a few of the regular faces, and to enjoy the taste of Peggy's own particular brand of hospitality. The place appeared to have been thriving for years, though there was nothing pretentious about either the place itself or the fare it provided.

The basic menu consisted of all-day-breakfasts, cheese on toast and the like, together with sandwiches, toasted or otherwise. Thick china mugs of tea so strong the teaspoon virtually stood up unaided, and slabs of home-made date or cherry cake so moist that most of the fruit had settled deliciously at the bottom, also encouraged a varied clientele, besides the impressive list of celebrities, made up of local people, travelling salesmen, lorry drivers and tourists. It was also a hotbed of gossip, not only local, but national and international, too. It was all quite amazing, really, for such a small and unassuming place.

I discovered more about the Brankstone residents in those first few days, from Peggy and her aged assistant, Rose, than I had known in all the years I had lived among them. I enjoyed liquid refreshment daily in the shape of tea or coffee, but in fear of regaining the pounds I had shed, I quickly and reluctantly made the difficult decision to pass on the cake. However, I quite liked the new svelte me, and felt the sacrifice was worth it.

Not looking forward to the evening ahead, due to the fact that the meeting that had ended in disarray had finally been rescheduled and was now imminent, I pulled into an inviting gap, with the promise that it would be a really quick cup of tea tonight.

'Hi, Peggy.'

I felt cheered the minute I walked through the door into the fugue of steam and delicious smells I had come to associate with the place. To my astonishment, it wasn't Peggy behind the counter, but swathed in Peggy's all-enveloping white linen apron was a very good-looking guy who, at a rough guess, was somewhere in his late thirties or very early forties.

Though he seemed quite at home behind the counter, he *looked* totally out of place. Top chef at the London Savoy Hotel might have suited him, but with his expensively-cut dark hair and immaculately laundered shirt, the role of counter hand in a café-come-tea-shop did not.

I had asked, 'Who're you?' before I even thought about how rude that sounded, and I apologised at once.

'That's okay,' a tanned and obviously professionally manicured – being the widow of a builder I always noticed such things – hand came over the counter and I found my fingers taken into a firm grasp and myself smiling up into a pair of twinkling brown eyes. 'Peggy's son, Sam Robbins,' he explained. 'I take over whenever Mum's not quite the ticket.'

He looked at me almost expectantly, as if he thought I might have heard of him. Perhaps he thought Peggy would have mentioned him, though I was sure I would have remembered if she had.

'Denise Moffat,' I said briefly and went on to query anxiously, 'Peggy's sick?' amazed by how worried I actually was. After all, I barely knew the woman. The state of her health was really none of my business.

'It's her angina playing up again and Mum, being Mum, has been playing it down for all she's worth. Cup of tea, is it?'

'Please, and a slice of bread-pudding.' Oh, dear, the latter request had slipped out before I could stop it. I always did eat more when I was worried. 'How bad is she? If you don't mind me asking.'

His smile was quite obviously forced, as he told me, 'It's going to mean a little stay in hospital this time, I'm afraid. Just until they've done a few tests, stabilised her condition, and sorted her medication out.'

'I'm so sorry. How will you manage? What about your own commitments?'

*

'You should learn to keep your nose out of other folk's business, Denise,' I chided myself as I drove the remainder of the way home. 'As if you don't have enough problems, you have to go and take on everyone else's.'

I couldn't believe I'd volunteered my services in the café every Saturday until Peggy was on her feet again, but once the words were said there was no taking them back. Sam – that was the son's name, Sam – was so obviously grateful, too.

The fact that he was charming, and rather nice-looking – well, exceptionally so, if I was honest – really had nothing to do with it, I assured myself. I *had* become extremely fond of Peggy in the short time I'd known her, and my only motive was to be of help.

Having said that, I found that I was looking forward to Saturday with far more enthusiasm than I normally reserved for my job with the Cheapsmart chain, despite the fact I'd always enjoyed my responsible and varied role in personnel management.

As I pulled into the driveway, I decided not to say anything at home just yet about my newly acquired Saturday job. Best to keep everyone's attention focused on the matter in hand – and that included my own.

'I've set the table up,' Bobbi informed me the minute I stepped inside the door.

'Great.' I tried to sound enthusiastic, but I have to say it wasn't easy. 'We'll get down to it, then, as soon as we've eaten and cleared away.'

The liberally peppered steaks Jason produced for supper were a sure-fire way of ensuring our temperatures were already close to boiling, and heartburn was threatening, even before we took our seats around what he had sarcastically termed the 'boardroom table'.

'I suppose you want to start with me again,' my mother said brusquely, and it wasn't a question.

'Not necessarily,' I tried smiling at her, but she refused to smile back, and I had a feeling she wasn't going to forgive me easily for not trying harder to see whatever point it was she was trying to make.

She took a deep breath. 'I know you all probably think I'm being ridiculous – at my age – to want to get out there and have a life,' she paused and looked around the table.

I felt like saying there was no 'probably' about it, but instead I said mildly, 'There are other ways to "get out there and have a life", than to throw all those years of marriage – and a good marriage at that – out of the window.'

'I might have known you wouldn't understand.'

The 'poor me' tone really got to me. I had to nip my tongue between my teeth to prevent the retort that struggled to be aired.

'Try me – us,' I offered.

She looked at me, studying my expression, apparently to see if I was serious. I willed the other two to remain silent and, thankfully, they did.

'I've never felt as if I really amounted to anything,' she began, and three pairs of eyes rounded in startled surprise. I, for one, was sure I had never met anyone with more sense of her own worth than my mother.

'But …' I began, but she held up her hand.

'Let me finish, Denise,' she said.

125

I was silent. Well, I was shocked really, and part of me was quite apprehensive about what was coming.

'I've watched you, over the years, gaining reasonable grades at school, and then eventually returning to education when Bobbi was still quite young, to get your personnel management qualifications and develop a worthwhile career.' She paused for breath, before continuing, 'I've watched Bobbi do similar things at school and then go off to study a nursing programme at university.'

Except Bobbi *wasn't* studying at university presently, and seemed unlikely to resume where she'd left off. I guessed we were all thinking it, but no one said a word, and simply waited for my mother to continue.

'I've done nothing with my life. Left school at fourteen with no qualifications, and worked at the Co-op on the bacon counter until I married. It was the sort of thing most of us did in those days. It was expected that we would work in a shop or factory and contribute to the family income until we snaffled a husband. Opportunities to better yourself were rare in those days, except through a good marriage.'

I was totally lost by this time. Was my mother saying she'd married my father just because he was good husband material? That she now wanted to ditch him and become someone in her own right? At her age, and without a qualification to her name, did she realise it was going to be a long old haul? Bobbi and Jason, still mercifully quiet, were obviously as mystified as I was myself.

'I just feel this need to be independent. To do something that doesn't rely on someone else providing for me. Yes, I know I'm living here and relying on your support,' she had clearly accurately identified my thoughts on the matter, 'but I needed time to think about the best way to go about it. I knew that if I didn't do something – and soon – it would simply be too late.'

It was a very odd moment for me. Probably one of the very first times that I had really understood my mother and saw how it must have been for her – but there was something ...

'But, Mum,' I said, 'you didn't have to leave Dad to change things. He'd support you in whatever you chose to do.'

'Yeah,' amazingly Jason chipped in, 'and even I know it's never too late to gain qualifications, Mrs J. People go to Adult Education classes, to college, and even to university, at any age.'

'There were some quite old people on my course,' Bobbi offered, and I just stopped myself in time from wondering out loud if they, at least, were still on it, as she continued, 'They seemed to do very well, often with a young family at home, and their husbands were mostly very supportive.'

Elaine looked thoroughly taken aback at our interest – and probably by encouragement she obviously hadn't been expecting.

'I've got a prospectus somewhere,' Bobbi recalled, 'I'll get it out for you, and we can send for information from the college and adult education, get some idea of what's on offer.'

This was obviously all too much for my mother, who turned a bit tearful, and looking round the table, she managed a watery smile, 'You don't think it's too late, and I'm just being silly then.'

'Of course you're not being silly, and it's never too late to study,' I told her seriously, 'but you should have talked this over with Dad. Surely you don't want to gain these qualifications at the expense of your marriage, do you?'

Elaine lifted her chin, 'I had to make him – and you – see that I was serious about this. Harry would have just thrown money at me. Told me to take myself shopping, offered another holiday to distract me, or got the decorators in. He's happy with the way things are – were – you see.'

'Perhaps now … ' Bobbi began.

My mother shook her head, 'I have to prove a point and to do that, I need to get a job as soon as I can,' she said, and three jaws hit the table simultaneously.

CHAPTER 8

'WELL, I DON'T KNOW HOW YOU CAN tear yourself away from home to come to work,' Jo marvelled, shaking her head and making the soft grey curls bounce. 'It's all happening at your house, isn't it?'

'It might seem that way,' I muttered, 'but it's like wading though treacle. Talk about a slow process. That's only my mother sorted, and only her aims and ambitions have been aired. There's still the situation with my dad. Oh, I can sort of see her point, now. He *is* quite set in his ways, but leaving him was a bit of a drastic move. I can't seem to make Mum see that by the time she's ready to go back home, and I'm sure she will be sooner or later, he might not want her there.'

Jo looked taken aback. 'Oh, but surely …'

I knew what she was going to say. That my dad doted on my mum, etc, etc, and I jumped in quickly to remind her, 'Good men are in short supply. You should know that, of all people. Leave him on his own too long – and who knows what might happen. I've got a bad feeling about this. There are some very attractive older women on the prowl at that golf club of his. Before you know it one of them will have stepped into my mother's elegant high-heeled shoes and then she'll find out what it really means to live alone.'

'Mmm, I get your point,' Jo mused, adding with a little half-smile, 'I always quite liked your dad myself.'

'Why, Josephine Farrell, what on earth are you saying?' I laughed lightly but, actually, I didn't find it very funny at all, because Jo had just proved my point. I suddenly knew without a doubt that, fond as I was of her, I didn't want Jo or even someone like her trying to take my mother's place. An irritating mother Elaine might be at times, but she was still mine.

*

Saturday morning saw me turning up at Peg's Place bright and early – accompanied by my mother. Well, she said she needed a job, Sam had said he needed help, and a word to him over the phone had sorted them both out.

'Just tell us what needs doing,' I told him when we presented ourselves in the kitchen behind the café, gowned up in crisp white overalls and, in my case, with hair tied back.

'I don't know where to start,' he admitted. 'I really appreciate your help, but I'm used to managing with just Rose and providing the basics for the few days which is all Mum's ever been off for. This looks like a longer job, and Rose has also decided to go off sick – probably in sympathy – so it will take a bit more organising. I'm also starting to run out of stuff, so a visit to the cash and carry looks like a necessity.'

'Look, Mum's a whizz in the kitchen,' I offered, and watching her face brighten, wondered how often any of us had told her that. 'Why don't you two work together there? You could make a bit of an inventory, see what's needed. I think I can manage at the counter if you give me a quick run though of what's what. I see you've got the coffee machine filled, and a good selection of sandwiches and rolls already on offer. Do these buns and scones need buttering?'

Luckily, as Sam pointed out, Saturdays were slower starting than weekdays, so I was broken in relatively gently before the rush. Elaine was amazing, whipping up egg and bacon, pasty and chips, scrambled eggs on toast, all to order, and all without working up a sweat or putting a hair of her liberally lacquered head out of place.

It was easy to see she was in her element, whereas I got hot and bothered making something as simple as a sandwich, being more used to dealing with paperwork. I could talk to the customers easily enough. I just wasn't very good at feeding them.

At the end of the day, Mum looked as if she had been working there all of her life, and was as fresh as when she'd started. All I had really learned was that cheese and pickle on wholemeal was the most popular sandwich, that it wasn't a good idea to wear high heels when you were on your feet all day, and that anything but underwear worn beneath the cotton overall was a bad idea considering the heat given off by all the appliances behind the counter. We got a wage packet apiece, and it was obvious to both Sam and I that my mother had more than earned hers.

'I'd love to offer you a permanent job if you were interested,' Sam told her in all seriousness, 'but, of course, that would be up to my mother. If you would agree to staying on and working with me on a daily basis, at least until she comes back, it would definitely be the answer to my prayers.'

Elaine positively glowed and, after accepting, she was quick to point out, 'I hope you don't mind me saying, but I did notice you were getting low on cake. Now, I know I don't have the benefit of your mother's tried and tested recipes, but I could whip up a few of my own basics tomorrow to tide you over the next few days. Denise will vouch for my fruit cake, and my carrot cake is ... '

'Stop,' Sam laughed and held a hand up. 'Take it from me, Elaine, I'll be more than grateful for anything you can come up with, but I really can't have you working on a Sunday.'

'I'd enjoy it,' she insisted and her enthusiastic tone ensured neither of us disbelieved her. 'I'll use Denise's kitchen, if she has no objection. I can make up a list of the things I'll need and perhaps you could drop the ingredients round, since we walked here this morning.'

*

Neither of us had the heart, after the short walk home, to tell Bobbi and Jason that the meal they were so obviously proud of having waiting on the table for us was the last thing we needed.

Elaine and I exchanged despairing glances, regretting Sam's generosity with the café's fare. I thought I'd burst wide open if I ate another thing, but dutifully sat down to sausage and mash with lashings of onion gravy.

'It's lovely, Bobbi. Isn't it, Mum?' I turned to my mother, who managed a nod as she forced another mouthful down.

'We cleaned the house, too,' Bobbi was quick to point out. 'Didn't we, Jase? Even the bathroom.'

'You've done a wonderful job,' I enthused, continuing, 'and it's so nice to come home to a delicious hot meal.' I then hurried on, before they could get the impression they were completely off the hook, 'If you've no plans for tonight, I thought we'd continue that talk.'

Bobbi and Jason exchanged a look, before nodding agreement, but without any real show of enthusiasm.

The phone ringing was a welcome diversion, especially when Jason, who took the call, returned to say, 'It's for you,' with a nod in my direction, going on to elaborate, 'some guy called Peter Farrell. I left the phone in the hall in case you wanted to be private.'

I expected a knowing look, or at the least a smirk with the information, and was pleasantly surprised when I got neither.

'Doesn't mean a thing to me,' I shrugged, and was halfway to the phone before the penny dropped. 'Petie,' I said into the receiver, 'is that you?'

'Uhuh,' he agreed.

'Nothing wrong with your Mum, is there?' It was the only reason I could come up with for him to be ringing me. He'd certainly never done such a thing before.

'No, nothing like that,' he said, sounding like he was smiling. 'I remembered you saying you liked eighties music and I just happen to have tickets for a show at the Winter Gardens. Mum won't go, I did ask her, but she's more into the sounds of the sixties.'

'Oh.' To say I was taken aback was an understatement, 'Well that's really kind of you.'

'I know it is,' he sounded remarkably chirpy. 'So you'll come then? It's two weeks today.'

'Er,' I couldn't actually think of a good reason to say no, and to be honest I didn't really want to. I *did* like eighties music and it *was* kind of him to think of me, when there must have been dozens of people he could have taken instead. 'I'd like that.'

'Good, that's a date then. I'll pick you up at seven-thirty – give us chance to have a drink first.'

Hardly a date, I thought as I put the phone down, but it just might be fun. It would certainly be different.

'Do you want the remainder of your meal heated up? It won't be very appetising stone cold.' Jason was the only one still in the kitchen, apparently making cups of tea for everyone. I didn't know how to say I didn't want it at all, and could have blessed his healthy appetite when he went on a shade hopefully, 'You *do* want it? Only, if you don't …'

'You have it,' I threw over my shoulder, as the phone rang for a second time and I went to answer it, blessing Petie's timing for saving me from a painful bout of indigestion, without having to offend anyone.

'You don't fancy coming to a wedding with me, do you?' It was Adam on the line and my heart lifted at the sound of his voice, especially because he sounded surprisingly cheerful. His tone was decidedly persuasive, as he continued, 'Only, I can't get out of it – and I really don't want to go alone. Please say yes.'

I felt for him – I really did – but a wedding. 'Oh, Adam, I don't …' I began, 'The last wedding I went to was …'

'With Rob,' he finished the sentence for me. 'I was there, too – remember?'

Of course he was. He was Rob's best friend and they had mostly the same friends, too. It had been the four of us, Rob, Adam, Lisbet and me. I could see us now, all dressed up in our finery. It had been beautiful and sunny, and Lisbet being on her best behaviour for once had pretty much ensured the success of the day.

'Please say you'll come,' Adam wheedled. 'You know you always say the first time for anything is the worst, and this will get the wedding situation out of the way. You told me avoiding situations doesn't help you to move on.'

'Adam Mitchell, are you quoting my own sentiments back at me?' I demanded, recognising my own words. 'That's coercion.'

'I don't feel any better about going alone than you would,' he reminded me, obviously quite prepared to use emotional blackmail to get his own way. 'I thought if we did it this time together, we would both find it easier another time.'

Funny that, but I'd never given any thought to it being as hard for a man alone to socialise, as it was for a woman. Admittedly, a man could walk into a pub, and even go to the bar with more confidence than a woman on her own ever could, but in a world geared towards coupledom, it was never going to be easy for either sex. You might as well wear a bumper sticker on your head stating, 'Yes, I *am* on my own. No, I *don't* have a partner.' It was almost as if you had to apologise for it.

Adam was still talking, and I cut across what he was saying to tell him, laughing, 'Okay, you don't have to go on. I'll do it. I'll go with you.'

'You will,' the relief in his tone made me want to smile and cry all at the same time. 'You'll come. Oh, Dee, that's great. You won't regret it – we'll have a great time, I promise.'

'Just as long as you're suitably grateful,' I laughed, liking the use of the shortened name he had given to me years ago that was peculiar only to him, '*and* promise to organise the buttonholes for us both. When is it anyway?'

I suddenly knew what he was going to say, and my heart sank to my aching stockinged feet, as I heard him confirm, 'It's two weeks today.'

I know I should have just told him I was already committed but, somehow, I just couldn't bring myself to do it. He'd been hurt enough by that wife of his already. Adam really didn't need me to reject him as well – because I was sure that was how he would see it, no matter how carefully I explained.

'I'd love to go,' I heard myself saying. 'What time is the wedding?'

I'd crossed my fingers for a morning slot at the church, hoping an afternoon reception would allow me – by some miracle – to manage both, but wasn't even surprised when Adam said, 'Quite late, really, four o'clock. At least it will give you plenty of time to get ready. Not that you need much time to look absolutely great,' he added hastily, 'That's not what I ...'

'Of course you didn't, Adam,' I soothed, wondering how many times he'd had his head torn off for making a similar remark to the gorgeous Lisbet, who did need hours of pampering to look her – admittedly stunning – self. 'I think we've been friends long enough for you not to feel it necessary to study your words for fear of upsetting me, don't you?'

'Mmm, sorry.'

'Or to have to constantly apologise.'

Adam laughed, and it was nice to hear him. He'd had precious little to laugh about lately – well, for quite some considerable time, actually. I couldn't let him down over this wedding, I just couldn't.

We spoke for a little bit longer. I had no idea what about because my mind was buzzing like a wasp trapped in a jam-jar, looking for a way out of the predicament I had allowed myself to get into.

I came off the phone no wiser. The thought of phoning Petie to cancel, after his kindness in inviting this widowed friend of his mother to a concert, when it was probably the very last way he'd really choose to spend an evening, made me feel awful.

He might feel only relief, but that wasn't the point. It was like throwing a gift back in his face – and I couldn't bring myself to do it. Well, I would have to do something eventually, that was for sure, but for the time being I decided to do what I usually did – absolutely nothing at all – and hope the situation would, somehow, resolve itself.

To my surprise the kitchen was deserted and the teapot missing. The lounge was empty, the TV silent when I wandered in there. Where had they all disappeared?

'In here,' my mother's voice guided me to the dining-room, to find Elaine, Bobbi and Jason – and a tray of tea and biscuits – all ready to pick up where the last discussion had left off.

'Oh,' I didn't try to hide my surprise. I hadn't expected anything like this much enthusiasm. 'You're all a bit eager, but you don't really have to feel obliged to sit in, Mum,' I told her. 'You've made a start with the job at the café.' I suddenly had a thought, and felt fragile hope begin to blossom. 'Unless you wanted to talk about going home to Dad.'

The cool shake of her head soon dispelled that little theory and I sighed inwardly, wondering why on earth *everything* couldn't just go back to the way it had been. Reality quickly stepped in when I realised that for that to happen, Rob would need to walk through the door, and even I knew that wasn't about to happen.

I blinked quickly, and forced my attention back to the group, telling myself fiercely I should just be grateful for their apparent co-operation.

'Granny still wants some help with choosing a course of study,' Bobbi pointed out, 'and, anyway, we sat in on her plans, so we thought it only fair she should sit in to hear ours, didn't we, Jase?'

'Yeah,' he agreed quite amiably, and then turned his whole attention to dunking a chocolate digestive.

The biscuit was almost completely immersed, and then swiftly transferred to his mouth before it disintegrated. I don't know who was more relieved when he achieved the intended result without mishap.

'It's a bit early for the autumn adult education brochures, but they might run a few courses during the summer – or at least that's what Sam said,' my mother confided happily.

Elaine showing an enthusiasm for something other than shopping was a real surprise. Apparently, she'd even been talking about it at the café – and to someone who barely knew her. I wouldn't have wanted to spoil that eagerness, but why on earth she couldn't share those plans with the husband who loved her was beyond me.

'Okay, so Granny's plan of action is to continue at the cafe as long as Sam needs her, and in the meantime we can grab any info we see available on summer courses around the area. I'd think the library would be the best place for those, wouldn't you? Perhaps you and Jason could have a look, when you do the grocery shop on Monday. The supermarket is practically next door.'

I met the indignant looks squarely. 'We have to eat, and you don't have any other plans, do you?'

'Actually, we do.' Bobbi had evidently been designated as the spokesperson.

'Oh?' came from my mother and me simultaneously.

'We've been talking ...' Bobbi began, 'Haven't we, Jase?'

He nodded, and my mind rushed into overdrive. I could hear myself silently pleading, Please, Rob, please make it be that she's seen the sense of continuing with her course – even if she transfers to a uni in this area. Please make Jason see the intelligence of such an action, and to understand that life isn't all about taking the easy ride, but about working for the future you want.

My late husband, bless his heart, obviously didn't hear a word I said. I was forced to recall times in the past when the footie had often taken priority over me, and I'd found that I was talking to myself. I supposed that wherever Rob was, he still had other priorities.

I almost envied him, as I listened to Bobbi say, in all seriousness, 'First we're going to find a flat and set up home together.'

Before I could ask how they intended to do that with no money for a deposit, and how they expected to live with no jobs, she continued breezily, 'and then we're going to try for a baby before I'm too old to conceive, aren't we, Jase? We read this article in the paper saying my age is the best time to get pregnant.'

All thoughts of Adam, Petie and the double booking went flying out of the window. This wasn't only serious, this was a potential disaster. A baby would tie Bobbi and Jason together permanently, it would also tie them to a future on the breadline as they struggled to raise a family at best on Jason's unskilled wages or at worst on income support.

Over the past weeks of having Jason live in my house, I had often seen a side to him that was really quite likeable. I'd been careful, up to a point, not to interfere in case I not only pushed them together even more, but drove Bobbi away from me. The stand-back-and-do-nothing Denise Moffat approach to life was rather hit and miss when it came to getting the result I really wanted, as I was beginning to find to my cost.

I supposed I'd been hoping that either they would get tired of each other – as often happened with a youthful and lustful love – or that Jason would wake up and smell the roses, get himself a life and encourage Bobbi to do the same. I really had no objection to them living a sensible life together – but this ... Well ...

'A baby..?' My mother and I must have sounded like a pair of parrots, but I totally failed to find the humour in that.

'Well, you know it's been in all the papers, and on the telly, about these career women who were infertile by the time they got around to trying for a family.'

'But you're only eighteen, Bobbi,' I pointed out, cursing those bloody newspapers that Jason – with far too much time on his hands – had obviously read from cover to cover and then, with great glee, spoon-fed certain of the contents to my gullible daughter.

'I'm old enough to know what I want,' she insisted stubbornly. 'What *we* want.' She reached for Jason's hand and he allowed her to take it, a familiar smirk on his face.

I was beginning to recognise that smirk. It seemed to appear whenever he had managed to get one over on me. In that moment I hated the sneering little bastard with his liberally gelled hair, his spots and his hold over my precious daughter. Looking into his face I was suddenly transported back years, and a glance in my mother's direction showed me that she, too, was remembering.

His name was Gerry. He, too, spent much of his time tinkering with engines, though his interest was in motorbikes as opposed to the cars that were Jason's passion, but there the similarity ended – apart, of course, from his aversion to work.

Gerry was tall, at least six foot, with curly hair and the beard that made him a man in my eyes, despite the fact that I was no more than a schoolgirl when we started dating each other, and he was barely eighteen himself.

I was sleeping with Gerry long before I reached the legal age of consent, and under his influence I left school with only a smattering of qualifications to my name.

Had things turned out otherwise than they did, I may have been with him still, living on the breadline, putting up with his affairs. It was the vivid memory of how one wrong move could send things out of control that had always made me tread softly where Bobbi and Jason were concerned.

Seeing my daughter apparently intent on repeating every mistake I had ever made, almost made me throw every one of my good intentions out of the window and totally lose it with the pair of them.

In my mind's eye I was already on my feet, hands jammed flat onto the table, leaning forward until my furious face was almost nose to nose with Jason's.

In my mind I was screaming abuse into his face, using words I hadn't even realised I knew. Telling him to get out of my house, to keep his filthy, disgusting hands away from my precious daughter, to get out of our lives and live with the little tart he had cheerfully cheated on my daughter with.

The 'friend' with the morals of an alley cat, who would have been his perfect match.

In my mind I had turned into my own mother, all those years ago.

CHAPTER 9

I DIDN'T KNOW HOW I DID IT, but somehow I remained totally calm and grimly determined not to repeat my mother's mistake. Interfering, or even showing disapproval now would almost certainly push Bobbi into the self-same course of action I had rushed headlong into years before. It would have been playing right into Jason's hands and was the very last thing I wanted.

I reminded myself – quite forcefully – that we had had this conversation, or one quite like it, the day Jason had moved in. Bobbi wasn't pregnant *yet* – or at least I had to hope against hope that she wasn't – and so there was still time to try and talk some sense into the pair of them.

Alienating either of them would have accomplished nothing, particularly in Jason's case. He had nothing to lose, obviously held the balance of power in that relationship, and would, therefore, dictate how and when things would happen.

'Well, I can't say I wouldn't have preferred you to wait until you were at least a little bit older,' I heard myself say, glaring at my mother, who appeared to be getting ready to voice an opinion she wasn't entitled to air.

Let me do this my way or accept the consequences, my look dared her. I was sure she knew what that meant, and was quite certain when she blanched and looked away.

'But,' I continued, 'I *can* see your point.'

'You can?' If Bobbi was surprised by my reaction, Jason looked totally taken aback.

Ha, not quite the reaction you were expecting, I wanted to say. I had difficulty hiding a smile, and had to remind myself grimly that this wasn't really at all funny.

'See,' Bobbi turned to Jason, looking inordinately pleased, 'I told you Mum would understand.'

'Of course, you'll want to look for that place of your own first.' I calmly poured fresh tea for everyone, hoping the tremor in my hands wasn't noticeable. 'There's not really room for a baby here, even if I decided to stay in the house, which seems fairly unlikely. The two of you in one small bedroom is one thing – having a baby in there, too, is entirely another. It would hardly be ideal for you to try and bring up a baby in those sort of cramped conditions – and certainly not fair on Jason to expect him live permanently with his mother-in-law. In fact it would probably be a recipe for disaster. Oh, no, I can quite see that you will need your own space.'

I was so grateful to Petie – of all people – at that moment, for having so recently pointed out to me that his Mum making him take responsibility for his actions – and probably trying, as I was doing with these two, to make it seem like his own idea – had been the beginning of the change in him.

Jason spoke up then. As well he might, I thought savagely, when he could see his nicely laid plans, and all the responsibility for them, placed firmly back in his lap.

'Well, we did think you might like having your grand-child around.'

That was clever, I admitted, recognising he was playing what he saw as his trump card. I'd love to have a grandchild around – one day – but I wasn't ready to be a grandmother yet. I didn't think my daughter was anywhere near ready to be a mother, either, and that had quite a lot of bearing on the matter – and on my reaction.

'It would be lovely,' I said, allowing a wistful smile to creep onto my face, and almost laughing at the confused expression on my mother's. 'But there's still the question of space.'

'Granny won't always be here,' Bobbi pointed out quickly, proving the matter had already been under discussion.

'I ... ' Elaine began, obviously indignant about having her future plans made for her.

'And nor will I.' I was determined to get in first. 'Remember, I talked about selling up. This is quite a big house to keep up, and I wasn't left well off.' I wasn't left badly off, either, but I wasn't about to get into a debate about my finances, which had nothing to do with any of them. 'It would be the sensible thing to sell up and move into something smaller, therefore cheaper, and also easier to manage. I don't want to be worrying about bills in my old age.'

'But that's how we could help out,' Jason said urgently. He was evidently upset at seeing all his carefully laid plans slipping away, I thought with great satisfaction, as he continued, not very convincingly, 'We'd contribute towards the bills and I can do maintenance around the house.'

Give him his due, he was trying hard, but he really wasn't stupid. Jason was wasting his breath, knowing as well as I did that his track record spoke for itself. He was an idle layabout with no notable skills. If he had any intelligence at all, and I thought he did – despite evidence to the contrary – he'd know I could see myself being taken for a complete ride for years to come.

Envisaging myself saddled with two feckless, not to mention jobless, youngsters, and possibly hordes of grandchildren that I would have to make myself responsible for, forced me to take the necessary stand.

'Oh, I couldn't let you do that,' I insisted. 'If I've learned one thing from being on my own for the past year, it's that we all have to take responsibility for ourselves and for our happiness. I shall manage very well alone, and leave all of you – including my mother – free to move on in whichever direction you choose.'

'But we don't have any money until Jason gets a job,' Bobbi wailed, finally beginning to see the real picture, and recognise the remote chance of their harebrained approach to family planning ever coming to fruition. Then she brightened perceptibly, and my heart sank as she said, 'There's the money Dad left to me, though, isn't there?'

'Oh, dear, that's all tied up in trust until you're twenty-one.' I recalled with relief what Bobbi should already know perfectly well, since the solicitor had explained it most carefully to her. 'Your Dad was very specific in his instructions and they are to be followed to the letter. If you are really determined to leave uni for good, even your allowance stops.'

I had forgotten all about that little clause right up until that very moment, and in that moment Rob was a hero – and even a saint – in my eyes. He'd obviously known his daughter a whole lot better than I suspected when he dotted all those i's and crossed all those t's so carefully in the solicitor's office all that time ago. I had thought him pernickety at the time, and now I humbly apologised under my breath for not recognising that he knew exactly what he was doing.

'But surely that would all change if Bobbi had a baby? Her Dad would want to make provision for his grandchild.' Jason again played what he saw as his trump card.

Talk about using emotional blackmail, I thought, acknowledging the deep anger I felt. Fancy using a child, not even conceived yet, never mind born, to pull first at my heart and purse-strings and then worse, trying to reach beyond the grave to Rob's.

'Since Bobbi planned to go into nurse training – from a very early age – a child wouldn't have been part of any plan she discussed with us. If the thought of a child had occurred to Rob, I guess he would have felt – as I do – that the baby's father would be ready and willing to provide for him or her.'

I watched a slow flush spread across Jason's face and thought, with real spite, Ha, you little bastard, finally beginning to get the message, aren't you?

*

Later, in my room, I couldn't even remember how the 'meeting' had ended. I was exhausted, both emotionally and physically and yet, despite taking myself off to bed early, I couldn't sleep. I was sitting up in bed staring, unseeing, at a magazine, when there was a tentative tap and my mother put her head round the door. Unlike me, she was still fully clothed and, apparently, as fresh as a daisy.

'What?' I didn't try to hide my annoyance, and didn't even care when she visibly shrank back at my sharp tone.

'I'm sorry to bother you, dear.'

'Then, why do it?'

My tone had involuntarily softened from abrupt to merely weary and, encouraged, Elaine came right in and closed the door behind her. When she sat on the side of the bed, obviously geared up for a heart to heart, I deeply regretted not telling her immediately and in no uncertain terms to go away.

'I couldn't believe the cheek of it … ' she began indignantly, preparing to launch into a scathing attack on Bobbi, Jason and their foolhardy plans for the future.

'I know what you're going to say,' I interrupted, 'and I don't want to hear about it. I'm certainly not prepared to discuss it with you.'

'Oh.'

'I've heard all of your plans now. What I never did hear, from any of you, was an apology for bringing them to my door and dumping them into my lap without so much as a by-your-leave.'

'I didn't …'

'I hope you're not going to say you didn't do any such thing.' I sat up as straight as the bed would allow. 'Are you going to say that you turning up here, complete with bag and baggage, gave me a choice? Not only that, but it gave Dad the totally wrong impression and allowed him to think I encouraged you.'

'Oh, but I ...'

'Didn't think,' my tone was rising. 'That's the trouble with all of you. You haven't thought – except about yourselves and your own precious plans. What about mine?'

Elaine was stunned into remaining silent, which I took full advantage of.

'You think I don't deserve a future – a life – because my husband died, is that it?' I demanded. 'I watched a future with *my* man die with Rob,' I went on savagely, 'and then had to watch *you* throw *yours* away on a whim, and break the heart of a good man, when you could have had it all just by involving him in your plans.

'I'm watching Bobbi throw her life away on an idle good-for-nothing, who sees me and my daughter as a ticket to an easy life and, somehow – *somehow* – you've all reached the impression that you're doing me a favour – a bloody *favour* – by descending on me and taking over my life and my home.

'You're *all* missing the point.' I felt like a volcano that, once it had begun to erupt, couldn't stop belching fire and molten lava, and wouldn't until it was all done.

'*I* have a future, too. I realise it's taken me a bit of time to see that, but I do still have a future. I don't know exactly how it will turn out yet. It will obviously be very different, because

150

Rob can no longer be part of it. Anything might happen, I *may* even meet someone else.'

I met my mother's shocked look straight on, 'Is it so hard to believe that I might? Mum, I'm a *single* woman. That status is not from choice, the decision was taken from me, but it *is* a fact.

'I don't plan to hold my breath or put my life on hold until, or indeed *if*, I do meet someone, but neither do I discount the fact that I might. You might not need love in your life, Mum – someone of your own to care what happens to you – but I think that I do and I think that I still have a lot to give, myself.' I gave her a very hard look before continuing, 'And, if I were you, I wouldn't discount the fact that Dad might very well be feeling the same.'

Elaine looked surprised and even a bit shocked. I felt as if I'd managed to hit a nerve and I was pleased about it. The thought of my father wanting anyone else had obviously never occurred to her. She was far too complacent about the situation, in my opinion. Too busy thinking of herself and what she wanted, to see that Dad might not put his life on hold until she came to her senses, saw what she was throwing away, and recognised that she really could have it all – with him.

'Anyway,' I continued, aware that Bobbi had come to stand in the doorway and was listening in amazement, 'aside from the fact that I may or may not decide to accept a date or two – if I'm lucky enough to be asked – I do intend to put my life back together. Others have done it before me, probably a piece at a time, a bit like making up a jigsaw. I know it won't

– can't – be the same, but though the picture may be different, it doesn't mean it can't be enjoyed and have meaning still.

'I've had a year on my own. A year to grieve for what might have been. A year to learn to accept what can't be changed, however much I might wish it could be otherwise. I'm not the first person this has happened to, I know I won't be the last, and I suppose we all have to learn to move on or sit trapped in the past until our life, too, is over.

'Life is a gift, isn't it? It was never meant to be thrown away or wasted on regrets.' I finally paused for breath.

'Is that supposed to be a dig at me?' Bobbi came right into the room and stood, hands on enviable slim hips, bare toes curling into the carpet, to glare at me.

'Hard as this might be for you to believe,' I told her tiredly, 'my whole life *doesn't* revolve around you. At this present moment I am talking about me, and my own situation, but perhaps you have something to say about that, too. Perhaps you don't think I have a right to a life of my own now that Daddy is gone.'

'That's a horrible thing to say,' she was indignant, and probably had every right to be. In truth, I did think she would back any plans I had to take charge of my life – as long as they didn't affect her very specific plans for her own life with Jason.

Jason's influence had changed her from the generous-spirited, clear-minded girl she had always been, and now it was all about pleasing him – doing what he wanted – whatever impact that had on her own long-held plans. I really didn't have any problem with him coming first in her life – if I thought it was a position he deserved, *and* if I thought she came anywhere near to first in his.

'I think,' I said, 'that we *all* have the right to make our own decisions, but I also think that it's too much for you to expect me to put my life on hold any longer while you make choices about your own.

'Mum, be free and single, if you think that's what you want, but do it in a way that doesn't compromise me. Find a place of your own, and take charge of your life. I won't be seen to be taking sides any longer. I'm going to talk to Dad and tell him straight that what you get up to has absolutely nothing to do with me – and that it never did have.'

'Well.' Elaine looked deeply affronted, but I quickly turned my attention to Bobbi.

'You are barely eighteen years old,' I told her, 'You can have a future and a good career and still have plenty of time left for a family, but – ' I held up my hand as she went to interrupt, determined to have my say, 'if you're bound and determined to have a baby now, then that should be *your* decision, and yours alone, since you'll be the one taking on most of the responsibility for it. Just make sure that it is – and that you're not compromising your happiness, to give someone else what *they* think they want right now.'

'I don't know what you mean,' she began.

'I think you do,' I said, meeting her indignant gaze full on and getting absolutely no satisfaction from the deep flush that flooded her lovely face, 'but I also think you will make your own choices and decisions without any help from me. I know that I did as I pleased when I was your age. Granny can vouch for that.'

Had I said too much, or not enough? My mother looked startled, and not a little afraid of the threat of a shameful family skeleton leaping out of a long-locked cupboard. I simply thought that perhaps it was time to open the door, but the moment passed when Jason issued what could almost be called a summons from the bedroom he and Bobbi shared, and with a sheepish glance in my direction she went to him.

'Don't say anything,' I ordered my mother as soon as she opened her mouth to speak. 'Just don't say anything. I know you have your version of events – and I have mine – it's pointless to argue about rights and wrongs after all this time. Just trust me to deal with this situation with Bobbi and Jason in my own way and using my own experience. You had your chance years ago.'

Elaine paled significantly, recognising a dig that had been a long time coming, but she simply said, quite mildly, 'Have it your way, Denise, I just hope you know what you're doing. Goodnight.'

The door closed behind her softly, and then I was alone with thoughts and memories I had refused to face for so many years, I had all but forgotten them. A few more and I would probably have managed to convince myself none of it had ever happened.

I didn't have to wait for the sounds of Bobbi and Jason's enthusiastic love-making to filter through the walls, to be reminded of how it had been for me and Gerry. At fifteen years old I had been ripe for his picking – and for his love-making. He knew all the right things to say and do to tempt me into his arms and into his bed. I just thought I was lucky to be the object of his attention.

I guessed we had both been lucky that Gerry's best efforts had failed to get me pregnant – until I was seventeen years old and beginning to recognise that there was actually more to life than Gerry. I suppose you would call that the 'sod's law,' we hear so much about.

I always thought, afterwards, that Gerry had recognised the fact that I was growing away from him and his influence, and that this had a bearing on his later treatment of me. Perhaps it was a form of punishment for daring to lose interest in him.

In spite of my doubts, I had allowed Gerry to persuade me that the baby was the best thing that could have happened, and together we had stood, defiant, to break the news to my parents.

They had practically recoiled in horror – and who could blame them. We had made such a good job of hiding our relationship that they were barely aware that I even *knew* someone like Gerry, let alone that I'd been sleeping with him.

'Pregnant?' they demanded, following that with, 'How long has this been going on?' from my mother, and a growing realisation evident in my father's eyes that the smirking man standing before him was responsible, not only for stealing his daughter's innocence, but possibly also for the poorer grades throughout the latter years of my schooling.

If I had doubts in that moment, and I did – very serious doubts about the wisdom and consequences of my actions – I refused to let them show. This was what I wanted, I insisted, what we both wanted.

I think my father would have remained calm, recognising the wisdom of allowing time to soften this blow and to dictate the best course of action. Unfortunately, the matter was taken completely out of his hands by my mother's words and actions.

'You stupid girl,' she had ranted, 'how could you allow yourself to get into such a position? You're no better than a slut from the bottom end of the town – and you,' she turned her ire upon Gerry, screaming obscenities, telling him to get out of the house – and to take his little tart with him.

From that moment I had no choice but to pack what I could carry and leave, to start a life with the man I was already having second thoughts about. I knew I would never ever forget the sound of my parents' front door closing behind me.

CHAPTER 10

I SLEPT FITFULLY, with unwanted dreams and memories of Gerry invading my mind. I had hated the sleazy bed-sit he took me to when we left my parents' house, even though I had spent so much time there in the past, loving the things he did to my body and the heights of ecstasy he took me to.

Sex was the very last thing on my mind as I hung away the few clothes I had brought with me, wondering what the future held for me and my baby, and if I could really trust Gerry to look after us both.

Looking at the unmade bed, the sink full of crocks in the curtained off 'kitchen', I knew I had grave doubts. Looking at Gerry, sitting in the only armchair, a can of strong beer gripped in one hand while he scratched his greasy curls with the other, I was suddenly terrified.

I was seven months pregnant when I knew, for sure, he was cheating on me, though I'd had my suspicions for some time. From wanting me practically every minute of every day, I had become lucky to get the benefit of his attention once a week.

His explanation that he was frightened of harming the baby didn't hold any water with me. I wouldn't have cared to be honest, since I no longer felt anything much for Gerry, but I did miss the sex. It was about the only thing that made me forget my surroundings, and was probably the one thing that he was really any good at.

As I said, I had my suspicions, and don't think I hadn't asked him more than once. His answer was always the same, 'I've got what I always wanted, you and our baby. Why would I bother to look elsewhere?' but somehow it failed to convince me, and he had been 'meeting his mates' more and more often of late.

However, I allowed myself to be lulled into a sense of false security when he swept me off to bed, quickly driving me into a frenzy of hot desire that culminated in the kind of throbbing orgasm that might have kept me his slave forever – if only I had been enough for him.

Of all things it was a hospital appointment that brought things to a head. It was just a simple antenatal check, but Gerry couldn't drive me there because he 'had something else on'.

I had the distinct feeling it was more that he didn't like to be seen with me, now that I was so obviously pregnant. It was probably bad for his image, but I couldn't find it in me to be bothered any more. I was just looking forward to escaping from the bed-sit for an hour or two.

The trip to the hospital involved catching two buses. One for the journey across town, and the second to reach the hospital on the outskirts. I was only halfway through the first stage of the journey, when the whole thing began to seem like a very bad idea. The motion of the bus was making me feel nauseous, to say the least, and my back was beginning to ache something awful.

Lumbering from the vehicle with the conductor's protests about this 'not being the right stop' ringing in my ears, I immediately vomited my lunchtime sandwich into the gutter, and determined to get a taxi straight home, despite the cost.

I was beginning to feel much better, and more than a little ridiculous by the time it drew up outside the shabby Victorian building that was a rabbit-warren of bed-sits just like ours. The sight of Gerry's battered Capri sitting in the drive brought me up short.

'Damn, damn, damn,' I muttered under my breath, as I paid my fare. I certainly hadn't reckoned on Gerry being back so soon.

He'd laugh at me for being such a sap, ask me how I expected to get through the birth when I couldn't even stand the discomfort of a bus ride across town. Still, I brightened at the thought he might still be able to get me to my appointment on time. It would save making another one.

Hurrying inside, I mounted the stairs faster than I normally would, taking little notice of the worn linoleum on the treads, the scarred and pitted walls that a thin coat of beige emulsion did little to improve. I did notice that a child had scribbled a picture near the top of the second flight, and found myself hoping we wouldn't still be living there when our little one was old enough to draw.

The battered door pushed open at my touch. I wondered if Gerry had seen me coming and opened it for me – and then I stopped wondering or thinking at all.

Whoever she was, she was naked, her long red hair fanned out on the pillow. She had pert breasts, an enviably flat belly, and she was writhing beneath Gerry's expert administrations – just as I had been doing only a few hours earlier that very same day.

Part of me noticed, in a detached kind of way, how hairy those pumping buttocks were, and how taut the cheeks became every time he thrust deeply into her body. It was strangely erotic, watching him do to someone else what he had done to me so often. I found myself becoming turned on, and even briefly contemplated joining them, until reality checked in and I found myself turning away with a strangled cry and running from the final proof that I had made the biggest mistake of my life.

I must have fallen down the stairs, of course, they were treacherous at the best of times. I don't know how I came to be in hospital. Not who had taken me there, or how. I don't know how my parents came to be there when I woke up, still sore from the emergency caesarean.

My little boy didn't even live long enough for me to meet him before he died – though the midwives were very good and brought his tiny, lifeless body to me, dressed in soft white baby clothes. I held him for hours, just looking at him. My eyes remained stubbornly dry, and though I had never known pain like it in my entire life, I refused, absolutely, to allow myself to imagine how it might have been if he had lived.

Eventually my parents took me home. I never saw Gerry again and, once the funeral was over, the whole sorry episode was never mentioned again. It was just as if it had never happened – until now.

*

Sunday morning dawned, bright and fresh, unlike me. My eyes were scratchy from lack of sleep and my head ached. Now that Pandora's box had been opened, by Bobbi's unconscious determination to repeat my mistakes, I didn't think everything would ever fit back into it again.

I felt a huge wave of guilt hit me at the realisation, previously left unacknowledged, that Rob had gone to his grave ignorant of the enormous amount of emotional baggage I had brought to our marriage. The scar was easily explained. He might have been the one person I would have been able to share it with, but I had always thought it all better left buried with the baby. After all, what good would talking about it do?

For the first time I wondered if it had been unfair to Rob to keep it all hidden. After all, my past must have had some effect on our relationship, for all that I'd tried to tell myself otherwise. Had he ever somehow known that for a very long time his tender love-making had left me cold? Had he been shocked by the times, few and far between admittedly, in those early days, when I had become a tiger between the sheets and enticed him to be the same, just so that I could reach the satisfaction that I craved?

It was something I would never know, but I gained some real comfort from the knowledge that, over time, we had eventually reached a satisfying and pleasurable intimacy in our sex life that had lasted right up until Rob's death.

Trying to put it all out of my mind wasn't easy. I did the best I could with my appearance, and when I went downstairs it was evident that my mother had tried to do the same. I only hoped my eyes weren't quite as red.

There was no chance of a quiet word, even had we wanted one, since Bobbi chose that morning to be up hours earlier than usual. I found myself wondering if it wasn't only my mother and I who had difficulty sleeping.

The chat round the table was desultory and mainly consisted of, 'Can you pass the milk, please?' and 'Would anyone like more tea?'

You could almost hear the secondary conversation that bubbled beneath the surface of these polite exchanges. All those questions that desperately needed to be asked, and answered, but, for the moment, remained unspoken.

Who could tell how long that would have gone on for, if Sam Robbins' arrival hadn't brought a flurry of excitement into the house and put everything else on the back burner.

Bobbi went reluctantly to answer the door, with a muttered, 'Who on earth can that be on a Sunday morning?'

She literally flew back into the kitchen and closed the door behind her with a bang that made Elaine and I pause in the individual acts of wiping the tops and loading the dishwasher, and turn round to face her.

Her eyes were round as she announced, 'It's Sam Robbins,' in the sort of tone usually reserved for Elvis Presley fans when they mentioned the King of rock and roll.

'Oh, ask him in,' I advised, with a pleased smile. 'I completely forgot he was coming.'

Bobbi didn't move so much as a step. 'Ask him..?' she squeaked. 'But it's Sam Robbins.'

'Well, we know that, dear,' my mother chipped in with a frown, 'but why have you left him standing on the step?' Gaining no rational answer, she stepped round Bobbi, with an impatient, 'Oh, out of the way, you silly girl. What on earth will he think of us making him wait on the doorstep? Come in, do, Sam,' she was cooing as she swept through the kitchen door, calling back to me, 'Shall I take him into the lounge, Denise?'

What a stupid question, when my mother knew full well he was bringing ingredients for her baking session and they all belonged in the kitchen cupboards.

'No, bring him straight in here. Come on through,' I called loud enough for Sam to hear.

The look on Bobbi's face was sheer, unadulterated horror. It might have been funny, if I knew what it was in aid of.

'In here, in the kitchen,' she hissed. 'What are you thinking about?'

She had no chance to say more, because Sam came in, loaded down with several bulging bags, advising my mother over his shoulder, 'I think I have everything you asked for in here, Elaine,' before he turned to smile at me and said, 'Hi, Denise.'

I defy anyone to receive a smile from Sam and fail to return it. You've heard of smiles that can light up a room; well, Sam's certainly did that – and it lightened the atmosphere no end, too.

'This is my daughter, Bobbi.' I put my arm round her to draw her forward and felt immediately how tense she was. I could see for myself how in awe of him she was. I half expected her to curtsey, though I had no idea why. It was only Sam from Peg's Place café, after all.

He was his natural, charming self, with a casual, 'Hello, Bobbi, it's nice to meet you, after hearing all about you.'

My daughter threw me a petrified look that wondered what on earth I had been telling him, and in the end I couldn't help myself, but simply had to ask, 'Is there something you haven't told us, Sam? Bobbi obviously knows something that my mother and I don't. You're not a film star or something, are you?'

Bobbi looked mortified, but Sam just threw back the attractive head that would have sat well on any celebrity, and roared with laughter.

'Mum, how could you?' my daughter demanded. 'I can't believe you don't know who Sam Robbins is. Granny, perhaps, but not you. You're not even that old.'

Then it was my turn to laugh, pleased that for once I wasn't being classed as too old for something, though I didn't know exactly for what.

I looked from Bobbi to Sam, and then back again. 'So,' I said, 'is someone going to put me – and my mother – out of our misery and tell us what this is all about?'

Before anyone could, the kitchen door opened – funny how it seemed to have almost taken on a revolving motion that morning – and Jason slouched in, only to come to a dramatic halt with an amazed expression on his face at the sight of Sam standing there, laughing, large as life.

I couldn't recall ever having seen Jason impressed by anything before, though I would say the shirt I'd bought him came fairly close. He was impressed to see Sam in my kitchen, no doubt about it.

He looked at me with brand new respect in his tone and in his whole attitude, as he said, 'Wow, I didn't know you knew Sam Robbins, Mrs M.'

'Will *someone* please put me out of my misery?' I demanded, beginning to get cross. To tell the truth, I was beginning to feel a bit of a fool, since it was quite obvious that Sam *must* be something of a celebrity and I didn't have a clue *who* he was, apart from the fact he was Peggy's son.

'Sam Robbins,' Bobbi explained loftily, the flushed face giving away the fact she was embarrassed by her mother and grandmother's ignorance, 'is only the owner of the biggest and best night-club in the whole of Brankstone.'

'You don't own DanzOn?' I have to say that in spite of myself, and my great age, I was impressed. I'd never been inside the place in my life – due to my advancing years I had never felt the need to frequent what was a young person's night-spot – but that didn't mean I had never heard of it.

' 'Fraid so.' Sam was still laughing, evidently finding it hilarious that we hadn't had a clue who he was when we were bossing him about in his mother's café.

'You should have said,' my mother reproved him. I doubt she had heard much about the club, but even she could recognise someone with a bit of a name when it was pointed out.

'It was actually quite nice to be liked for myself and not for who I am.'

Sam looked straight at me, and the look left me in no doubt that he wanted me to like him for himself. I felt myself blushing rosily and wondered why someone like Sam would care two hoots about the opinion of someone like me.

'How rude of us.' I became suddenly very busy to hide the confusion I felt. I didn't want to acknowledge, either, that I did like him. I liked him quite a lot – which was ridiculous, of course, because I barely knew him. Rushing to put the kettle on, I offered, 'Tea, Sam, or coffee? But perhaps you're too busy to stop.'

'Mu-um,' Bobbi protested, 'don't drive him away. We've got a million things to ask him, haven't we, Jase?'

Sam sat down happily to answer the barrage of questions fired at him by a previously tongue-tied pair of youngsters. My mother examined the contents of the bags, piling the stuff onto a worktop and checking them off the detailed list she had given Sam the day before.

All of a dither, I had made instant coffee in mugs before I realised real coffee in cups would have been much more suitable and, at about the same time, remembered there were only a few broken biscuits at the bottom of the tin thanks to Jason's voracious appetite.

The next minute I was suddenly cross with myself for getting into such a state – and about a man I hardly knew, for heaven's sake. Anyway, he hadn't come here to see me, I reminded myself sharply, but to bring baking ingredients to my mother. It was quite enough that she was fluttering all over him, not to mention Bobbi and Jason hero-worshipping him, without me getting in a state, too.

I banged the mugs down in front of them a bit harder than would have been polite. The effort was wasted, because no one noticed, they were so engrossed. The only real satisfaction I got was from realising the mug in front of Sam bore a graphic slogan referring to flatulence.

Taking myself off in a fit of very childish pique, I had dusted the whole of the downstairs and was roaring up and down the lounge with the Hoover when Sam finally came looking for me. Not that I wanted him to, of course, I assured myself, switching the machine off with a great show of reluctance.

'You're off, then, are you?' I said brightly, feigning surprise that he was still in the house at all.

'I was actually hoping to have a word with you.'

'Oh.'

'Yes,' he smiled, and my stomach flipped in a way it hadn't done for years.

I was suddenly very, very glad that I had made the attempt to hide the traces of my sleepless night with carefully applied make-up, that my fair hair fell loose to my shoulders, and that I was wearing new jeans that fitted and a pretty and trendy little top. The look in his eyes told me every little bit of the effort had been worth it.

'I wanted to thank you for your help yesterday, and for getting your mother involved, too …'

'It was nothing, really, we both enjoyed it.'

'And,' Sam continued, as if I hadn't spoken, 'for being a friend to Mum before that. I know she's become very fond of you in a very short time because she was always talking about you.'

'Oh, I liked her, too.' I suddenly forgot to be self-conscious and remembered to be concerned. 'How is she?'

'Doing well,' he suddenly sounded relieved and I knew very well how worried he had been. 'You wouldn't..?' he began, and then looking at the Hoover, the handle of which was still grasped in my hand, he said, 'But you're busy, of course. It's bad enough that I'm taking up your mother's spare time.'

He was going to ask me out. I was suddenly sure of it, and my heart started thudding with anticipation and nerves, before I had even decided if I would go.

CHAPTER 11

'AND – AND ... ?' Jo's egg and salad sandwich remained untouched on the plate as she prompted, 'Go on then, go on.'

She was leaning across the lunchtime table, so eager was she to catch my reply. It was a long time since I'd seen her so excited, especially at the start of a working week.

'He wasn't asking me on a date,' I told her ruefully, still remembering the feeling of being let down, no matter how many times I told myself I didn't care – and that I wouldn't have gone anyway. 'I don't know why I thought that he might. He's really not my sort at all – and I'm quite sure I'm not his. The Peter Stringfellow of Brankstone is hardly going to be desperate to date a widowed mother-of-one, and one who is almost certainly older than he is.'

'Oh.' Jo sank back into her chair like a deflating balloon, and compensated herself with a huge bite of her sandwich. As she chewed, she managed to ask, 'What *did* he want, then?'

'To see if I would visit his mother with him.'

'Oh,' she said again, 'and did you?'

'Mmm-mm,' I nodded, going on to elaborate, 'She's in the private Brankstone Heights Hospital. You know, that brand new private one, where all the posh folk go.'

Jo couldn't fail to be impressed. We'd both heard it was like a five star hotel with bathrooms en-suite and an à la carte menu, not to mention staff who looked like something off ER, if our source was to be believed.

'I felt a bit out of place in my jeans,' I confided, 'but I was glad I went.'

'With him?' Jo asked nosily, as only a friend is allowed to do, prompting, 'He took you in his car, did he?'

'Yes,' I grinned. 'In his brand new, probably top-of-the-range, navy blue Jaguar.'

'Wow.' She was suitably impressed. 'With real leather seats, no doubt.'

'Now you sound like Jason, or Petie,' I reminded her, 'but I have to say it *was* a very nice car – and I was glad that I went – not just for the ride, either.'

I was, too, and pleased to have my mind taken away from family problems, and memories I would much sooner forget. Sam was good company and it had been lovely to see Peggy sitting up in bed, looking as if she didn't have a care in the world – never mind a serious health problem.

He hadn't given me time to change, insisting gallantly that I looked just great as I was, which was why I was still wearing the jeans. Stopping at a florist on the way, it was clear that Sam had previously ordered the huge bouquet, which was all ready for collection. I insisted on purchasing my own small bunch of freesias, seeming to recall that Peggy loved those little flowers, as turned out to be just the case, as was proved by her evident delight.

'How lovely to see you both.' Peggy's smile was as warm for me as it was for Sam, and it encouraged me to kiss the wrinkled cheek in a way I would normally only do with someone I had known for a lot longer.

How we had met came out in the course of the conversation, and Sam was suitably horrified. I was able to laugh and dismiss it as 'nothing really', though the memory still gave me unpleasant nightmares. I explained about the mobile phone, which was now working with the aid of a new sim card and twenty pounds' worth of pay-as-you-go. Sam insisted on taking the number, though I couldn't think why he might need it.

Sam told Peggy I had been helping out at the café and that I had also volunteered my mother's services, which would prove invaluable given her talent for cooking and all things domestic.

'Oh, I am pleased.' There was no doubting Peggy's sincerity and she confided, 'To tell you the truth, I could do with a bit more help than I've had with just Rose. She's nearly as long in the tooth as me, and a martyr to her varicose veins. You don't think your mother would be interested in a more permanent job, do you?'

This was exactly the result Sam had been hoping for, as he confided to me later. He gave me a swift hug when we left the hospital, just a friendly one. As friendly as the casual arm draped around my shoulder as we made our way to the car.

He couldn't have known that it was so long since I'd been that close to a man, that it did the most amazing things to my equilibrium. I was far more conscious of the warmth of his body and the smell of his expensive aftershave than was good for me. It was almost a relief to arrive home, and I couldn't get out of the car fast enough. I didn't invite Sam in – he would probably have refused if I had.

*

My main concern, as the week passed – apart from the worry that the lively sex life Bobbi and Jason made no secret of was going to result in the pregnancy they desired – was finding some way of sorting out the double booking for the following weekend.

I didn't know if Jo was aware of Petie's kind offer, and didn't know, either, how she would feel about my letting him down, so I said nothing. I also *did* nothing, as per usual, holding out on the grim hope that something would miraculously come along and solve the matter for me. Cowardly, I know, but if the wedding was cancelled, or the concert postponed, then I would have been worrying all for nothing. Stranger things had happened, after all.

My mother worked daily in the café with Sam, with the added benefit of Rose and her veins returning during the week. I'm sure trade would have been a lot busier if more people were aware that a local celebrity was serving behind the counter, but the fact appeared to go almost entirely unnoticed. Somehow, I thought the regular clientele would be more interested in the quality of the food they were about to eat than in the identity of the person serving it, and it seemed I was right.

My father, apparently, had begun taking some of his meals there, and there was a noticeable softening of my mother's attitude towards him, so that I was building up high hopes of a good result there, eventually.

I was so wrapped up in my own concerns for once, that I don't quite know when I became aware that all was not sweetness and light in the Bobbi and Jason part of the household. When I did notice I simply assumed it was no more than a lover's spat and made a point of showing no interest, even when they were pointedly making barbed comments at each other across the meal table.

The weekend prior to the wedding was almost over before I actually got dragged, unwillingly, into the dispute. It appeared there were several issues involved.

'Well, I think it's pathetic,' Bobbi was almost snarling as they came into the kitchen, pulling chairs up to the table in preparation for the roast beef with all the trimmings I had spent the afternoon preparing. 'Do you want us to get a place of our own, or not?'

The buzz of the electric knife slicing through a nice piece of topside almost drowned out Jason's reply, but by straining my ears I could just make out part of it.

It went something like, ' ... one chance. Spare tick ... Why should I ... ?'

'Oh, please yourself,' Bobbi stormed, her raised tone loud enough for me to hear every word and the scrape of her chair clearly as she leapt to her feet. 'You usually do.' The slam of the door as she left the room punctuated the end of her angry accusation.

I waited for Jason to go after her, but he remained seated, so I calmly carried on slicing, and then moved on to straining cauliflower and carrots, before turning my attention to the gravy.

'Will Bobbi be back, do you think?' I queried, 'or will I put her dinner in the microwave for when she's ready for it? It's no problem, I'll be doing the same with my mother's.'

I knew Elaine was going to be late because she'd already said that after seeing my father for a light lunch, she was going to visit Peggy at the hospital to let her know what had been happening at the café that week.

Jason heaved a heartfelt sigh, before dragging himself reluctantly to his feet, and with a last longing look at the steaming dishes of food, he said, 'I'll go and get her.'

They were both back within minutes, but Bobbi still looked angry and close to tears, and Jason was sullen and uncommunicative. It didn't make for a very comfortable meal, but I was hungry and had my own problems, which made it easier to ignore theirs – whatever they were.

It wasn't so easy to ignore whatever was going on when, during the apple crumble and custard dessert, tears began to run unbidden down Bobbi's pale cheeks.

'Come on, love,' I pleaded, casting a look of dislike in Jason's direction, quite certain this had *something* to do with him, if not everything. 'It can't be that bad.'

'It is,' she hiccoughed, pushing her dish away with the pudding barely touched.

Jason looking at it longingly didn't help my mood at all, but I was determined to remain neutral. Just as determined that he shouldn't have the left-over food, though, I collected the dishes as I waited developments and scraped the contents into the bin. Very petty, I know, but very satisfying.

'You'd just as well tell her,' Jason sneered. 'I know you're dying to.'

He might just as well have added, See if I care, because he sounded childish enough and extremely defiant.

When Bobbi remained silent, I lost patience a bit and said bluntly, 'Well, perhaps one of you will tell me what's going on. Who knows? I might even be able to help.' I said the latter in the kind of tone that showed them I knew they would think this was unlikely, but as they appeared to be running out of options it had to be worth a try.

'He's been offered a job,' Bobbi said, and began to cry even harder.

'But that's good – isn't it?' I must have looked as confused as I sounded.

'It would be, if he was taking it.' Sobbing into a paper napkin, my daughter was the picture of heartbreak, and even Jason was beginning to look worried.

'Come on, babe,' he reached out clumsily.

His hand was flicked savagely away with an abrupt, 'Don't you touch me,' from Bobbi.

Well, this was proving interesting, to say the least. I had to say, I had never seen these two have a serious falling out. Mainly, it must be said, because whatever Jason said, and whatever Jason did, had always seemed to be fine with Bobbi in the past.

Admittedly, he had come unstuck for a time after the episode with Bobbi's 'best' – and I use the term with reservations – friend, but even that he had managed to talk his way out of eventually.

'It's at B and Q. You know the …'

Jason was obviously about to launch into an explanation of the well-known company for my benefit, when I interrupted him with a dry, 'Yes, Jason, I do know, and is there a good reason why you aren't able to take it?'

'Well, they want me to start straight away,' he said, as if that were reason enough.

I refrained from stating what was in my mind, which might have been something along the lines of, So, what are you waiting for? Get your skinny little arse down there without delay.

Instead, I was immensely proud of my forbearance, when what I actually said was, 'And is there a problem with that?'

'Yes,' Bobbi spat, 'there is. He's been invited to go on a stag weekend in Amsterdam with his mates, next weekend.'

Several things popped into my mind, so to give myself time to think before I spoke, I busied myself for a moment, putting the kettle on. Then I thought better of it and reached for my emergency bottle of wine at the back of the baking tin cupboard instead. This was obviously an occasion when a drop of the harder stuff might be beneficial.

As I handed Jason the bottle and opener, I wondered simultaneously three things about this weekend he seemed so determined to go on. What was he going to use in the way of money? Who were these mates? And, finally, after making it seem so important that they spend twenty-four hours a day together, what about Bobbi? The impact this weekend would have on the job offer didn't immediately occur to me, I have to say.

'Oh,' I said finally, 'You mean they might not like you having time off, when you've only just started the job.'

'And weekends are their busiest time,' Bobbi pointed out, before blowing her nose hard into her serviette.

I took a minute to feel relief that we weren't using linen napkins that day, and then said, 'Do you *want* the job, Jason?'

'Oh, yeah,' was his immediate response.

Mine might have been, but not enough to forego this drunken weekend with the boys, eh? He couldn't have made it clearer where his priorities lay. No wonder Bobbi was upset after what she had given up for him.

I could feel myself getting angrier by the minute, but I put all of that to the back of my mind, and said simply, 'Couldn't you have just tried asking? They might be more understanding than you think about a prior engagement.'

By the surprised looks I received from the pair of them, this had obviously not occurred to either one of them.

'Well, the worst they can say is "no".' I shrugged, 'They might just say, "yes". It must be worth a try.'

'I'll phone them tomorrow,' Jason promised a now radiant Bobbi.

I wondered why on earth I seemed to be so hell bent on helping to sort out their problems, when, in doing so, I was keeping them together. In my heart, however, I knew that if I tried to part them it would one day go against me. I didn't want Bobbi carrying around the kind of memories that haunted me. Kids of Bobbi's age won't be told anyway, they simply don't listen to what they don't want to hear. I should know.

It didn't occur to me that there might be another good reason to encourage Jason to go on the weekend. When it did I was careful to keep it to myself until the very last minute, though I realised I was taking a huge gamble and could become seriously unstuck.

In the end, it all worked perfectly, with Jason taking himself off in the early hours of the Friday morning. A tearful Bobbi crept into my bed, and after I had patiently listened to how he didn't even *want* to go on the weekend, but felt he couldn't let his 'mates' down, and how he would never *dream* of looking at another girl while he was away, never mind touch one, I was ready to scream.

However, my patience paid off. When I worried aloud at the breakfast table about the mess I had got myself into by unwittingly double-booking myself the following day, Bobbi didn't hesitate.

'I could go to the concert with Pete,' she said, trying to hide the eagerness which became more apparent when she added, 'I've liked Duran Duran since I was a baby. I used to pinch your records when I was little, remember?'

I did remember, and had actually been counting on the fact that *she* would remember, and sure enough, she had.

'Oh, would you, Bobbi, love?' I didn't have to feign my relief. 'You'd be doing me *such* a favour. You wouldn't rather go to the wedding with Uncle Adam, would you?' I held my breath, because it would be so much more appropriate the other way round.

'Not unless you really want to go to the concert.' Looking suddenly anxious, she said, 'You don't think Jase will mind me going, do you? It's just a concert. I hardly know Pete Farrell and wouldn't fancy him in a million years.'

The thought that she might change her mind about that last statement filled me with euphoria for a long moment. Then I realised that the changes to Petie's old ways were relatively new, still subject to the occasional hiccup, and may not even be long-lasting. Sometimes it really was better the devil-you-knew. At least with Jason I thought I had a damn good idea of what I was dealing with.

'I'm sure Jason wouldn't grudge you a couple of hours of enjoyment,' I assured her, making my tone very definite. Though knowing Jason as I did, I was quite sure he would object strongly, and come up with a valid reason to stop her going into the bargain, while being careful that his disapproval of her enjoyment didn't involve him giving up any of his own, of course.

'You can always ask him when he rings,' I pointed out, and then interpreting the doubtful look on her face pretty accurately, I thought, I added, 'Or you can wait till he comes home, and then tell him it was very last minute and you only went to help me out.'

'Yes, I could, couldn't I?'

Given the relief this suggestion was met with, I began to wonder if Bobbi didn't know Jason very well, after all. I had no doubt in my mind that if he'd been around there would have been no chance in the world of Bobbi going anywhere near this concert, and nor would she have considered the possibility. He certainly wouldn't have suggested taking her himself, for the simple reason it wasn't something he would have chosen to do.

*

'Jo?' For once it was me putting my head round her door at lunchtime that same day. 'Can we forget the sandwich for once? Would you mind?'

'Moi?' she feigned surprise. 'With my size eight figure,' she patted her well-padded hips, 'isn't it obvious that I often skip meals? Don't tell me you've had a better offer?'

She was all agog, probably under the misapprehension that men were queuing round the block to take me to lunch, despite me pointing out, time and again, that I'd not been asked on one single date in the whole of the past year.

'I wish,' I said, 'or should I say *you* do. No, but I've got this wedding tomorrow and I *know*, without looking, that there's nothing suitable in my wardrobe.'

'Ah,' she nodded, 'this full social calendar of events that led to my precious boy being side-lined.'

I'd finally got round to telling her about the double-booking but only, in my usual cowardly fashion, that very morning when it was all sorted out satisfactorily.

'I think he's come out of it pretty well, actually,' I said ruefully. 'I wonder now whether Adam would have liked the same option. Going out with a lovely little chick or an old broiler, what do you think?'

Jo snorted, which could have meant anything, and then she said, 'You'll have a job to pick an outfit in your lunch hour, especially if you want something a bit special.'

'Actually,' I came back, a bit sheepishly, 'I was thinking of taking the afternoon off. I'm owed enough time, when all's said and done, and you're right, it might well take more than an hour – especially as I was going to try and get my hair done, too.'

That wasn't strictly true, because I hadn't given a thought to my hair until the words popped out of my mouth, but now I'd said it, I realised it was a damn good idea. I thought I might even get my nails manicured, too, and then admitted I was being a bit unrealistic with the time I had.

'Bugger it,' Jo pushed back her chair with defiant air and snatched up her handbag from under the desk. 'I think I'll come with you, for an hour or so, at least. Might as well make use of the temp for the short time she's with us. I wouldn't mind something new, myself, and I hate shopping alone.'

We walked out of the building, arm in arm, and laughing – straight into Sam, who was obviously waiting for someone, and even I didn't think it was for Jo.

CHAPTER 12

I STUMBLED, CLUTCHING AT JO'S ARM. She caught hold of me, and stared at me in surprise, and then at the tall, and exceptionally good-looking man who stepped forward. It didn't take more than a minute for her astute brain to work out, first, that we knew each other and secondly, that he was waiting for me.

This was a guy who looked great in his mother's apron, and gorgeous in jeans, but seeing him all dressed up in fabulous charcoal grey suit and immaculate shirt of a slightly lighter shade was a revelation. It took a minute or two for me to realise I was gaping at him, mesmerised, like a rabbit caught in a car's headlights.

I searched for a voice and finding one that didn't sound a bit like mine, I said, 'Sam. Oh, what a surprise. I didn't expect to find *you* here.'

I was trying to get it across to Jo both who he was and also that this meeting hadn't been pre-arranged, but realised immediately that I was being too heavy-handed, as in 'methinks thou do'st protest too much'. I also sounded incredibly breathy and girlie for a woman of my mature years, so I took a quick grip of my senses and started again in a far more sensible fashion.

'Jo, this is Sam Robbins, remember I told you about Peggy's son?'

I could have kicked myself for not wearing one of my smart new and far more trendy suits that morning, and vowed to fill a charity bag with every baggy outfit I owned that very evening. I could grab handfuls of this skirt, and it was ridiculous to keep something that no longer fitted just because it had once cost a lot of money.

'You certainly did,' Jo responded in a very dry tone that let me know I hadn't told her nearly enough about him – and that she would be asking me why later.

I carefully ignored all the hidden innuendo and turning to Sam, I said, 'Sam, this is Jo Farrell, she's a work colleague and very good friend. We were just off to do some shopping. Can I do something for you?' and belatedly, as a thought struck me, 'It's not Peggy, is it? She hasn't had a relapse? Not after doing so well.'

He smiled, and I could see that the flash of perfect teeth, the twinkle of dark eyes, had exactly the same effect on Jo that they always seemed to have on me.

'No, Mum's fine,' he sounded pleased. 'She should be out at any time, and I'm much happier about that now I know your mother will be sharing in the running of Peg's Place.'

'Then..?'

'Lunch,' Sam said hastily, 'I was going to offer to take you – both,' he added gallantly, 'to lunch.'

*

'Well,' said Jo, as we carried a plate and glass apiece to our usual table in the corner of the Harvester, 'I don't know whether to be flattered that you chose my company over Super Sam's, or bloody miffed that you talked us both out of a lunch. It would obviously have made these,' she waved a disparaging hand over what were actually perfectly accep-table, freshly-cut and tastefully arranged tuna and sweetcorn sandwiches, 'look like curled-up leftovers from a vicarage tea-party.'

'Mmm,' I could see her point, 'but he really *should* have phoned, you know. It was a little bit presumptuous of him to assume I wouldn't have any other arrangements or that, if I did, I would simply drop them when he appeared. Anyway, it would have taken far too long to have a proper lunch, and the whole point of having a quick sandwich was to leave us time to look for my wedding outfit. It *is* tomorrow, you know.'

'Okay, okay,' Jo laughed, 'it's your lunch.' We chewed companionably for a moment, and then she added with a little satisfied smile, 'I reckon he had the shock of his life, having you turn him down without a second thought. I bet it doesn't often happen to a man like that.'

I was surprised and knew that it showed on my face as I pointed out, 'It's only Sam.'

'Only Sam,' she chortled. 'Listen to yourself. You must be the only woman in Brankstone who hadn't heard of Sam Robbins, prior to meeting his mother. There are posters of his nightclub all over town, and his picture is always in the paper, at charity events, involved in this or that big deal. He's practically the face of this town – a bloody good-looking one at that – and you just turned down a date with him.'

'It was *not* a date.' I knew I must look indignant, I certainly felt it. 'What is it with everyone lately, convincing themselves that every time I go out of the door I must be on a date?'

*

I said the same to Adam, the following day, when we set off for the wedding in the black BMW he had acquired at great expense, and only a few months before, to please Lisbet.

'Are you *sure* he wasn't after a date?' he swivelled slightly in his seat, as we reached the crossroads at the end of the road, and gave me a straight look. Then he added obscurely, 'Are you sure *I'm* not?'

'Don't you start,' I tried to laugh it off, but had to tell myself that this sudden obsession that everyone seemed to have developed with my personal life was really beginning to get on my nerves. 'Sam's just a friend, and so are you. I *am* allowed to have friends of the opposite sex you know,' I said forcefully, and then, letting that go, I remembered a promise I had made earlier in the day. 'Oh, Adam, I almost forgot, can you slow down as we pass the café, and toot the horn, just so my mother can get a glimpse of me in my finery? She'd gone this morning before I'd even started getting ready.'

'I can do better than that,' he sounded enormously pleased at having spotted an empty space right outside, and had swept neatly into it before I could stop him.

'Oh, I didn't mean … '

It was too late and Adam was already out of his side and round to open my door with a flourish.

To say I felt silly walking into Peg's Place was a real understatement. It was mid-afternoon on a Saturday, but the place seemed to be full of people and, without exception, they all stopped eating and drinking as we stepped through the door.

There was worse to come. Sam was standing behind the counter instead of Rose or my mother as I'd expected, and for the longest moment our eyes met and held. I wanted to look away, but try as I might – and I did – I couldn't tear my gaze away from his.

'Wow,' he said, finally, adding over his shoulder, 'Elaine, you'd better come and get a look at this.'

She came bustling out, and even in my embarrassed and confused state I couldn't help noticing the very real change in her. She looked as busy, fulfilled and happy as, I had to admit, I hadn't seen her looking in a very, very long time. She stopped short at the sight of me.

'Oh, Denise, oh.' She seemed totally lost for words and even lifted the corner of her apron to touch her eye.

Her reaction and Sam's was making me feel ever more silly. I wanted to say, Hey, it's only me, just Denise, scrubbed up and dressed up for a wedding. Let's calm it down a bit here, shall we? Let's get things into perspective.

'You like the outfit then?' I quipped, trying to lighten the atmosphere, 'and what about Adam, handsome, or what, in a real state of the art designer suit in a fetching shade of navy? Don't leave him out or he's bound to sulk for the rest of the day and accuse me of trying to outshine him.'

Everyone laughed, the tension eased perceptibly. I breathed a sigh of relief and told myself I had either imagined the over-reaction to my appearance or just misread it.

'You do look stunning, darling.' My mother was effusive in her praise, but seemed genuinely impressed with my appearance. 'The black and white together is very eye-catching, and I adore the hat. A hat finishes off an outfit, I always say.'

As we made our way back through the café, between the tables, there were various comments from the customers, all of them complimentary. I began to accept that the effort made the day before, the trekking from store to store, had really paid off and I mentally thanked Jo, once again, for her patience and determination to help me find just the right outfit.

It was an ensemble that had been made up bit by bit, and shop by shop, but it had finally come together in exactly the way we had envisaged. I knew I looked the part, from the top of my black hat with its neat white trim, right down to the heels of my eye-catching black and white shoes.

I turned as Adam held the door open, to give a final wave to my mother, and again found my gaze clashing with, and held by Sam's. Something in that dark look sent a shiver the length of my spine, and I felt something that could have been anticipation, or it might have been foreboding.

It wasn't until we had pulled into the carpark at the side of the church, that Adam turned to me and said, 'That guy – Sam, is it? – looked at you as if he could eat you.'

All the protestations and dismissive jokes died on my tongue as we faced one another across the interior of the car. This was my late husband's best friend, my good friend for more years than I could remember, and I didn't feel I had to deny or hide anything from him.

'I think you're reading him all wrong, Adam. Don't forget you said something just as ridiculous about Petie and he's not much more than a boy. Sam's just never seen me dressed up before and possibly thought I scrubbed up rather well. I think he is grateful for my interest in his mother – especially while she's been so poorly. He treats my *mother* in much the same way as he treats me.'

I wasn't sure if I was trying to convince myself, or Adam. Even as I was speaking, calmly and seriously, part of me was imagining that Sam really did want me – in every way – and wondering how it would feel to be with him like that – and suddenly wishing, far too hard, that it might happen.

It had been too long. Too long since I had been with any man, but suddenly the prospect was far too appealing, and I wondered if I was turning back into that sex-mad teenager who had fallen such easy prey to Gerry's well-honed and practised sexual skills all those years ago. I felt very certain that Sam would be every bit as good in bed – better, probably – and I felt again that frisson along my spine.

'Oh, my God.' All thoughts of Sam went out of my head as I suddenly sat up straight and peered through the windscreen, squinting against the bright sunlight. 'Is that Lisbet going into the church?'

I stared at the vision in a white silk trouser suit, all honey tan, skinny limbs, and golden curls, hanging possessively from the arm of someone who looked liked a candidate for Mr Universe – and a serious contender for the title at that.

'Mmm,' Adam sounded doleful, 'I thought she might show up. She has every right to. The couple *are* mutual friends and I guessed we might both be invited.'

'Why didn't you tell me?' I knew I sounded indignant, but I just hadn't been prepared. I had no reason to fear meeting her, but Lisbet wasn't the easiest person to be around at the best of times, and I had an uneasy feeling she wasn't going to take kindly to seeing Adam and me together – however innocent it was.

'Would you have come if I had?' Adam already knew the answer to that, was probably reading my mind all too accurately, and he continued, 'I needed a friend today, Dee, and I don't have a better friend than you. The fact that you look absolutely ravishing is an enormous bonus, given the fact she's here with the Adonis she left me for.'

'All brawn, no brains and obviously nowhere near as nice as you,' I dismissed staunchly, suddenly feeling much better.

I was obviously here for a reason, and I was flattered that Adam felt he could count on me in what was bound to be a difficult situation. It made me determined to hold my head up and give Adam the support he needed.

Adam laughed, 'You say all the best things. Let's make an entrance, young lady.'

Make an entrance, eh? That brought back memories. When I was younger, in the early days of my marriage to Rob, I'd loved to shop for clothes and cosmetics, loved to dress up and go out socially. We'd had the money for luxuries and the energy to socialise on a regular basis, and I'd used to spend ages on my appearance, whether it was for a party, trip to the theatre or even a meal with friends.

I guessed all the effort I made had something to do with Gerry and the way he had knocked my youthful confidence. Looking good and feeling great was very important to me, back then. It had done my marriage no harm at all, because Rob had adored having a well-groomed lady on his arm and he never hesitated to tell me so. I'd had a favourite saying then, and now it came rushing back to me.

'I don't go places to be ignored,' I'd used to say, believing anyone could look ordinary – and that it was entirely up to the individual how they presented themselves. I'd wanted to stand out, and had taken great pains to ensure that my appearance always warranted a second glance – from both men and women.

Looking back, I could see I was probably strongly influenced by a mother who was always meticulously turned out. Though, back then, I'd have vehemently denied that I was anything like her.

I guessed I had changed a little over the years. Rob's love and a long marriage had built my confidence, so the need to be noticed had diminished somewhat. I thought he would appreciate the fact that the vanity was back and could imagine his warm smile of approval.

'Okay.' I said it with a confidence that was still only partly pretend, but I straightened my back, tweaked the white jacket I wore over a sleek black dress that Jo swore had skimmed my newly defined curves in the most flattering manner, before tucking my hand into the crook of Adam's arm and walking into the church.

I felt as if every head turned to look at us, but they were probably looking for a glimpse of the bride and I was just flattering myself. We took our seats in a pew on the bridegroom's side, as indicated by an usher sporting a flamboyantly embroidered waistcoat and silk cravat in the same shade of green as the bridesmaids' dresses, and it wasn't long before the actual arrival of the bride took any attention away from us.

The wedding ceremony was a bit of a blur. To be honest, I was too busy with a mis-match of thoughts, feelings and memories to really feel part of it all. I was also very concerned about how Adam must be feeling with his wife – because she still *was* his wife – sitting somewhere behind us. I would have liked to take his hand or arm again, just to show my support, but was all too aware of how that might be misconstrued to actually do it.

I stood back during the photo session, because although I did know the happy couple vaguely, I was quite sure they could do without me smirking out of the group pictures for the next lord knows how many years, invoking a, 'Who *was* that woman in the black and white hat?' every time they opened their wedding album.

'Well, you didn't waste much time?'

My thoughts scattered and my back stiffened perceptibly. The day had warmed up nicely, just in time for the late afternoon ceremony. I'd been enjoying the peace, and the shade offered by an oak tree.

Recognising the voice, I forced myself to turn slowly to face Lisbet for what – judging by her tone – promised to be a confrontation of some sort.

'Hello, Lisbet. How are you?'

She ignored the greeting, but looked me up and down. I could tell by her expression, she didn't much like what she saw. I forced myself to stand tall and straight and to look her right in the eye.

Despite the tan and the heavy make-up, I thought she looked quite haggard. Thin to the point of gaunt, she looked as if a puff of wind would blow her away. She certainly didn't look very happy.

'Couldn't wait to get your hands on him, could you? I bet you clapped your hands with glee when I took myself out of the frame.'

Anger stirred, but I ignored it, along with the urge to justify my reasons for being with Adam that day, saying instead, quite civilly, 'I beg your pardon, Lisbet. Are you saying you have a problem with me being here with Adam?

'Only,' I continued quickly before she had a chance to say a word, 'just remind me. It was you, wasn't it? You, who took yourself "out of the frame" – as you so charmingly put it – to go off with "Mr Muscle-bound-and-masculine", over there? That being the case, I don't think you can have anything to say about what Adam does, or who he does it with. He's a free agent now, by *your* choice.'

The crimson tide of colour that swept Lisbet's tanned cheeks told me I had scored the intended point and, satisfied,

I turned on the heels of my smart new shoes and swept across the lawn to join the rest of the wedding party.

'I saw Lisbet approach you,' Adam looked a bit worried. 'She wasn't hassling you, was she?'

'Oh, I think we understand each other perfectly now,' I told him calmly, slipping my arm through his and suddenly feeling very determined to enjoy the rest of the day. 'Let's make our way to the reception, shall we? I think the bride and groom will be a little while yet.'

*

'I had a great time last night, did you?'

The question came from Bobbi. She smiled on her way to the fridge, and after pouring herself a huge glass of orange juice – carefully replacing the now empty bottle back in the fridge – she joined me at the table.

'You didn't tell me how nice Pete was,' she accused, taking a huge slug of orange and wiping the tell-tale moustache away with the back of her hand. 'In fact, you gave me the distinct impression he was a right tearaway who gave his mum a really hard time.'

'Well, he was, and he did,' I confirmed, pointedly removing the bottle from the fridge and rinsing it ready for recycling, 'up until quite recently. He finally seems to have turned the corner, accepting that he must assume responsibility for his own actions. Petie reckons it was Jo getting tough and refusing to help him out any more that brought about the change.'

'Mmm, perhaps that's what you should have done sooner with me and Jason, and with Granny,' Bobbi sounded thoughtful.

I was surprised by the comment, but tried hard not to show it. 'What? I should have barricaded the door and refused to let any of you in, you mean?' I tried the humorous approach, and it seemed to work, because Bobbi smiled.

'I almost wish you'd turned me round and sent me straight back to university,' she said it lightly, but sounded wistful. 'Listening to Pete made me feel that I've messed up nearly as badly as he did.'

'Except,' I pointed out, 'that Petie started "messing up" a lot sooner than you. You still have your school qualifications behind you. Good GCSE and A level results that no one can take away from you. Petie really has to go back and start from scratch, and hold down a job while he gains the qualifications he needs to get what he wants from his future.'

'I still want to be a nurse,' Bobbi said, and I felt my heart leap in my chest with suddenly rekindled hope, especially as she continued thoughtfully between mouthfuls of greedily spooned up cereal, 'I don't want to start all over again in a few years, when I'll have the added responsibility of a family to make it that much harder. I want to do it now. It's what I've always wanted and I don't really know why I let Jason convince me otherwise.'

I decided to leave Jason out of this and took a sip from my rapidly cooling cup of tea to give myself a minute. 'Perhaps,' I suggested carefully, 'it's not too late.'

Bobbi stared at me, her eyes wide and suddenly bright. 'You mean,' she said, 'that I might be able to go back and pick up where I left off, or transfer closer to home, or something?'

I smiled, 'Well, those things have always been a possibility. You knew that right from the start.'

'But I just left, without a word. I've never contacted them, or tried to explain.'

It was now or never, so I took a deep breath, seized the moment, and admitted, 'I did.'

'You did?' The spoon clattered into the now empty cereal bowl.

I waited for the accusations. I had interfered, something I had always promised myself I wouldn't do, but it had seemed so important to give Bobbi time. Time to think about the reality of throwing away the chance of the career she had always wanted. Time to think about the realities of life with a child and a feckless partner, while she was still so young. Time to reflect on whether Jason really wanted what was best for her, or just what he thought was best for himself.

I'd had all the best of intentions, but I had still interfered in her life, and Bobbi had every right to be very angry with me. I waited for her wrath, accepting that I deserved everything she would level at me.

CHAPTER 13

LONG MOMENTS PASSED, Bobbi remained silent, and gradually I let out the breath I hadn't realised I was holding in. Perhaps Bobbi wasn't as angry as I thought she'd be about me going over her head and getting in touch first with the course administrator and then, through her, with a Senior Nursing Lecturer.

On the other hand, perhaps Bobbi was absolutely furious – as mad as hell with me. I really didn't blame her, despite the fact I had acted with the best of intentions.

'I'm sorry.' I thought the apology was due, anyway. I *had* interfered, something I had always tried not to do. 'I know I shouldn't have poked my nose in.'

I could suddenly tell Bobbi wasn't really listening, and this was proved when she asked eagerly, 'What did you say to them? What did they say?'

'Well,' I began, and continued quickly, 'I pointed out that you'd had a hard time of it recently, and that starting a three-year course within such a short time of losing your dad probably hadn't been a very sensible course of action.' I hesitated, and then hurried on, 'I didn't mention the problems you'd been having with Jason and … Well, you know. I thought they'd probably have more sympathy for a bereavement than a broken romance.'

'Oh,' was all Bobbi said and my heart sank.

'You're cross with me,' I said, 'and I don't blame you.'

'You did what you thought was best.'

I was surprised, and I expect I showed it. 'Well, yes,' I admitted, wondering what was coming next.

'What did they say?'

'I was passed from administrator to tutor – someone quite senior apparently – I'm afraid I can't remember her name, but she was very nice. She said that, fortunately – unlike some students in your year – you were always very up-together with your assignments. An extension for extenuating circumstances is sometimes permitted, and as long as you didn't take too much more time off she thought it might be arranged for you to make up any time missed from your placement.'

Bobbi stared at me, and then she jumped up so quickly that her chair toppled backwards with a crash. I waited for the wrath that would surely pour onto my head, and was stunned when she dragged me to my feet and forced me to polka around the kitchen.

'What on earth is going on?'

We skidded to a halt in front of my mother, who, unlike us, was all dressed and ready for the day ahead. Going out, too, if the light jacket and large handbag were anything to go by.

'Oh, you've had your breakfast, shower, and everything, then,' I uttered stupidly. 'I didn't hear you get up.'

'Well, unlike the pair of you,' she said, a shade bitterly, I thought, 'I wasn't out gallivanting half the night – or sleeping halfway through the following morning.'

'I saw you'd been busy.' I indicated the various tins and Tupperware boxes piled on the work surfaces. An earlier peek at the contents had proved that Peg's Place would be well catered for on the home-made cake front for the next several days. 'You've obviously got plans for today.'

'I'm meeting your father,' she said, and then hurried on to say, 'It's important that I talk to you, Denise, before I go. I'm sure Bobbi won't mind.'

She gave her granddaughter a pleading look, and Bobbi immediately turned towards the door, saying, 'I'll go and get a shower.' Before she could disappear, I reached out and caught her arm.

'Bobbi might not mind – but I do,' I said firmly. 'We were actually having a pretty important talk of our own. We hadn't finished, so whatever it is you want to discuss with me will have to wait till later. I'm sorry, but that's how it is right now.'

It had to be said. Bobbi was in the right frame of mind – at that precise moment – to make a decision that was going to reach far into the future. Left till later she might well make the wrong choice, and I couldn't take that chance.

More gently, I asked my mother, 'It *can* wait a while, can't it?'

The look on her face almost made me change my mind. For a moment I was completely torn between my mother and my daughter, and then my mother managed a strained smile, and said, 'Yes, it can wait,' and was gone, in a flurry of perfume, silk scarves and air kisses.

'Do you think you should have talked to her?' Bobbi looked quite concerned. 'She looked a bit upset. Didn't you think so?'

I refused to feel guilty, telling her, 'Right now, you're my main concern. Granny is big enough to stand on her own two feet.'

'And I'm not?' Once that might have been a sarcastic remark, but Bobbi's tone indicated that, for once, she was happy to accept my support, and she confirmed that by adding, 'No, I know I'm not. I do need your help and I do need your advice.' She shrugged, 'I obviously don't take after you for common sense. Your life's all been plain sailing hasn't it? Great career, great marriage, great life – at least until Dad died, and then if that wasn't enough for you to deal with I messed up and dumped all my crap, and Jason on you. I've been an idiot and I'm so – so sorry.'

The next moment Bobbi's face crumpled, and the minute the tears rained down her face I felt my composure crack. That was when I knew it was time to tell her about my past – all of it.

*

'All of it?' my mother faced me across the kitchen, looking horrified – as well she might.

'All of it,' I confirmed, pausing in the act of tidying up before taking myself off to bed, 'and do you know what? It was actually good to talk about it – to bring it out into the open. We never did that, did we? It was the family skeleton, pushed rattling loudly into a sound-proofed cupboard, and locked away so firmly it was just as if it had never happened.'

'But I – we – thought it was for the best.'

'*You*, thought it was for the best, and we went along with it,' I told her firmly, but with no malice. 'We had little choice,

Dad and I. We never could stand up to you, either one of us. I never even told Rob, because you thought it best, and that's something I would bitterly regret if I didn't feel so strongly that regrets are a waste of time.'

'He,' my mother obviously couldn't bring herself to utter Gerry's name, 'was a youthful mistake. I thought it best – yes, I did and I admit it – to leave him in the past where he belonged.'

I stared at her. It obviously counted for nothing that, mistake or not, Gerry had been my first love and was, therefore, never going to be easy to entirely forget. 'And the baby,' I said. 'My little son, *your grandson*,' I emphasised, thought I saw her flinch, and was glad, 'and Bobbi's brother. Is he best left in the past? I've spent most of my adult life pretending he never existed, but he did. He does. Here,' I indicated my head, 'and here.' I placed my hand on my heart and felt the tears well up in my eyes.

'But I thought …'

'That I'd forgotten.' I shook my head. 'Oh, no, not a day has gone by that I haven't thought of him and wondered what might have been. He'd have been a young man now. Almost thirty years old. Do you even remember his name?'

I watched my mother's composure slip. I couldn't ever recall seeing her cry and it was a most disturbing thing to see. I can only compare it to watching a charming painting disintegrate or the façade of a building begin to crumble. As the immaculate mask slipped, the mother I had known – or thought I had – disappeared in front of my eyes.

'You think I didn't care. You think it didn't tear me apart to see my daughter's life in ruins, to watch that tiny baby's life slip away before my very eyes.' She was sobbing and I stared at her in amazement. 'You think it didn't rip the heart from me to see everything you went through and to know that a lot of it was down to me.'

'Down to … ?'

'To me, yes,' she repeated. 'You think I didn't know that I handled things badly, that by losing control, the once, I pushed you into that – that monster's arms. I've been dreading watching history repeat itself with Bobbi and that – that boy. I've been so proud of you, watched how hard you've tried. If that girl's life turns around, Denise, the credit all belongs to you for being a better mother than I could ever be. His name,' she added, without an explanation being wanted or needed, 'was Jack.'

For the first time in so many years that I couldn't even remember, I walked into my mother's arms. She wrapped them tightly around me, and all the barriers, walls, fences and gates we had erected over the years came tumbling down around us.

'Now then,' she began, when we'd composed ourselves enough to sit back and enjoy a cup of tea, and an understanding that was probably commonplace in the majority of mother/daughter relationships, 'about Bobbi.'

'Well, it seems,' I told her, 'as if getting her to attend the concert with Petie in my place was a real stroke of genius. I think she was probably already having second thoughts about the wisdom of giving up on the nursing course, and

Jason taking himself off to Amsterdam has given her time to think, away from his influence. Listening to Petie's regrets about his wasted years, and the struggle he faces to make something of himself now, was just what she needed to hear – at just the right time.'

My mother's expression was a picture, full of hope, as she queried, 'So, she's going to phone the university tomorrow? See what can be done?'

'Better than that,' I told her, trying not to sound too gleeful. 'I confessed to her that I'd already been in touch, offered reasonable excuses for her behaviour, which were accepted. They said they would have been "sorry to lose her from the course", and also said, she'd "been doing so well up until she left", etcetera, etcetera, so the door is already open for her to return.

'Now, I know – and she knows – that the minute Jason arrives home tomorrow afternoon he'll do his damnedest to talk her out of either going back or even transferring closer to home. To put it bluntly, he wants her here, with him, and preferably pregnant. It's not in *his* best interest to see Bobbi make anything of herself.'

'Because he'll never make anything of himself,' my mother finished astutely.

'Exactly.' We both nodded. 'So,' I went on, 'I'm driving her up to the uni. It's only a two and a half to three-hour journey. We're setting off at the crack of dawn, and by the time Jason arrives home it will be too late for him to do a thing to stop us. She's in bed now, and I'm going to take myself off shortly.' I reached out and touched my mother's hand. 'I'm sorry about this morning.'

She looked surprised, and repeated, 'This morning?'

'You wanted to talk to me,' I reminded her, 'and I had to put you off. I'm sorry about that, but you can see how important it was that I strike with Bobbi while the iron was hot. I waited up for you. Do you want to talk now?'

Elaine looked as if she was going to say something, and then she obviously thought better of it, because she shrugged and dismissed lightly, 'Oh, it was nothing that can't wait.' She flapped her hands at me, 'Go on, off to bed with you. You'll need a good night's sleep with that journey ahead of you tomorrow. I'll see you in the morning, before you set off.'

I kissed her goodnight for the first time in years and, once in bed, I found myself wondering about that look, the way she'd hesitated over her answer – and about the length of time she'd been out with my father that day. It had to be a good omen. I could feel myself smiling in the dark. They must be getting back together. In fact, I was almost sure of it.

If that really was the case, with Bobbi and my mother settled, all that left was to get Jason out from under my feet, and then I could concentrate on my own future – at long last.

For the first time in a very long time I went to sleep smiling.

*

My mother was up to wave us off in the morning. I had no doubt that she was extremely relieved that she was working in the café all day, and so wouldn't be in obliged to face Jason on his return.

I'd already decided I would cross that bridge when I came to it, which seemed be working a treat so far. You only had to look at the way everything was sorting itself out, quite satisfactorily, with only a very little intervention from me in the end.

The sun was shining as we hit the motorway. A good omen, I thought, since we'd had a typical British summer so far, with only the odd warm day to boast of, despite the fact we were now well into July.

For some time we drove in silence, each busy with our own thoughts. I knew that Bobbi had left a letter of explanation for Jason, and she must have been thinking about that. She'd be wondering if she'd done the right thing, and whether he would ever forgive her.

She would also be apprehensive about the day ahead, and what sort of a reception awaited her. She had behaved unacceptably – you didn't just take off like that when you had committed yourself to a three-year course – and she must face the consequences of her actions. I thought at the end of it all, she would probably have grown up quite a lot and learned a few lessons.

We spoke about this and that, about everything and nothing, stopped at the services, glad to stretch our legs, and enjoyed, if that was the word, a weak tea apiece and a shared sticky Danish pastry.

'Thanks, Mum.'

We were turning into the road Bobbi had indicated and that I vaguely remembered led into the sprawling campus. The site was a maze of mismatched buildings, each one built for a different purpose, and all erected in different decades, making the end result interesting, to say the least.

'For what, love?' I kept my attention on the signs, looking specifically for those indicating visitors' parking.

'For – for – everything.' Bobbi hesitated then, before continuing in a rush, 'You won't be too hard on him, will you?'

I didn't have to ask who she was referring to, and I didn't actually have to try too hard to be kind about him. Jason wasn't *all* bad, after all. Even I had come to realise that – despite the odd altercation – I had even become fairly fond of him, in my way.

I did my best to say as much, and then we were parked and making our way towards the building where the teaching and administration of Bobbi's nursing course, and various others of a similar nature took place.

'They may not be able to see you today,' I warned, already nervous for her. 'After all, we've come without an appointment, and you can't just expect to walk back in the way you walked out.'

'I presume I still have my room at the nurses' home in the hospital,' Bobbi said, looking grimly determined. 'If I have to I'll go there, but I'm staying up here now until I have something sorted out. Whatever they want me to do to put matters right, I'll do it.'

The automatic doors swished back, and we had no sooner stepped into the reception area than a cheery voice called, 'Bobbi. Bobbi Moffat. I hope you're looking for me.'

Apparently this was the administrator for Bobbi's course and in no time she had everything under control. I was directed towards the refectory, and Bobbi was swept off to 'see what could be done', because, apparently she 'couldn't have chosen a better day to get this sorted out'.

In the large refectory I purchased a cappuccino from the machine and a pre-packaged cheese and salad sandwich from the counter, and found myself a table that wasn't occupied by a gang of laughing chattering students. Some of them, I was amazed to note, were as old as me – older even in some cases.

I rang Peg's Place on the mobile phone Jason had insisted I have – one of the few times I had ever used it – to tell my mother what was happening.

'Peg's Place.'

Sam's voice was deep in my ear and I felt the hairs lift on the back of my neck. I hadn't expected him to pick up the phone, though I didn't know why, since he was still helping out prior to Peggy's return the following week.

'Oh, uh,' I fumbled for something to say, suddenly tongue-tied and foolish, without really knowing why. 'It's Denise. I ... '

'He-*llo*.'

I shivered deliciously, and then gave myself a good shake. I was almost forty-seven for God's sake, not a teenager. I had no business getting all stupid over someone who was, quite obviously, out of my league.

'I just wanted to let my mother know that Bobbi and I have arrived safely and that everything seems to be going well, touch wood.' I touched the Formica-topped table superstitiously, and went on, 'Is she there?'

'She's popped out for a minute, to post a letter, I think. Hey, are you on a mobile, because I can ring you right back. She won't be a minute.'

'Oh, no, there's no need if you can just tell her what I said – so she doesn't worry.'

'What about me worrying?'

I could hear a smile in Sam's voice, and repeated, 'Worrying – about me? I don't understand.'

'No,' he said wryly, 'I don't think you do. I worry that the time is never going to be right to ask you out, because if it's not one thing it's another with you. I've never met anyone with so many calls on their time. I also worry that you might turn me down.'

'Ask me out,' I repeated stupidly. 'What do you mean? Like a real date?'

'Oh, yes,' he said, his voice deepening with more than a subtle hint of promise, '*definitely* like a real date. So … ' he seemed to hesitate, sounding unsure and quite unlike his normally confident self, 'are you going to say yes?'

'Oh, uh, I've got to go. I'll speak to you later.' I fumbled and then hit the end call button and sat back in my chair shaking.

Oh, my God. He had asked me out – Sam – on a real date. I couldn't believe it. He was too young for me, too good-looking for me, obviously way out of my league. Was I flattered? Was I scared? You bet I was.

Then all thoughts of Sam went out of my head, because Bobbi returned, with the administrator, and they were both smiling. Bobbi was going to stay, at least for the moment. It wasn't all done and dusted, and there were still a few people for her to see, but it was looking 'very promising', in the administrator's own words.

Bobbi came with me to the car to collect her bag, and we hugged for a long moment. It was what we both wanted, but that didn't make it any easier to say goodbye.

'Let me know how you get on, Bobbi, but I feel sure that everything will turn out all right in the end – hopefully for Granny, too.'

The latter was added as she began to walk away, and pausing, she turned and said, 'Yes, I'm sure she'll be all right. I know she was the one to walk out, but it must have been a bit of a shock for her, though, finding out Granddad had got himself a girlfriend.'

CHAPTER 14

BOBBI WAS WRONG, OF COURSE, but she was gone before I could tell her so. My father, my lovely dad, who had always been totally devoted to my mother, would never even look at another woman? It was unthinkable. What on earth had made Bobbi say such a thing?

My head was buzzing, full of possibilities, followed by immediate and fierce denials, and I was halfway home before I realised it. What was worse, I had no clear idea of the journey thus far, and that was more than a little scary, especially given the fact the majority of it had been accomplished on a motorway.

Becoming conscious of the whizzing traffic surrounding me, and the speed I was travelling at, I eased my foot from the accelerator and indicating went over to the inside lane. I stayed there until I finally left the motorway and joined the familiar streets of Brankstone.

Was that what my mother had wanted to share with me the day before, when I had rebuffed her in order to give Bobbi all of my attention? I'd had no choice of course. Bobbi was my child and was, therefore, my priority. She was still young enough for errors of judgement to be understandable, while my mother would appear to be old enough to know exactly what she was doing and should have been prepared to accept the consequences of her actions.

I knew I shouldn't feel guilty, and as if I had let her down – but I still did. Perhaps I should have taken just a minute or two to listen. Was I starting to believe what Bobbi had said about my Dad was true, after all? I was very much afraid that I was, and part of me felt strongly that my mother had brought this on herself. Hadn't I seen this – or something very like it – coming?

How was she feeling? I found I had absolutely no idea, but if she was so keen to move on with her life, perhaps she actually *preferred* to do it alone. On the other hand, she may well be shocked by this sudden turn of events and be wondering what on earth to do next.

She could have talked to me about the wisdom of abandoning her husband and her marriage, *before* she took that first step into the unknown. She could have, and she should have. She really should have asked me, her own widowed daughter, of all people, about the reality of living life alone, and yet she never had.

Some people cope perfectly well with a solitary existence, many may even prefer it: others, like myself, are obviously cut out to be one of a pair and find life alone extremely hard, if not almost impossible to deal with.

I could have told my mother that losing Rob had left me feeling only half the person I'd used to be. It was as if I had lost, not only my soul-mate, but my whole identity when he died. We had been 'Denise and Rob' for such a long time. It was who we were, who I was. At work I signed everything Denise or D Moffatt, and everything in Rob's building business was in his name, but at home everything was a joint venture. I had always signed cards from us both and when suddenly there was only me, just Denise, I was afraid that no one would know who I was any more.

I could just imagine the scenario that first Christmas. Someone opening my festive greeting, and saying, 'There's a card here from Denise. Denise who?' which would be met with a shrug of complete indifference and result in the card being tossed to one side.

Everything we'd planned together for the foreseeable future died with Rob. I'd found it difficult, if not impossible, to get motivated about anything, particularly in the early days. Plans for the house, the garden, for holidays, eventual retirement, meant nothing at all without him. Even simple things like pub lunches, a trip to the cinema, a walk along the beach, lost all their appeal when they had to be done alone. It was all made that much harder by a world that seemed to be geared almost totally towards couples.

My mother just couldn't see how lucky she'd been to still have my dad. He was a gem of a husband, and that wasn't only my opinion. Rob had used to say he was a saint, though I wouldn't quite go that far. He was just a normal, kindly man, one who had always loved his wife dearly, despite all her little foibles and tantrums, showing limitless patience with all her demands and often incredibly silly ways. Harry had known Elaine inside and out – and he had loved her anyway.

I felt I'd had a love like that with Rob, counted myself lucky for it and grieved every day for all that I had lost – all those years we might have shared. My mother – well – my mother had simply thrown everything she had away, and I guessed she was probably only just beginning to realise it.

I couldn't talk to her at the café, pointless to even try at that hour of the day, when everything would be geared towards getting late lunches out of the way before the afternoon tea rush began.

And there was Sam. He would be there. I shivered deliciously at the thought of the promise in his deep tone and wondered, a bit worriedly, if he was playing games with me. He might just see me as lonely, vulnerable and available. I was very different from his normal choice of companion, I would have thought, and therefore something of a challenge. I didn't know if I was prepared to be his little taste of something different.

All thoughts of my mother and Sam shot out of my head, however, the minute I reached home. Pulling into the driveway I was confronted by Jason's battered red Escort, parked on the grass in his usual careless fashion.

For once I wasted little concern for the state of my lawn beneath the wheels. My heart sank to the soles of my comfortable driving shoes as I acknowledged that I hadn't been expecting him to arrive home so soon. Knowing he was inside and must have already read Bobbi's letter made me feel at a distinct disadvantage. I had expected to be there first, ready and waiting and fully prepared to deal with the rage and recrimination that would undoubtedly be my lot.

Oh, well, it was my fault for allowing Jason to get his feet under my table, though I admit I hadn't reckoned on Bobbi giving him her front door key. However, I had known when I encouraged her to leave in his absence that this moment would have to be faced, so, having no one to really blame but myself, I straightened my back, took a deep breath, and went inside. I was determined that, no matter what, I would keep my calm and have the least favourite of my uninvited guests out of my house within the hour.

With this all organised in my head, and having hyped myself up for the storm that I was sure was about to break over my head, it rather took the wind out of my sails when the house was still and ominously silent. Even the slight slam of the front door didn't bring Jason thundering down the stairs to confront me.

I had to confess to feeling a little let down. Had Jason gone out then? On foot? How very odd. I took a step towards the kitchen, and halted as I heard a slight sound upstairs.

I paused, torn between the desire to put off the confrontation and enjoy a nice cup of tea, or getting it over and done with. Part of me was even desperately wishing I *had* gone to the café first. Facing Sam and my mother really was preferable to this.

I sighed deeply before changing direction, and made my way slowly and hesitantly up the stairs. I went up those stairs sometimes a dozen times in a day, usually they were climbed at a run, always in a hurry, I couldn't recall ever using them so slowly that I really noticed the state of them.

The carpet was good quality, in a neutral beige colour, and barely worn at all. Vacuumed fairly frequently but, as was obvious on close inspection, always carelessly, if the accumulation of fluff in the corners of the treads was anything to go by.

My feet moved soundlessly upwards a step at a time. Once at the top I could see Bobbi's bedroom door standing open, and Jason inside – packing. He had his back to me and all of his attention was focused on what he was doing. He obviously hadn't heard me come in.

'Jason.'

The sound of my voice took him by surprise and he straightened up and spun round in one swift movement. He turned away again just as quickly – but not before I had seen the tears on his unshaven cheeks.

To say I was shocked was an understatement. I felt as if I'd been punched in the stomach and winded. Whatever I was expecting his reaction to Bobbi's simultaneous defection and departure to be, the very last thing was tears. Had I been pressed, I think I would have cheerfully and confidently stated that Jason was incapable of showing any emotion, except perhaps anger, and yet here he was crying his heart out because my daughter had left him.

I tried to harden my heart, to tell myself that he was crying at the loss of a meal ticket, a roof over his head, but I had seen the heartbroken expression on his face and didn't believe any of those things was the cause.

Keeping his back to me, and his tone carefully flat, he said, 'It won't take me long to finish here, and then I'll be out of your way.'

He didn't add that he knew I'd be glad to see the back of him, and I didn't say it would be good riddance, but the words hung in the air between us. I wondered why I felt slightly ashamed, feeling sure I had no reason, that I had been more than fair to him during his stay – uninvited – in my house.

'Where will you go?' I heard myself ask. 'Will you go home?'

What the hell did I care where he went? I couldn't believe I was asking. This was exactly what I had wanted all along, and I knew it, so why the sudden concern?

'Not home, no,' he said evenly, adding almost as an afterthought, 'probably to a mate's.'

I went further into the room, until I was close enough to look into the tattered rucksack that Jason had come with. Most of his clothes had been tumbled in any old way, it was a typical bloke's effort at packing, but right on top, and folded with infinite care, was the Ralph Lauren shirt that I had bought for him. The sight of it proved to be my undoing and I, too, began to cry.

'I'm sorry, Jason,' I said through my tears. 'I'm sorry it didn't work out for you and Bobbi.'

He looked at me then, for the first time. A crooked smile crossed his face as he said, without rancour, 'Liar.'

'Okay, then,' I corrected. 'I confess I'm not sorry she's made the decision to return to uni to complete her studies. It's what she's always wanted, to be a qualified nurse and, therefore, what I've always wanted for her, too. I can see that you're hurting, though, and I understand that you care for her. What I can't understand is why you thought there had to be a choice made between a career or you.'

'Because you had a supportive husband?' Jason queried. 'One who had a career of his own and was able to feel good about himself?'

'Rob, you mean?'

He nodded.

'Yes,' I agreed, 'he was everything you say, though he was always the first to say that he was the brawn and I was the brains of our relationship. He was man enough not to have a problem with that, recognising that it didn't make him inferior, that we all have different skills to bring to a partnership.'

I found myself continuing, talking quickly, before I could change my mind, 'But in my life, before Rob, there was Gerry, who was quite the opposite. You don't know about Gerry, Jason. I only recently told Bobbi about the man who tried to control my life and all but ruined it. It took me a long time after Gerry to feel really good about myself again.'

'You're saying I was like this – this Gerry?' I could see he was waiting for me to confirm it, was even prepared to accept that it was so.

'I'm not going to insult you by saying that, Jason,' I surprised myself by saying. 'You've been living in my house for a while now, and I feel I've gotten to know you a little better than I ever did. I actually think there's a lot of good in you, and I wonder why you try so hard not to show it.'

Jason stood very still, his head drooped and his hands hung limply at his sides. He looked at me thoughtfully, 'This – this Gerry, who made you feel so bad about yourself, he sounds a lot like my Dad. I come from a family of six brothers and not one of us has amounted to anything. My Dad made it clear he didn't expect us to, told us we were all just like our mother, who took herself off out of it years ago.'

'Oh, Jason,' I said sadly, because I knew how much it hurt to have someone you love belittle you so much that you ended up believing everything they said.

He screwed his face up, confessing, 'I never really thought about it till now. Never thought about *why* I messed about with other girls, when all I wanted was Bobbi. Why I could love her so much and still be determined to stop her being the girl I knew she could be – independent and strong. I guess I knew in my heart she was always too good for me and that one day she would realise it and leave me.'

'Other girls.' So there had been more than one, then. Well, that was between him and his conscience, and Bobbi – if he ever told her – if they ever got back together.

'People like your dad,' I told him, 'people like Gerry, are to be pitied, because they'll never learn that to keep love you have to be prepared to let it go. If love is real it will always come back to you, if not, then it was never yours to keep in the first place. Loving someone means wanting what's best for them – and that's not always necessarily what *you* think is best for them, or for you.'

Jason laughed, and the sound was harsh to my ears, 'Yeah, well I wish someone had made me see that sooner.' He hefted the bag up on his shoulder and said, 'I'll be off then. Thanks for having me stay. It's been …' he hesitated, before adding surprisingly with a genuine smile, 'good.'

*

I finished relating all this to my mother later, as she stood in the kitchen and watched me clear away the remains of what had obviously been a meal for two people.

After listening carefully, she asked in a puzzled tone, 'So, why is he still here, then?'

' 'Cos she thinks she can do something with me,' Jason's voice came from the open doorway, 'i'n't that right, Mrs M?'

'That's me,' I admitted with a wry twist to my lips, 'a glutton for punishment. Just as I think I'm beginning to get rid of you all, I go and shoot myself in the foot.'

'Is Elaine off, then?' Jason queried, and then demanded of my mother, 'Off back to the old man then, are you?'

I cringed and put in quickly, 'She's just told me she's been offered the flat over the café, actually. It's where Peggy's been living, but apparently Sam's having a granny annex built at his own property. There's plenty of room, so they won't be on top of each other, and it'll be custom built and therefore more labour-saving, with no stairs.

'Whether my mother decides to take the flat,' I put in, before he could make another thoughtless comment, 'is none of your business or mine. Now, go and tidy that room up before I change my mind about letting you stay.'

My mother didn't say anything, when he'd taken himself off, but gave me a look that spoke volumes.

'You needn't look at me like that,' I said. 'I'm just giving him the same chance as I gave to you and Bobbi. Time and support while you sorted out what you wanted to do with your lives.'

'But he's not …' she began.

'Family? Not my son? No, he's not, but Jason *is* someone's son – he might easily have been my son's friend, if things had turned out otherwise. He's only a little bit younger than Jack would have been – and I happen to think he deserves a chance. It's up to him what he does with it. Now,' it was my turn to give her a look, 'wasn't there something you wanted to talk to me about?'

*

I was glad to get back to work the next day, and told Jo as much over the inevitable lunchtime sandwich.

With yet another new recruitment drive currently in progress at Cheapsmart it was the only chance we got to really talk. Even that would have been impossible without the co-operation of a very efficient temp, who was more than happy to hold the fort for an hour.

'Let's have a glass of wine with this, for a change,' I suggested. 'I could do with one, I don't know about you?' I took a good look at her for the first time that day. 'Actually, you *do* look as if you could use one. Is it work, or something else you want to talk about?'

'Yes, to the wine,' Jo smiled wanly. 'You first for the talk, mine can wait, it isn't going to go away.'

I thought it was a funny thing for her to say, but decided to leave prodding her until she appeared to be good and ready to share whatever ailed her.

'So,' she prompted, 'Your Dad's got himself a lady friend. I have to say I'm not surprised. He's actually quite a catch, as I've said before. How did you know?'

Christ, I suddenly had an awful thought. It wasn't her, was it? Not Jo who had willingly confessed to always having a soft spot for my Dad.

I relaxed suddenly, feeling the tension ooze out of me, as I remembered aloud, 'It was Bobbi who told me. She and Jason saw them out together, and Jason, at least, was most impressed. Twenty years younger than himself and 'fit' was his description of the female hanging from his arm. I had to warn him not to go blathering about it to my mother, especially in such graphic detail.'

'I wonder where he found her?' Jo wondered out loud, 'I could do with finding the male counterpart – and so could you.'

I felt myself colouring up at words spoken partly in jest, and took a huge slug of wine to hide my confusion. Jo was on to it in a minute. Nothing much escaped her, as I had often has cause to regret.

'You're blushing – look at you – right to the top of your head. Come on – tell. What have you been up to and – much more important – who with?' She looked at me closely, and I could see her mind working overtime. 'It's Sam, isn't it?'

'Well … ' I began reluctantly, 'it is, and it isn't.'

'You've had contact with him since Friday, I take it?'

'Only on the phone,' I hastened to explain, 'but – well – he, sort of, asked me out and,' I went on in a rush, 'I don't quite know what to do about it.'

'Does it have to be a problem, then?' Jo looked completely mystified, as well she might, I admitted. 'He wants you to go out with him. Either you want to go, in which case you say yes, or you don't, and the answer is no. How difficult is that?' She thought for a moment and then added, 'If the answer is no, I suppose you could pass him on to me.' She thought again, and then continued, 'On second thoughts, don't bother, he's way out of my league.'

'And mine.'

'Ah, so that's it, then.'

'Well, you said it.'

'No,' Jo contradicted. 'I said he was out of my league. I'm fat, middle fifties and fading, you're fit, forties and feisty, there is a vast difference, Denise.'

'You're not fat,' I said the first thing to come into my head, 'and I don't know if I want the complications that seeing someone like Sam would bring.'

'It's just a date,' she pointed out calmly, 'not a full-blown affair or even a relationship at this point. It's up to you whether things go any further than that.'

'But is it?' I asked urgently. 'I do quite like him,' an immense understatement if you like, 'and a date sounds – well – nice,' another huge understatement, 'but what will he expect in return, and how will I get rid of him if I don't want to see him again? Oh, Jo,' I wailed, 'it's been *forever* since I went out with a man. It just scares me to death – the very thought of it.'

'I'd quite like to have those sort of worries,' Jo said, without smiling, 'and, unlike you, I haven't had a good relationship to use as a measuring stick.'

I stared at her in surprise. I'd never heard her sound so sorry for herself before.

'Jo, I'm so sorry. I'm being totally thoughtless, not to mention so shallow you couldn't paddle in me.'

She laughed then, looking and sounding much more like herself, and I was almost light-headed with relief. She was having a bad day, that was all – 'feel sorry for yourself' day. We all had them at some time or another.

'No,' she said, '*I'm* sorry. If I was asked out by a gorgeous man, I'd have a few concerns, too, but at the end of the day, it's just a night out initially, and worrying ahead is a bit pointless. I think it was you who told me that.'

I could see that she was making a real effort to be more her old self, but I was beginning to get the distinct impression that something was far from right with her. Was she ill? I looked at her closely, over the rim of my wine glass; a little pale, perhaps, but not unusually so.

Could it be Petie, up to his old tricks again? No, I dismissed that notion out of hand. He'd only been out with Bobbi on Saturday night, and she hadn't mentioned anything about problems. In fact, I had Petie to thank for helping to steer Bobbi back onto the right pathway.

Looking at her again, I decided there *was* something wrong. Jo definitely wasn't her usual self and it had to be something fairly serious because she was normally so good at hiding any problems she had.

'Jo,' I said hesitantly, 'you can tell me to mind my own business but …' I paused, and then rushed on before I could change my mind, 'I feel as if something's really bothering you. If you want to talk … If I can help … Well, I just wanted to say I'm here for you – just as you're always been there for me.'

There, it was said. She could laugh and dismiss it as nothing. She could say it was nothing and simply clam up, or she could …

Jo burst into noisy tears and I immediately realised it was the one option I hadn't been prepared for. I didn't recall her ever doing such a thing in all the years I'd worked with her. In fact, I was so shocked that I almost joined her and had to fight back the tears welling up into my own eyes.

'Oh, Jo, love,' I pushed both of our paper napkins into her hand. 'What is it? What's happened? How can I help?'

As was usual in such a busy place, no one was taking much notice of us. I guessed the staff had seen it all before, and the customers were too busy catching up on the weekend activities of friends and colleagues to worry about the two middle-aged women in the corner having some sort of crisis.

'Jo?'

She hadn't answered, being too concerned with mopping her face, and pretending that nothing had happened. Her furtive gaze flicked round the room, and I wanted to tell her they didn't matter – just as she'd told me a dozen or more times during those early grief-stricken days after Rob's death.

'It's Petie,' she said finally, and I felt my jaw drop.

Despite everything that had happened in the past, I'd truly believed that this time he had changed. Hadn't I seen him with my own eyes? Listened and approved of his plans?

Seen his determination influence my own daughter into taking stock of her life and turn it around.

Jo laughed a trifle grimly at my expression, 'See. He even had you fooled.'

'But what has he done? It can't be that bad, surely? Non-payment of fines, no MOT on his car?'

I trawled round in my mind for some of his misdemeanours of the past, all of them bad enough for a law-abiding citizen like me, but fairly run-of-the-mill for someone like Petie – or even Jason.

Then I remembered. He had a drink-driving rap hanging over him. Again, bad enough, but a ban and a hefty fine would have sorted it out – unless … ?

'He was caught drink-driving again last night. One of his "friends" phoned me. He's up in court today and this time, Denise, this time I'm sure he's going to prison,' and then we both burst into tears.

CHAPTER 15

MOPPING AT MY EYES FRANTICALLY, I demanded indignantly, 'What on earth does Petie think he's playing at. Drink-driving is such a serious offence. One charge is bad enough, but to do it again. After all he said, too, Jo.'

'See,' she said, managing a watery smile. 'You're beginning to feel the way I feel – and he isn't even your son.'

'But he might have been, Jo,' I admitted, and then it all came pouring out. It was as if telling Bobbi about her brother had opened the floodgates. I wanted to tell all my nearest and dearest about my little boy – not to have to keep his birth and death hidden away like some shameful secret. I'd been doing that for far too long.

My son might have behaved just like Petie or Jason, had he lived to become a young man. Like Jo, I knew that I would have loved him, no matter what. Unlike Jason's mother – who must have had her reasons, I allowed – I felt sure that I could never have abandoned him. In my heart I somehow knew that feeling had a bearing on my treatment of Jason the day before. Every child, good or bad, young or grown, deserves the unconditional love of at least one parent.

Jo was amazed, more than anything, because I had managed to keep it such a well-kept secret for so long, I think. We didn't have to say it aloud for it to be understood between us, that a living son, no matter how badly behaved, was still a blessing. Losing a son temporarily to prison was infinitely preferable to losing one permanently to death.

'You should have taken the day off,' I told Jo, suddenly horrified that she'd had to work when she should have been there, supporting her son in facing a fight for freedom that was probably doomed, from what I'd read and heard.

'I've been there and done that more times than I care to remember,' she told me sadly. 'This time he must stand on his own two feet and take responsibility for his actions alone. I've thought and thought about this – all through the night, actually – and I've finally accepted, allowing him to witness the grief and pain his actions cause me is not going to change him. It never has before, has it? Oh, I don't doubt that he loves me, in his own way, but never quite enough to change his behaviour for my peace of mind.'

I could see Jo's point. I didn't know if I could have stuck to the decision to stay away as she had, but I admired her for taking this stand, and I said so.

It didn't stop her breaking her heart, probably with relief, when the news finally filtered through that Petie had escaped the custodial sentence she had been fully expecting him to get. However, a three-year ban on him driving meant he would undoubtedly lose his job, leaving him with no way to pay the hefty fine that was also imposed on him.

Convinced he would still end up in prison eventually, anyway, for non-payment of the fine, Jo became so distraught that I had to send her home by taxi. If I hadn't already taken the previous day off with the plea of a crisis at home, I'd have gone with her. I promised to go there right after work, ignoring all her protestations that she'd be all right.

I snapped at two younger colleagues from another department, when I caught them gossiping in the corridor later that afternoon, obviously having heard about Petie on the grapevine.

I firmly reminded them that when they became parents they would realise that child-rearing is not easy – and nor is the outcome certain – and that being the case, they could well find themselves the subject of someone's gossip one day. Asking them how they would like it sent them slinking back to their desks with their tails – metaphorically – between their legs.

Feeling totally exhausted and emotionally drained by the end of the day, I sighed deeply when the phone rang as I was putting my jacket on, and thought more than twice about answering it. My reluctance must have been apparent in a tone that was normally determinedly up-beat and efficient.

'Rough day?' came a sympathetic voice, and I felt my heart lift just a little. Of all people, I was never so pleased that it was Adam on the other end of the line.

'You don't know the half of it,' I told him. 'What can I do for you?'

'I was hoping I'd catch you before you left. Don't fancy a drink, do you?'

'Oh, Adam, you don't know how wonderful that sounds, but I'm sorry, I really can't.'

'That's okay,' he said quickly – too quickly – and I knew that he, too, had something on his mind.

I had to make a decision, in a hurry. Jo and Adam were both my very good friends. They were friends I had relied on heavily over the past long, lonely months. They had never let me down and I knew I simply couldn't let either of them down. There was only one thing for it.

'I have to go to Jo's,' I told Adam. 'Something has come up – something awful – but why don't you come with me? She likes you, Adam, and I'm sure she won't mind you being there. Perhaps we could have that drink later, when we see how it goes.'

'Don't worry about me,' he said immediately.

But I insisted right back, 'Come with me,' and this time he didn't refuse.

A quick phone call home advised Jason to expect me when he saw me, to give the same message to my mother, and to sort himself something out to eat.

'No worries,' he said.

He didn't mention Bobbi or whether she had been in touch, and I realised belatedly that she hadn't let me know how things were going up there. Realistically, she probably wouldn't have phoned home, just in case Jason was still there, but she could have contacted me at work. No doubt she would when she had something definite to tell me. I'd keep my mobile switched on, just in case, and my fingers crossed for her. I'd perhaps ring her on her mobile later or tomorrow.

Adam and I reached Jo's block of flats at the same time and he followed me up the two flights of concrete stairs to her door. The door was slightly ajar, which I half expected, because she obviously knew I was due to arrive, and I walked straight into the familiar lemon-washed narrow hallway. What I *hadn't* been expecting was a delicious smell of cooking to greet me. Surely, with everything she had on her mind she hadn't felt obliged to cook a meal?

'Jo,' I made my way to the kitchen, 'what on earth do you think you're doing?'

'You know I'm better keeping busy at times like this.' She turned from stirring the bubbling contents of a saucepan with a fleeting smile.

'I've brought Adam with me,' I told her, and he popped his head round the door behind me and greeted her warmly, as I added, 'I hope that's not going to cause a problem with whatever you've prepared?'

'No, I've made plenty. Hello, Adam. Nice to see you. I hope you like tuna and pasta bake.'

'A home-cooked meal, whatever it is, sounds like heaven to me, but tuna pasta has always been a particular favourite of mine. Will it have the crunchy, cheesy topping?'

When Jo promised that it would, and that she would ensure he got the lion's share, Adam didn't even try to hide his delight, which made us both smile, just a little bit. He didn't protest or offer to go away, either, and I felt that Jo was as glad to have him there as I was. We all had our share of problems after all.

We were all kept busy for a while, with Adam laying up the table in the homely lounge-cum-diner, having been provided by Jo with cloth, napkins and what looked suspiciously like her best cutlery. I was given the task of preparing a green tossed salad, and Jo carried on with the pasta, finally transferring the whole dish to the oven for browning.

'And now this,' Jo whipped a chilled bottle of white wine from the fridge. 'It's very low alcohol,' she explained in answer to my quizzical look, 'but quite delicious, and we can pretend, can't we?'

'Of course,' I agreed, adding under my breath, 'I hope you didn't mind me bringing Adam. He phoned just as I was leaving, I think he wanted to talk and I didn't have the heart to put him off.'

'Poor you,' Jo returned, 'landed with not one, but two lame ducks.'

'The same ducks,' I reminded her firmly, 'who had no hesitation about tucking me under their wings, not too long ago.'

'Can I carry anything through?' Adam was back in the doorway, and then, looking puzzled, he added, 'I thought we were having tuna – not duck.'

The off-hand remark made us giggle a bit, and lightened the atmosphere considerably. I think we all felt more at ease by the time we sat down around Jo's minuscule dining table and, as we ate, we shared just general small talk about work in general and newsworthy items from the papers.

It was quite difficult for me to try and steer the conversation round to those things that really needed to be aired. A good drink of something stronger would have loosened all of our tongues and made it that much easier all round.

'Adam doesn't know yet,' I began awkwardly, 'about Petie. I wasn't sure if ...'

'No point trying to keep it secret,' Jo said bravely. 'I'm sure it will be common knowledge before too long and,' she interpreted my downward gaze accurately, 'by the look on your face the news has already reached the office.'

'Well, I soon put the gossips back into their place,' I assured her, indignant all over again as I remembered. 'None of us has the right to sit in judgement.'

'I know,' Jo agreed, 'but we all do it.'

'Whatever it is will be a nine day wonder,' Adam put it, 'just as my divorce will be.'

That stopped us in our tracks, two jaws practically hit the table simultaneously, and Jo and I gaped at him.

'But I thought ...' Jo began.

'Are you sure you know what you're doing?' I couldn't keep the concern out of my voice. I really couldn't believe Adam was giving up on his marriage without a fight, not when he'd invested so much time, patience, and not to mention money, all to keep Lisbet by his side.

'I really appreciate your concern,' Adam smiled at us both, 'and I can see now why women – most women,' he corrected, 'make such good friends. Even I, however, can finally see that I'm banging my head against a brick wall.'

I wanted to shout, hallelujah, but didn't think it was quite appropriate, given the circumstances. There was no doubt that Adam had always adored Lisbet, and it must be tearing his heart out to admit defeat.

'Sometimes,' he said, and I found he was echoing my thoughts, 'it's easier to admit defeat and start over. Yes, I might eventually win Lisbet back from muscleman, but then it will just be someone else she sets her sights on. It's humiliating, to say the least, and you can hardly call it love, can you?'

It was a bit telling that neither Jo nor I disagreed with him. In the end, I just reached out, took his hand, and said, 'I'm so sorry, Adam,' and I was – for him.

'That's how I feel about Petie,' Jo told us, and quickly sketched in what had happened for Adam's benefit. 'He's probably out tonight celebrating his lucky escape, though he seemed quite confident he wasn't going to prison anyway. I suppose he should know, having a better knowledge of the judicial system than I possibly could, given my unblemished character.

'It all seems to be water of a duck's back to Petie, I'm the one lying awake at night worrying. I feel I must cut my losses, stand back and just let him make his own mistakes – and take full responsibility for them. I've tried everything, and whatever I do, it changes nothing. Perhaps an eventual spell in prison will achieve what I can't.'

'I hope it won't come to that,' Adam said seriously. 'I really liked your son, Jo, and I feel sure that in the end he will turn around. In fact, I'm so sure of it, I'm prepared to put my money where my mouth is and offer him a job, if he wants it.'

Jo was delighted, and she said so, taking Adam's hand and looking into his eyes as if he were some sort of god. He didn't take his hand away, and for a minute or two they remained like that.

I felt very much the outsider and wondered why I wasn't more pleased to see them close like that. It was what I'd always wanted, wasn't it? Or was it?

Wasn't someone like Jo just what Adam needed? Okay, she was a bit older, but she would take care of Adam as no one else ever had. They would be ideal together, I told myself staunchly, but in my heart the idea did nothing for me and I wondered why that was.

I quickly pulled myself together and said, 'I didn't tell you, Jo, that Petie was instrumental in getting Bobbi to rethink her future and make that snap decision to return to university.'

'No.' To my relief she let go of Adam's hand and turned to face me with her eyes bright.

Adam looked mystified, because, of course, I hadn't had time to tell him everything that had happened since the wedding. Was it really only on Saturday? Lord, it seemed a million years ago.

'Petie had invited me to a concert,' I explained quickly, 'on Saturday, but as it clashed with the wedding we went to, he kindly took Bobbi instead. Jason was away,' I added, as if that explained everything, which, of course, it did. 'Petie was talking to her about regretting never gaining any real qualifications, and how that had always held him back. According to Bobbi, he seemed determined to go to college, evening classes or something, and to start all over.' I paused, and must have looked confused – as indeed I was. 'I wonder what changed between Saturday night and Monday night.'

Jo looked rueful, 'He'll have realised the effort it was going to take,' she said sadly. 'He's great on theory, but low on effort and commitment. Petie never liked the fact that the good things in life just don't come easily.'

'Well, I'll always be grateful that his comments brought home to Bobbi what she was throwing away,' I said staunchly, 'I'm hoping to hear that they've allowed her to go back and take up her place on the course, and make up her placement time at the hospital.'

'What about the boy?' Adam asked, 'Jason, wasn't it?'

'Yes,' Jo looked at me closely. 'You didn't get as far as telling me all this at lunch-time. I'm really pleased about Bobbi – especially about Petie's part in it all – but you've still neglected to mention what you've done about the lodger from hell.'

'I've let him stay – for now,' I told her reluctantly, and seeing the two looks of complete horror, I added in what I recognised was a very defensive tone, 'He's not *that* bad and, anyway, if I don't give him a chance, who else is going to?'

'You're not on your own in the house with him, are you?' Adam was obviously concerned with my safety, though whether the concern was for my physical or moral welfare, I had no idea.

I found his anxiety laughably over the top, and said so, 'For heaven's sake, Adam, he's not *dangerous.*'

'Perhaps not in the way that Adam means,' Jo agreed, 'but he can still break your heart, Denise. He's not *your* responsibility. You don't have to put up with the kind of grief I get from Petie, Jason is not your ...'

'Son?' I finished for her, and saw the expression on her face change as she accepted that at least one of the reasons I was doing this for Jason *was* my own son. 'I know,' I continued, hoping she wouldn't say more, since Adam, like Rob, had never known anything about the child I'd lost, 'and I'm grateful for your concern, both of you – really – but you're just going to have to let me do this and trust that I think I know what I'm doing.'

*

I had a rare moment of feeling that I was doing the right thing – at least by Jason – when I arrived home. He had his music on louder than I would have liked, but turned it down the moment I walked in the door, and he even hurried to put the kettle on.

'Bobbi phoned,' he told me, his attention on warming the teapot.

My heart sank. Bobbi now knew that Jason was staying, without me having the chance to explain why. What on earth would she think of me? Would she understand my reasons for allowing him to remain?

'What did she say? What did you say to her?' I said carefully, and then asked indignantly, 'Why didn't she ring me on my mobile?'

Jason laughed, 'Hark at the lady who definitely didn't ever want or need a mobile phone.' Then he was serious. 'It's okay, I didn't have a go at her.' Seeing my doubtful look, he insisted, 'Honestly, Mrs M. They're letting her continue, and I wished her well, and said I hoped we could be friends. I was wrong before. I know that now. I told her that, too, and that I was beginning to understand the true meaning of family.' He poured the tea out, still without really looking at me. 'She asked would you ring her on her mobile. She said she didn't ring yours because it's less expensive to ring a land-line.'

'I'll ring her now,' I said, itching to hear her news, and wanting to get explanations I owed her about Jason out of the way. 'I'll go and change my shoes while I talk to her, I won't be long. Why don't you get some bourbons out to go with the tea?'

In the peace of my bedroom, the background noise of the pub or club Bobbi was in sounded extra loud.

'Hi, Mum.' She sounded more cheerful that she had in weeks. 'Did Jason tell you my news?'

'He did, love, and I'm so pleased.'

'Yeah, it means I won't get much of a summer break, with having to make up placement time, but I'm just so happy to be back. I'm having a drink or two with my mates to celebrate.'

'I didn't get a chance to talk to you …' I hesitated, 'about Jason.'

'It's just typical of you, Mum,' for a moment I thought she was about to criticise, and then she continued, above the hubbub, 'to be thinking of someone else when you really should be thinking of yourself. Jason was amazed, though he's always been pretty impressed by you, and he's promised me that he won't let you down.'

'So you don't mind, then?'

'I'm really pleased – honestly. I felt really bad about baling out like that, and I *was* worried about what would happen to him, even though I couldn't let it stop me from coming back here. He's not all bad, Mum,' she said, echoing my words to Jo and Adam earlier in the evening.

'Well, we'll see,' I said cautiously. 'Perhaps I'll make a ruling like *Big Brother* on television, as in three strikes and you're out.'

We both laughed, and I noticed how carefree Bobbi sounded, and I thanked God that she, at least, appeared to be back on the right track.

Back downstairs again, I told Jason about Adam's divorce. There seemed to be no harm in that since it would obviously be common knowledge soon enough.

'That's a shame,' Jason surprised me by saying. 'He seemed like a fair guy. What was *her* problem?'

I shrugged, 'Who knows?' Then a thought struck me. 'Where's my mother? It's getting late for her to be out, she doesn't even drive.'

'I gave her a lift, as it happens,' Jason said surprisingly, adding more typically, 'She had to let me have some petrol money, of course, 'cos I was running on empty.'

'Of course,' I said faintly, wondering what having a lady of Elaine's vintage years in his car had done for his street cred.

'I said I'd pick her up if she rang.'

'That was nice of you, but where did she go?'

'Well, to see your Dad about this other woman, I think, and by the look on her face when I dropped her off, I don't think that Adam chap is going to be the only one looking for a divorce.'

CHAPTER 16

I WAS GLAD OF JASON'S COMPANY as I waited for my mother to come home. I realised she was probably still out with my father, but it felt strange, a real case of role reversal, to be waiting up for a parent who was out after bedtime. No wonder she'd been concerned when I'd stayed out late as a teenager all those years ago.

In the end it got so late that Jason took himself off to bed, at my insistence. It was no good two of us losing our sleep and that's what I told him.

'But you've got work,' he protested, 'and I haven't.'

I nearly said I didn't need reminding that the job at B and Q hadn't worked out, but carefully refrained from comment. Working in a personnel department, myself, I could hardly blame them for thinking twice about employing someone who showed such a lack of enthusiasm for the job offer. He must have made it all too obvious that he preferred a weekend jaunt to Amsterdam to a good job and a regular wage.

'You've got a date with the job centre,' I insisted, 'Remember? The early bird catches the worm, Jason, where jobs are concerned. No one is going to come knocking at the door to offer you work.'

'Mmm,' he looked thoughtful for a moment. 'I don't suppose that Adam has any jobs going for someone like me, or what about Cheapsmart?'

I tried not to look horrified, stared at Jason, and then, remembering his own words just in time, I reminded him, 'You said you wanted to work with cars, remember?'

'Yes, but …'

'What did we say about settling for less than you really want from your life? I've never heard you express any interest in building or shop work. You'll be much happier doing a job you really like, won't you? Be honest, now.'

I knew acute lack of confidence when I saw it, and it showed on Jason's face and was apparent in his words, when he said, 'What if I'm not good enough? I don't have any real experience, do I?'

'You've kept that old banger outside going,' I pointed out, 'and even patched up the bodywork reasonably well. With proper training I think you'd be great. Please, Jason, give it a go for me, will you? If all else fails, I promise I will have a word with Adam for you.'

I hoped he wouldn't notice that I'd left Cheapsmart out of the equation. I really thought expecting me to recommend him for a job there was carrying this whole un-family support thing much too far.

'Well, all right,' he said grudgingly, and I wondered if I had pushed too hard with the car thing – until I caught the glitter of tears in his eyes as he walked to the door and realised that, apart from Bobbi, I was probably the only one who had given a damn about what he did or didn't do with his life.

'Goodnight, Jason,' I said.

'Goodnight, Mrs M,' he replied softly, and the door closed on a barely distinguishable, 'thank you.'

*

'Where have you been?' I asked my mother, when she finally walked in as the clock in the hall struck two.

'Is it very late, dear?' she asked, as if she had no idea.

'Cup of tea?' I offered, recognising what was obviously barely hidden distress, in spite of the immaculate appearance that was always so much a part of Elaine.

'No tea, dear,' she refused. 'I'm very tired, I think I'll just go on up.'

It was the first time I had ever seen her look anything like her age, but she suddenly looked old and weary, and I found that incredibly scary.

'Do you want to talk?' I offered.

'I think it's too late for talking,' she said, scaring me even more. 'He's got someone else, you know – Harry.'

'Bobbi told me yesterday,' I admitted, 'but I wasn't sure that I believed her, though I couldn't think why she'd want to lie about it. With everything going on I never found a chance to talk to you. It's true, then, is it?'

Elaine nodded silently, and then, her tone accusing, she suddenly turned on me and demanded, 'You must have known this would happen. When I arrived here why on earth didn't you just turn me around and send me back home where I belonged?'

With that parting shot, she turned on her elegant high-heeled shoes, and was gone, closing the door with a decisive little click behind her. I was left behind, still trying to gather my scattered wits together and wondering how everything had suddenly become my fault.

*

'It's just so unfair of her to blame me,' I told Jo, who had courageously returned to work determined to face the inevitable gossip sooner, rather than later, and with her head held high.

By then, the whole department, and probably the whole of the company, for all I knew, must have been aware of the court case and the result of it. Some colleagues were supportive and openly sympathetic, others found it easier to ignore the episode, a few muttered behind their hands but *they* were in the minority, I was pleased to note.

'Unfair, yes, but easier for your mother to blame you, than to take responsibility for her own actions. You see, Denise,' she said, 'it all comes back to the same thing in the end.'

She was right, of course, but that didn't stop me smarting with self-righteous indignation. Hadn't I tried to show my mother that she was taking things too far, that she could have had a new independence *and* kept her marriage to my father safe – if she had only started by simply telling him how she felt?

'The only way to deal with it, is to refuse to accept any of the blame,' Jo advised. 'Don't be like me. I spent months – even years beating myself up over Petie and wondering what I could have done differently. Don't allow yourself to follow that route. Your mother is an adult, for heaven's sake, she's a lot older than you, and she made her own choices – without consulting you at all, if my memory serves me right.'

Changing the subject abruptly, she went on, 'Wasn't that lovely of Adam? Fancy him offering to sort Petie out with a job. He's offered to take me out for a meal tonight, too, "cheer us both up," he said ... '

Jo went on in the same vein for what seemed like ages. She was obviously excited about going out socially for a change, and wondering about such things as what she should wear, where they might go, and whether she ought to offer to go Dutch with the cost.

I hope I was encouraging, cheerful and helpful with my replies. I certainly tried not to feel dog-in-the-manger about them spending an evening together. I was pleased for them both, I really was, but I suddenly felt friendless and a bit redundant, too, if I was being honest. If they were supporting each other, they obviously didn't need me.

I went back to my office in a thoughtful frame of mind and tried to knuckle down to the pile of paperwork that waited for me there. It wasn't that easy to concentrate and I welcomed the phone ringing – until I realised who was on the other end of the line, and what she wanted.

'Well, I hope you're satisfied with yourself.' The tone was needle sharp and it took me a minute or two to place it.

'Janice? Is that you, how ni ... '

'Never mind the pleasantries,' she cut in swiftly, 'I've been talking to Lisbet and she told me ... '

'I didn't know you knew Lisbet,' I put in, recalling belatedly that they'd probably met at barbecues and the odd social occasion, when Rob would issue invitations to Janice and her family in an effort to maintain even spasmodic contact with his only sibling. As I recalled, the effort had always been pretty one-sided.

'She told me,' Janice went on forcefully, 'that Adam wants a divorce – and that it's all your doing.'

I was speechless, and in my job, dealing with sometimes very difficult people, that didn't happen very often. In fact, I was so shocked at the blatant untruth of the accusation being levelled at me, and the venom in the tone used, I almost dropped the phone. That last remark completely took my breath away, but I could tell that Janice was waiting for my reaction.

'And how did she come to that conclusion?' I was really pleased that my tone sounded so even and as if I was completely calm.

'Apparently, you were all over Adam at some wedding on Saturday, and it's obviously no coincidence that within forty-eight hours he's threatening divorce.'

'I was not,' I protested vehemently before I could stop myself, 'and Adam deciding he's had enough of Lisbet's well-documented extra-marital antics has absolutely nothing to do with me.'

'Well, you would say that, wouldn't you?'

'Yes, I would,' I said, beginning to get very angry, 'if it was the truth.'

'Rob must be spinning in his …' she began.

'*Don't. You. Dare.* Bring Rob into this.' I could hear the ice in my tone, but despite the fact it would have frozen boiling water, there was no stopping Janice.

'Hardly been gone five minutes. Any bloke will do, even someone else's. Not the first time … seen in a public house with him.'

At that point I realised trying to argue was a waste of time. Janice had evidently been waiting for something – anything – to pin on me. I'd never been good enough for Rob as far as she was concerned, I'd always been well aware of that, and now she was going to fight his corner – whether he would have wished it or not.

No matter that I was totally innocent of every accusation Janice had thrown at me – in her eyes I would always be guilty of daring to live when her brother had died. It would have been laughable if it weren't so sad, because the fact they hadn't been close when Rob was alive had never seemed to bother Janice, though it was something her brother had regretted.

I took a deep breath, went to say something, thought better of it, and put the phone back onto its receiver, very, very gently. When it rang again, almost immediately, I let it ring until it was picked up by the voice-mail system.

I was shaking and, of course, once I'd disconnected the call I came up with a million and one answers to each of her accusations. It would have been pointless to argue back, I knew that, *and* that I had no hope of convincing her that she was very wrong. Janice didn't want to hear the truth. She had just what she wanted, a stick she thought she could beat me with, after months of waiting, and she wasn't about to let it go.

Normally, I would have run to Jo, or phoned Adam, but I'd have felt very uncomfortable discussing this with either one of them. Adam would be embarrassed at Janice's insinuations, I was sure, and Jo might just have thought there was an element of truth in there, somewhere, given the interest she had suddenly developed in Adam herself.

The phone ringing again was a distraction I welcomed. I just hoped, fervently, that it wasn't Janice.

'About that date,' said a deep voice. The invitation and the tone were enough to send my temperature soaring and my pulse racing and, after my sister-in-law's spite, it was just the soothing balm I needed.

'I'd love to go out with you, Sam,' I said, without pausing to allow myself any misgivings, and I knew that I meant it.

*

Jason's reaction was just what I needed. He was on a high, anyway, having landed a trial with a local car repair bodyshop, working for them initially through an agency for a trial period.

'Good on you, Mrs M,' he chortled, tickled pink. 'Get out there and strut your stuff on the arm of the most eligible bachelor in town, why don't you?'

He was exaggerating, of course, but I had concerns nevertheless. 'You don't think I'm too old for him, do you?' I queried anxiously.

'Too old. Nah, you're fit. That Pete guy didn't think you were too old for *him* and *he's* only twenty-something.'

I stood stock still, and stared at Jason. 'What on earth do you mean?'

He was still grinning. 'Bobbi was telling me about the concert, on the phone last night, and about how he went on and on about you. She said it wasn't very flattering to be compared to her mother all night, and that it was quite obvious Pete would have preferred it to have been you there with him.'

'Don't be silly.' I laughed, too, suddenly sure he was having a joke at my expense, but also certain that I had to prove a point to a few people – and also to myself.

This was *my* life. Mine to do with as I pleased. I didn't interfere much with the way those around me chose to live their lives, and I wished they would all give me the same courtesy. I *hadn't* chosen to be single again, but it was a fact of my life, now, that I was. It was time to move on, to live again, and that was just what I intended to do.

My mother maintained a dignified silence for the most part through the remainder of the week. Perhaps she was intending to keep it up until I apologised for allowing her to set up home in my house, without so much as a by-your-leave. She had a very long wait ahead, but I had no intention of telling her that, or anything else. I was done with explaining myself.

She did unbend a little on Saturday when I picked her up as she walked home from Peg's Place on my way home from town. She followed me into the house, watching me drop a pile of slithering carrier bags in the hall with a good attempt at disinterest, but I could tell she was itching to say something.

'Have you had something done to your hair, Denise?' she eventually enquired stiffly. 'It looks a little different.'

'Just a couple of highlights and a blow-dry,' I dismissed a three-hour session at the trendiest salon in town as if it was nothing, despite it having cost me the equivalent of a whole arm, plus half a leg. 'I'll just pop a frozen lasagne into the microwave, for quickness, shall I? Only I'm going out tonight.'

I watched her jaw drop, but didn't wait for any further reaction, or indeed any comment, before making my way upstairs to hang my purchases away.

A few moments later, when I went back downstairs intending to throw together a salad to go with the lasagne, I was surprised to hear Jason fighting my corner. So surprised, in fact, that I stopped, unashamedly, to listen.

'How can it be her fault?' he was demanding fiercely. 'Did you ring first, ask your daughter if you could come and stay? Did you even trouble to let her know you weren't happy with your life before you upped sticks and landed here? No,' he went on furiously, 'I didn't think you did. I don't suppose you mentioned it to poor old Harry either.'

My mother spluttered a bit, but Jason was already continuing indignantly, 'Stop trying to shove the blame anywhere else but where it belongs. *You* walked out on a very nice life. Yes, you did. No one made you, did they?'

There was more muttering, but my mother was showing signs of knowing when she was beaten, though she did make one final attempt to shed some of the blame.

'You and Bobbi ... ' she began.

'Shouldn't have taken advantage, either. I'll tell you straight, I don't know how Mrs M put up with me. She didn't deserve what we dished up, *and* at a time when she was still having real trouble getting her life back on track. Looking back, I'm ashamed of myself and my behaviour – and so should you bloody well be.'

I crept back up the stairs, just about halfway, and then made a lot of noise about coming back down. Supper, I have to say, was a much friendlier affair than any of the meals that had preceded it through the week.

*

Sam's club 'DanzOn' was the first nightclub I'd been into in more years than I cared to remember. As a child of the eighties, brought up around the time of discos, the sophistication of the place was completely unexpected.

The theme was appropriate to a club situated in a seaside resort, with realistic sand dunes in unexpected corners and what looked like genuine bathers of both sexes – surrounded by similarly realistic fish – swimming behind the floor to ceiling glass walls that surrounded bar and dance areas. I had to make a concerted effort not to appear completely gauche and lacking in sophistication by gawking, but it wasn't easy to behave as if such sights were an everyday occurrence in my mundane life.

'We won't stay,' Sam had promised, as he ushered me from his dark blue Jaguar saloon to the club door with a protective arm around my waist. 'Only I usually show my face at some point during the evening – just to keep the staff on their toes,' he'd added with a bit of a smile, so that I wasn't sure if he was joking or not.

'Don't apologise,' I managed before we were caught up and swept along by a wave of chattering, laughing people all apparently wanting a piece of Sam.

For someone who had barely been out socially for many months, and who even before that had tended to live the quiet life, it was a frightening yet exhilarating experience. Sam never let go of me, not even for a moment, introducing me to this person and that, pointing this way and that at things he particularly wanted me to notice. He was obviously very proud of his club, and with good reason.

Even at that relatively early hour in the evening the place appeared to be heaving. Mainly with youngsters, it had to be said, but there were a few groups of people in their thirties, forties, and possibly some into their fifties, too. I didn't feel out of place, thanks to Jason's advice on what was acceptable wear in these sort of places.

Not for me the cropped top, pierced naval, or trendy tattoo, but in a pale pink sequinned vest and matching trousers and with the aid of an application of fake tan, I felt quite part of the scene. It seemed as if anything went, though dressing up appeared to be the order of the day as opposed to dressing down.

Looking round, I did take a moment to wonder what on earth Sam was doing here with me, when he could probably have his pick of the luscious young lovelies who crowded the place. Then I shrugged, mine not to reason why, after all. He'd asked me, I'd accepted, and I was here to enjoy myself, not to question Sam's motives.

True to his word, Sam was ready to leave within a short time, to the very evident disappointment of his army of hangers-on. I didn't miss the curious and frankly envious looks that followed our departure, and the murmured, 'Who *is* that?' from the feminine contingent.

We went straight to a restaurant that I was unfamiliar with, though I had probably passed its discreet doors a hundred times. It wasn't the sort of place Rob and I would have frequented on our rare nights out. You could tell, without setting foot in the place, that the prices would probably make your eyes water. Its huge bay windows looked out across Lower Brankstone's small, but very well-kept park, and inside the atmosphere and ambience encouraged a very select clientele. Sam, it quickly became apparent, was a regular.

We were shown, without delay, into one of a number of booths that took up all of the centre of the main body of the restaurant. Built of dark wood, and with high sides, these afforded total privacy to the occupants. It was as if Sam and I were quite alone, a fact I found quite disconcerting at least initially.

The menu was all in French – with no sub-titles – and I thanked heaven for a strict French tutor at school all those years before. I had carried a smattering of the language with me, courtesy of her determined teaching, ever since. The prices were every bit as steep as I'd expected but I resolutely followed Sam's lead and ordered exactly what I wanted.

It was a very long time since I had been out on anything that could be termed a date, and this odd feeling that I shouldn't be there persisted. Perhaps that was because inside my head I was still a married woman.

Rob wouldn't have been at all comfortable in such a place: the thought crept into my head unbidden and stayed there. He'd been a plain man, with plain tastes. A good steak, without all the fancy sauces, would have been more to his liking. I worked harder at dismissing the thought and tucked into my *steak bordelaise* with gusto, reminding myself that was then, this was now, and I was here to enjoy myself.

'You don't know how lovely it is to find a woman who enjoys her food,' Sam said suddenly, and as I paused with a forkful halfway to my mouth, he laughed at my expression, and added, 'Everyone's on a diet these days. It can get very boring. Eat up, eat up,' he encouraged. 'They do the most wonderful choice of sweets here.'

I relaxed, understanding that he was only speaking the truth. He was his mother's son and would appreciate anyone with a good appetite. There was no hidden agenda in his smiling words.

Recalling that the majority of females in the club – especially those surrounding him – had been thin to the point of emaciation, I could well believe that a good cooked meal – especially any that came complete with a rich sauce – would be abhorrent to them.

We talked about this and that, about everything and nothing at all. He knew about my remaining lodgers, obviously from my mother or his, and expressed concern about the fact that Jason was still in my house. I was surprised when he pointed out that with Bobbi gone and my mother now considering moving into the flat above the café, I could find myself the butt of idle gossip.

I could have made a joke about the fact that I already was, but in the light of realising that folk really *will* make something out of nothing, I determinedly laughed it off instead.

'I would certainly have to have an inflated idea of my own charms to think Jason would look twice at me,' I smiled, 'and I'd probably be incredibly flattered to think that anyone else would assume such a thing – though I doubt that he'd find it so amusing.'

'I think,' Sam said, looking right into my eyes, 'that you have no idea how attractive you really are – to men of all ages – and I find that absolutely refreshing.'

In my confusion I dropped my fork, and Sam laughed softly as, with a flick of his tanned fingers, he had the waiter bring me another one.

When we left the restaurant he had his arm around me. I felt quite comfortable with that, and most of the other diners took absolutely no notice. There was one person, female, however, who appeared to be taking a great deal of notice.

She looked thoroughly disapproving and she also seemed vaguely familiar.

It wasn't until Sam had assisted me into his car – his attentiveness all too apparent not only to me but to interested onlookers – and we were driving away, that I recalled when I had seen her last and why she had seemed familiar then.

CHAPTER 17

WHEN I PLACED THE WOMAN GLARING at me so censoriously in the restaurant, I immediately understood the animosity emanating toward me. She was a friend of my sister-in-law, Janice, one I had met probably only once or twice in the past. As I remembered I recalled, in an instant, having her glare at me in a similarly disapproving fashion on another occasion only quite recently.

She'd been in the pub the night I'd arranged to meet up with Adam. In all innocence – given the fact that he clearly wanted to talk, and the state of great chaos reigning at home at that time – I had deemed it a more suitable choice of venue. After all, what harm could there be in meeting an old and dear friend in a crowded pub? In some people's eyes, quite a lot it appeared, and it all suddenly made perfect sense of Janice's 'not the first time' remark.

My God, they would have a field day with this one. My ears would be burning by the morning, that was if she could even manage to wait that long. My reputation was going to be in tatters, at least in their fraternity, but I found to my immense surprise that it didn't bother me in the least. They should really get a life, perhaps then they would realise that I was entitled to one. In any case, everyone who cared for me knew me well enough to know the scarlet woman label was just not the real me.

'Do you want to go home yet?'

Sam's voice scattered my thoughts, and I turned to him with a smile. 'What did you have in mind?' I said, before I realised how that might sound and went on hurriedly, 'What? A drink somewhere, dancing, something like that?'

'We-ell,' he drawled softly, his eyes on the road, 'we could go back to the club if that's what you fancy. My preference would be to have you to myself for a bit longer. It's a lovely night, what about a walk along the beach?'

I turned in my seat to face him, and laughed delightedly, 'I'd like that of all things. It's what Rob and I ... ' I bit my lip and cursed myself for being so tactless. Sam didn't want to hear about Rob and I. He knew I was widowed, he didn't need me to rub it in.

I had begun to turn away, feeling remarkably foolish, when Sam pulled swiftly into the kerbside and stopped the car. With a finger under my chin, he lifted my face until I was forced to meet his serious gaze. His eyes were very dark.

'Denise, I won't throw a wobbly if you mention your late husband's name. I really don't mind if we sometimes go to the same places. You had a long life together, I wouldn't like you to try and pretend it never happened for my sake.'

I stared at him, beginning to see there was more to Sam than a good-looking face. 'Thank you,' I said.

*

'Walking on the beach, Denise?' my mother repeated, when I told her where I'd been. 'Do you think that's wise?'

'Wise? What's that supposed to mean? Wise?'

I stared at her. I'd only been talking about my evening, not really inviting her opinion or asking for her approval, but somehow her manner took the shine off what had been an enjoyable experience.

I wondered why she'd bothered to wait up to hear about it if she was merely going to find fault with the way Sam and I had spent our time. What on earth was her problem, and did I really want to know?

Jason had been busily dunking digestives in his mug of tea, one after the other, but now he looked up, first at my mother and then at me.

He said nothing but began to sing softly under his breath the words of a very old song, *Walkin' in the sa-a-and*.

I recognised the words of an old Shangri-La's song, and began to realise just what they were both getting at. I glared at him and then, even more forcefully at Elaine.

'Have you two got a problem?' I demanded.

Jason held up his hands quickly. 'Not me,' he said, 'but I think Mrs J is thinking, *From Here To Eternity*, and all that sort of stuff.'

I guessed, pretty accurately I would have thought, that a picture of Deborah Kerr and Burt Lancaster rolling in the surf immediately sprang unbidden into all our minds, and I was incensed.

'Thank you, Jason,' my mother said sarcastically. 'When I need your help I will ask for it.'

'I think he's put it very well,' I replied tersely, 'though I'm amazed he's familiar with such an old film.'

'It was one of my mum's favourites,' he offered unexpectedly. 'She thought it was romantic and we know you ladies are suckers for a bit of romance, don't we? Nothing wrong with that.'

'As long as you don't get carried away,' Elaine put in nastily, adding, 'It's not only teenagers who get pregnant, you know.'

She'd gone too far, way, way too far. I knew it, by the expression on his face Jason knew it, and a rough guess said my mother knew it, too. I was so angry, I seriously doubted if I could be civil to her, yet somehow I had to try.

'How *dare* you?' I demanded furiously. 'What the hell is your problem, Mother? Do you begrudge me a bit of happiness? Is that it? I'm trying to get my life back together here, to pick up pieces and try to put them back into some sort of order. I'm entitled to a social life – and yes – even a bit of romance isn't too much to ask. Perhaps if you'd made some attempt to keep the romance in *your* life your marriage wouldn't be in tatters now.'

A stunned silence met my harsh words. Even Jason appeared to be lost for words. The next minute my mother was gone, slamming the kitchen door behind her so hard that the whole room seemed to shake. There was the sound of her footsteps drumming up the stairs at a speed that belied her age, and then the harsh slam of her bedroom door.

Jason stared at me, and I stared back at him, and then he asked softly, 'Cup of tea, Mrs M?'

'Thanks, love.' I slumped onto a chair, all the anger was gone as suddenly as it had come. I could see that I'd over-reacted quite considerably and I said so.

'I think she asked for it,' Jason said quietly. 'If you don't mind me saying so, she's been a bit of a cow since your Dad found himself this woman.'

'She *is* going through a bad time,' I was beginning to feel really bad. 'I should try to have more patience.'

'Bull,' he said mildly, but quite forcefully. 'She's doing what you said we shouldn't – what I used to do – and blaming everyone but herself. She's cocked up and she knows it.'

He was probably right. I think we both knew it and I expect my mother did in her heart of hearts. She'd been trying to make a point, but had taken a sledge-hammer to what was only a tiny nut. I was sure she didn't want the separation from my father to continue, would probably have gone home before this, but my father meeting someone else was a development she, quite simply, hadn't allowed for.

'What can we do?' I sipped my tea, staring at Jason over the rim of the cup, thinking how nice it was to have him there and surprising myself by saying so, right out of the blue.

He went very red around the ears, then smiled and told me, 'You're a great person, you know. Don't worry too much about your mum, she was asking to be told, you know. Haven't you heard the saying that you have to be cruel to be kind?'

'Mmm,' I murmured, 'but they are my mum and dad and I'd quite like them to stay married, if that's possible.'

'Perhaps you could start by talking to your dad, then,' Jason suggested. 'At least you'd know if this woman was a real threat, and whether there's any point trying to get him and your mum back together. If it's a lost cause, you might just have to accept it, mightn't you?'

'I'll phone him tomorrow.'

*

I was riddled with guilt the minute my father picked up the phone, because he was so obviously pleased to hear from me. I'd been avoiding him because I hadn't quite known what to say to him. I still didn't know what to say, so I started by apologising.

'I'm sorry, Dad. You must think I've been trying to avoid you.'

'No such thing, love,' he contradicted, the cockney twang my mother had spent her life trying to eliminate still very apparent in his deep tone. I loved my father's voice and always had. It reminded me of rich, dark chocolate.

'Can we meet?' I thought I'd get right in there and not beat around the bush.

'Today?'

The urgency must have shown in my tone, but I said the next day would do just as well, gaining the feeling that his Sunday was already arranged. Trying not to wonder what was arranged and with whom, I agreed quickly that would be great if it would be possible to meet at lunchtime.

'Can you get out to the golf club in the time they allow you for your break?' he queried. 'Any time from twelve-thirty. Say no, if you can't and I'll cancel my game with Tom Greening. He won't mind too much.'

I couldn't help laughing, knowing that his old friend Tom would be absolutely furious. He hated being 'messed around,' as he put it.

'I can get there,' I said, 'Would one-ish be okay?'

I dialled Jo's extension as soon as I got into work next day, glad of a real excuse not to have to meet her for lunch as usual. I couldn't ever recall feeling like that about meeting Jo, but selfish as it seemed, I really didn't want to hear about what she and Adam had been up to over the weekend. I was well aware I was being a complete dog in the manger, but that didn't change anything, I just couldn't seem to help myself.

'Give him my love,' she said sweetly, then offered, 'I can pop in for a coffee later, instead if you'd like.'

'Bit busy, actually,' I excused. It wasn't a lie but I immediately felt like a complete bitch anyway.

What on earth was the matter with me? Why couldn't I just be happy for Jo – and for Adam, too. They were my closest friends, it would be ideal if they found happiness together. They certainly deserved it more than most and I *should* be delighted.

It wasn't as if I was Nelly-no-mates, sitting at home with no invitations, I thought as I drove through the lunch hour traffic to the golf course which was set conveniently just on the edge of town. From what everyone told me, Sam was quite a catch. He was a really nice guy, too, and very fanciable. I couldn't quite work out yet what exactly he could see in me, but he'd seemed very keen – flatteringly so, in fact – to arrange another date as soon as possible.

Our first date had been a complete success from every point of view, or at least as far as I could tell. From being very nervous, understandably, I had relaxed more and more as the evening had progressed. We had talked easily throughout the meal, about anything and everything, tasting morsels from each other's forks, and finding lots to laugh about. The perfect end to a really pleasant evening had been the walk along the seashore.

We hadn't been the only couple with the same idea. It felt so nice to be half of a pair again, and I'd enjoyed the warm feeling of having my hand taken and held. The kiss, when it came, was hardly unexpected, and I hadn't demurred, though it had been a little strange, and quite unlike the comfortable, familiar kisses that Rob and I had shared during the later years of our marriage.

I found myself smiling. Sam certainly did know how to kiss. Well, he probably had quite a reputation to live up to. He hadn't put a foot – or a hand – out of line, either, but had just held me close with his fingers splayed across my lower back and kissed me as if his life depended on him getting a reaction.

I gave myself up to the feeling his kiss evoked. As he tempted my lips apart, and the kiss had deepened, a warm feeling spread right through my body, until it felt as if every bit of me was on fire and my bones had turned to liquid. I was so turned on that, had we been somewhere more conducive, one thing might well have lead to another. It had been a very long time, I had missed such intimacy, and I was only human, after all.

I'd moaned against his mouth, and he'd pulled me closer yet, until every inch of us was touching, my breasts crushed to the hard wall of his chest. When he released me, we were both out of breath, as if we'd been running, and I could hear my own heartbeat drumming loud in my ears.

'You,' Sam had tilted my chin up and looked deep into my eyes, 'are one very sexy lady.'

We'd both laughed softly and continued on our way, arms entwined. He didn't kiss me again – perhaps it was just as well. Perhaps, too, my mother's comments hadn't been so wide of the mark, though she'd be totally horrified if I'd told her as much.

I smiled again. It was nice to be told you were still desirable. I'd almost forgotten how it felt to be a woman – never mind a sexy one. I must remember, though, that there was no rush. It was one thing to be out there in the world and dating again, but it was quite another to be thinking of a full blown sexual relationship – even if one was on offer. I was quite certain I wasn't anywhere near ready for any such thing.

'You should wait to be asked, young lady,' I advised my reflection in the rear view mirror, once I'd parked the Metro rather conspicuously among the selection of top of the range motors already in the golf club car park.

I was smiling as I walked towards the imposing wooden clubhouse door, turning just as I reached it, to continue on to the entrance of the connected restaurant that was used, not only by golf-club members but also by guests of the hotel that was all part of the same complex.

'Darling.' My father had obviously been looking out for me, and came out into the reception area to greet me, holding me close for a minute.

I breathed in the familiar smell of him. The Old Spice aftershave, the hair preparation he used, and a hint of tobacco from the occasional cigarette he still smoked in secret. Harry's face was tanned from his regular games of golf and, as always, smoothly shaved. He was dressed as impeccably as ever: grey trousers with knife-edge creases, immaculate navy blazer, sober patterned cravat tucked into the neck of a beautifully ironed white shirt.

Since my mother had always looked after his wardrobe, this begged the question, was his current pristine appearance down to him, or did it denote another feminine involvement?

'You look absolutely stunning,' he exclaimed, holding me at arm's length. 'What have you been doing to yourself?'

I felt embarrassed and pleased all at the same time. 'Oh, you know,' I dismissed, 'new hairdo, fresh make-up and a new outfit can work wonders for an old bag like me.'

'Well, you look gorgeous. Now, let's go and eat. I took the liberty of ordering because I know you don't have too much time. Just something light. Is that all right with you?' He stopped again, and pulled me round in front of him. 'You're really going to be okay now, aren't you, darling? I can see in your eyes that the worst is over for you.'

He walked on, pulling my arm through his and nodding to this one and that as we made our way through the surprisingly busy restaurant. It was obviously a popular lunchtime venue with golf-club members and holidaying hotel guests alike, midweek.

'My daughter,' he offered, once or twice, by way of explanation, and with a clear note of pride in his voice.

We sat and smiled at each other, and I wondered why on earth I'd been so reluctant to see him. Unlike my mother, my father would never try to involve me in any conflict – he certainly wouldn't blame me for the break-up of their marriage.

'What about you, Dad?' I questioned, 'How are you doing? It must have been so hard for you?'

I didn't get the chance to hear his reply because a vision in pink swanned up to the table, and leaning over, kissed my father full on the lips, enveloping us both in clouds of not very subtle perfume. I hated the woman on sight, and seeing her so obviously familiar with my dad took my appetite clean away.

From a distance she might have warranted the 'twenty years younger and fit' description Jason had attached to her. Up close she had the look of a woman, much more my mother's age, who was overly familiar, not only with the surgeon's knife, but every other age-defying remedy known to man. The result was not always as successful as it might have been – though she did have a figure to die for.

'Miriam.' Ever polite, my father rose to his feet. 'How nice to see you again. This is my daughter, Denise.'

I could tell that the feeling of dislike was entirely mutual. Our greeting was polite on the surface, glacial beneath and I was horrified when my father offered, 'Won't you join us?'

Of course, she – Miriam – didn't need asking twice. Accepting with alacrity, she had pulled up a chair and had soon managed to make it clear that I was the one in the way.

My father seemed completely mesmerised by her and as a result I found lunch that day something of a challenge.

*

'She's just awful, Jason,' I whispered, as I set the table in readiness for the 'spag bol' that was pretty much the sum total of his culinary repertoire. I'd had it in mind to widen his horizons by a simple dish or two, but there just never seemed to be the time.

Conscious, as I was, that my mother could come through the door at any time, Jason gave the sauce a stir and came over to stand next to me, to whisper conspiratorially. 'Are you sure she's "the one"?'

'Well, she obviously thinks so,' I muttered crossly. 'She had her feet under that table before you could say knife, and I wouldn't be surprised to find her slippers under my parents' bed at any moment – if they're not there already, and if someone like that even possesses a pair.'

'You didn't like her much, did you?' Jason's tone was dry.

I opened my mouth to detail just what exactly was wrong with her. Then I closed it again with a snap, because I knew, and even Jason knew that, had she been perfect – and she was far from that with her over-bleached hair and toothy smile – she still wouldn't have been good enough for my father. She wasn't, after all, my mother, was she?

There had to be something I could do to make them see the damage they were doing to each other – and to me. Old as I was I had no intention of becoming a child from a broken home, and so I would tell them if I had to. There must be something I could actually do, besides banging their stupid heads together.

My mother and I were very sheepish around one another at supper that evening, both very aware that we had gone too far. I didn't mention that I had seen my father, confining my conversation to trivialities and encouraging her and Jason to talk about how their day had been.

Jason didn't take much encouraging. It was quite obvious that this job could be the making of him. I hoped his enthusiasm would be noted by the powers-that-be in the company, and more than make up for his lack of experience. I had my fingers firmly crossed that working through the agency would lead to something more permanent eventually.

The change in him was remarkable and just went to show what could happen when you gave someone a chance. Why, he even *looked* different. I risked a surreptitious peek, and though he hadn't been in long from work, noted that he was already showered and dressed in clean clothes. The gel had been discarded, leaving his hair much fairer than before and cut to a length even I could approve of. He had also made himself familiar once more with a razor and he was clean-shaven.

He looked – I realised with a wry grimace – just like the sort of young man I'd have been happy to see Bobbi bring home. Funny how things could change.

I was on my way upstairs when the phone rang, and I called out, 'I'll get it,' thinking it might be Sam. My stomach did a little somersault with the anticipation of hearing his deep voice as I lifted the receiver.

'Hi, Mum.'

It was Bobbi, of course, and I carried the phone upstairs, talking as I went, asking how it was all going, if she had settled back into the course, caught up on her assignments and was back out on placement yet. It was a minute or two before I realised I was doing most of the talking. Registering the subdued edge to a tone that had been full of enthusiasm only a day or two earlier, my heart began to sink.

She was regretting going back, having second thoughts, was missing Jason. All of this rushed in and out of my head in a matter of seconds. I'd wait for her to tell me. Yes, that was what I'd do, and then we could discuss her options.

'Mum, I've got something to tell you.'

Yes, here it was. Well, whatever it was it wouldn't be the end of the world …

'I think I might be pregnant.'

CHAPTER 18

EVERYTHING STOPPED AND THE EARTH TILTED ON ITS AXIS. I almost fell into my bedroom and quickly sat on the side of the bed, doubting that my legs would have supported me for a moment longer. All the strength seemed to have gone right out of them.

I heard my daughter's voice in my ear, it was barely more than a whisper as she repeated, 'Did you hear me, Mum? I said, I think I might be having a baby.'

Bobbi having Jason's baby? I couldn't believe what I was hearing. It was so unfair. That this should happen now, of all times, just when I seemed to have got the pair of them sorted out. If it was true, this was going to change everything – for all of us.

Keep calm, I advised myself. I knew I mustn't lose it now, because it definitely wouldn't help. I actually had no idea what *would* help in a situation like this, so I took a deep, steadying breath and asked, 'Are you sure, Bobbi? Are you quite sure?'

'I'm late with my period – about two weeks – but I only just realised, with everything that was going on.' Her voice rose to a wail, 'Oh, Mum, what am I going to do?'

I felt like saying, *you're* asking me? You got yourself – yourselves – into this mess and now you think *I* can come up with a solution that will magically make everything right. Just like that.

Well, casting blame wasn't going to help, I did know that much. I clamped my tongue firmly between my teeth and thought so hard my head hurt with the effort.

'Have you done a test?'

'A pregnancy test? Ooh, no.' Bobbi sounded absolutely horrified. 'What if it's positive?'

God, give me strength, I thought, exasperated beyond belief by her head-in-the-sand attitude – even though I knew exactly where she got it from.

'What if it's not?' I asked, amazing myself with the patience in my tone.

'Oh, you think I might not be, then?' Bobbi's voice brightened perceptibly.

'I've no idea – and neither have you, yet. Shall we quit worrying ahead until we find we have something definite to worry about? It's the best advice I can offer, for now.'

'Should I go and get the test now?' she asked, obviously waiting for me to tell her what to do. 'Only ...' she hesitated and then continued in a rush, 'I promised to meet some of the other girls for a drink in half an hour, and they'll wonder where I am if I go off looking for a late-night pharmacy.'

Christ, talk about getting your priorities right, I thought furiously, seriously in danger of losing my temper with her. Still, I calmed down almost immediately, one more day wasn't going to make a scrap of difference, one way or another, was it?

'Tomorrow will do just as well.' I agreed, wondering if I was going to get a wink of sleep that night. 'Ring me at work straight away. Oh, and Bobbi, do you want me to say anything to Jason?'

'Yes. No. Oh, I don't know, what do you think? Oh, I'll leave it up to you.'

'Did you want to..?'

'Talk to him?' she finished, and then called to someone at her end in response to a clearly heard knock at the door, 'Come in. Oh, Mum, I'll have to go. I'll speak to you tomorrow.'

I stood, deep in thought for a long moment, and then turned round and started visibly when I found Jason leaning against the door-frame, watching me.

' "Say anything to Jason" about what?' he queried quietly, explaining, 'Sorry, I wasn't earwigging. I was just passing on the way to my room.'

'Um, it was Bobbi,' I said unnecessarily, knowing he knew full well who it was, but playing for time in order to give myself more.

'Well, I guessed that much.' There was just the teeniest touch of sarcasm in his tone, and he repeated, ' "Say anything to Jason" about what?'

Still I hesitated uncertain just how much it was wise to tell him, when it could all just be a false alarm, and then we'd all be worrying unnecessarily.

'She's found someone else. Right?' It was a statement rather than a question and there was no trace of either anger or annoyance in his voice that I could detect. 'Don't worry, you can tell me. I won't lose it,' he sketched some sort of salute, 'Scout's honour. It's probably no more than I deserve anyway.'

I suddenly became conscious that if Jason had overheard my conversation with Bobbi, my mother probably had as well. She was probably all ears at that very moment. If I asked Jason to come in and close the door it would arouse her curiosity even more. I wouldn't put it past her to put a glass to the wall, and though I was probably maligning her good character by even thinking such a thing, I really couldn't take the chance.

The less anybody – even my mother – knew of this, the better. There'd be time enough to broadcast the news when we knew for sure there was something *to* know, and since as far as I could recollect I hadn't actually mentioned the words 'pregnancy' or 'baby,' the secret was safe for the moment.

'Actually,' I said, 'I could do with a cup of coffee, I don't know about you.' Jason looked at me as if I'd gone mad and I didn't really blame him, but I rushed on, 'Did you want a cup, Mum?'

Her immediate, 'That would be nice, dear,' confirmed my suspicion, and understanding dawned on Jason's youthful face in a minute.

'I'll do it,' he offered, adding a touch louder, 'I'll bring you a cup up, Mrs J.'

I listened to him making his way down the stairs, and then going to the door of my mother's room, I said, 'I was going to have a shower, but I'm not in a hurry, so did you want to go first?'

I knew she would accept with alacrity and I was right. Elaine hated the fact that one bathroom in a shared household often meant an inconvenient wait. As soon as she'd gone in and locked the door I made my way downstairs.

Jason had made the coffee, the real coffee that he had come to appreciate, along with the regular meals and freshly laundered clothes that the rest of us took for granted. He poured two cups out and placed them on the table in front of us as we both sat down. He looked at me and I looked at him. I tried to feel it in me to be angry with him, to recall that this was exactly what he'd wanted only a very short time ago. I wondered if it was going to be what he wanted right now.

'So are you going to tell me what this is all about, then?' he raised his eyebrows and then calmly took a sip of his coffee.

Damn it, I felt a swift flash of irritation. Why should it be just Bobbi and me worrying? This was Jason's problem, too, so why was I trying to protect him – of all people?

I answered my own question before I answered his. I was trying to protect him because he had come so far in such a short time, and what I didn't want was to see a return of his old irresponsible self. Something like this could be all it took.

I was also trying to protect him because he wasn't Gerry and shouldn't be compared with the likes of him. The biggest reason was that I found I was thinking of Jason's mother, who must wonder and worry about him sometimes, surely. I hoped that someone would have made some effort to protect my son – to think of his thoughts, feelings and future – if he had lived and I wasn't around to support him.

'Bobbi thinks she might be pregnant.'

He was appalled, and there was no doubt about it. I could tell it was the very last thing he had expected. If I'd punched him hard in the face he couldn't have looked more stunned. He stared at me for a long, long moment, and then he closed his eyes and put his head in his hands.

I felt sorry for him, I really did. Realising he and Bobbi had brought this on themselves didn't even make me harden up. I recalled, only too well, being in this self-same position and was grimly determined to handle the situation with kid gloves. Screaming and throwing accusations – as my mother had done all those years ago – would not help. It could affect my relationship with my daughter for years to come, as I was only too well aware.

'This couldn't have happened at a worse time, could it?' Jason groaned, his head remained buried in his hands, and I sensed he couldn't bring himself to look at me. 'Why didn't we listen to you?'

'Well,' I patted his arm,' it's always easy to be wise after the event, isn't it?'

'Why are you being so understanding?' he looked up, finally looking me straight in the eye. 'Why aren't you throwing me out onto the street? I wouldn't blame you, at all. I can see now that I've abused your hospitality in the worst way and have since the day I moved in – uninvited. I don't understand why you're not throwing things at me.'

'It's a long story,' I murmured, 'but – at the end of the day – it really wouldn't solve anything. I think it's called shutting the stable door after the horse has bolted. This may well, also, be a false alarm. Bobbi hasn't done a pregnancy test, but she's going to do one as soon as she gets a kit in the morning. She's going to phone me at work.'

Sam phoned me, then, and my mother came downstairs. If I were honest I would admit that I was in the mood for neither Sam's sweet nothings, nor for my mother's continuing hard done by attitude. However, I found myself agreeing to attend a charity event with Sam at the weekend and, as soon as I came off the phone, giving some serious thought to what a bit of interference from me might manage to achieve in my parents' present situation.

Playing loud music was obviously going to be Jason's way of dealing with what possibly loomed for him, and I flatly refused my mother's demands that I, 'get that boy to turn down that racket right now.'

'Leave it,' I ordered harshly, when she showed signs of marching upstairs to do it herself. 'It won't hurt, just this once.'

She glared at me, and the set of her mouth was an indication that she was verging on pulling senior rank and going up to hammer on his door anyway. I met her look steadily, daring her to do such a thing, and something in my eyes must have made her think better of it.

'I'm going to talk to Peggy, see if I can't get a definite date to move into that flat.' She threw me a look of complete disgust, snatched a jacket from the hat stand in the hall, her keys from the hook, and she was gone.

She must have been annoyed, I realised, because the jacket she'd taken was one of mine, and not her style at all. Add to that the fact that it was badly creased, being only recently retrieved from days spent on the back seat of my car under items of paperwork and shopping, and you got some idea of her state of mind.

Something had to be done about her and my Dad, I decided, going back to my earlier thoughts, and sooner rather than later. Left to their own devices, it was quite clear that my father would soon be bulldozed into living over the brush with the dreadful Miriam, and my mother would be ensconced in the flat over the café and prey to all kinds of unscrupulous men.

Giving that particular matter careful thought achieved its purpose, because it not only took my mind away from the threat of an unwanted pregnancy, but pretty soon a plan began to formulate in my mind.

The situation would need delicate handling, I realised nervously, and the timing would have to be exact, or it could well achieve the opposite result to the one hoped for. On the bright side it may well work like a dream – and I was always one to look on the bright side whenever possible.

That being the case, I woke up in the morning in a positive frame of mind, the way that you sometimes do when the sun is shining and you have slept particularly well. My mood rubbed off on Jason, and promising to ring him as soon as I heard any news sent him off to work happily enough. My mother caught the tail end of this conversation and viewed us both with suspicion.

I just called, 'See you later,' to her as I followed Jason out of the door, and hoped against hope there would be absolutely nothing for her to know, or for us to worry about, by the time we all met up again at the end of the day.

Paperwork, meetings, and phone calls kept me fully occupied during the course of the morning. By the time the phone call came through from Bobbi at almost mid-day, I'd convinced myself that it had all been a false alarm. She would surely have phoned long before if she had anything to tell. I was wrong on both counts and I knew it the minute I heard her voice, thick with unshed tears.

'It's positive, Mum. What am I going to do?' and then she was crying as if her heart would break, and tears were streaming down my own face, too.

How I kept my voice steady I'll never know. I just knew that one of us had to remain strong, and that as I was the adult, it would have to be me.

'It will be all right,' I said calmly. 'Trust me. This doesn't have to be the end of the world.'

'Abortion, you mean, but … ' hiccoughing, sobbing and sniffing made it impossible to make out any more of what Bobbi said, but I could guess the gist of it.

'You have various choices,' I told her, working hard to keep my tone soothing. 'It will be for you and Jason to decide what's best – for both of you and the baby – together. I just want you to know that I will be here for you, whatever you decide.'

No one had warned me he was coming and I hadn't heard a knock at the door, but when I looked up Jason was standing in front of my desk. We stared at each other. It was obvious he knew what was happening. He looked totally gutted and I wouldn't have been at all surprised if he had burst into tears as well. He held out his hand for the phone.

'Darling,' I whispered to my daughter, 'Jason is here, he's just come in. He'd like to talk to you.'

Without waiting for her reply, I handed the receiver to Jason and standing up, made a motion toward the door with my hand, indicating that I would leave. He shook his head emphatically, so I just busied myself with a bit of filing.

The young man who had been a thorn in my side for longer than I cared to remember, had gone up in my estimation in recent days, but never more than during the course of that conversation.

He willingly accepted all of the blame for the situation that he and Bobbi found themselves in, saying he was older and should have had far more sense, and more respect for her right to have the career she wanted.

Jason said he would drive up to see her, at a time and place of her choosing, that they would talk this through, discuss all the options, but that he would abide by her final decision – whatever that was.

By the time he replaced the receiver, he was crying, I was crying, and I had no doubt at all that Bobbi would have been crying, too.

'Thank you,' I murmured, going across the room to hug him.

After a moment's hesitation, Jason hugged me back, but he told me, 'I don't think you have *anything* to thank me for.'

Holding him at arm's length so that I could look into his face, I said, 'I have a feeling that one day I'll have a lot to thank you for. Do the right thing by my daughter – whatever that is – and you will always find a friend in me.'

'I just don't understand … ' he began.

'Perhaps one day you will,' was all I was prepared to say, acknowledging that my past could have no bearing on their future – except perhaps in the way *I* handled things. 'Can I buy you lunch?'

That made Jason smile at last, as he protested, 'You already made me sandwiches this morning.'

I smiled, too, 'And I wouldn't be at all surprised to discover you've eaten those already.'

I paused only to let the temp know where I was going and we were both laughing when we left the building. I hoped that Bobbi had someone she could confide in where she was, and promised myself to phone her that evening, perhaps persuade her to come home for the weekend.

As soon as we walked into the bar I saw Jo. She was sitting on her own in our usual corner, and I knew I would have no choice but to join her. It might not be so bad with Jason there, I acknowledged, and pointed him in the right direction, saying, 'I'll get the sandwiches, any preference for filling? Drink?'

'Tuna and sweetcorn and a coke, please.' He put his hand in his pocket and offered, 'Let me get them.'

I gave him a little push. 'Put your money away, I think you're going to need it.'

By the time I reached the table, he and Jo were talking easily. I knew I didn't have to warn Jason not to mention anything about the current situation. It may well become common knowledge in time, but for the moment it remained personal and private.

If Jo had realised I'd been avoiding her, she didn't say anything, and any awkwardness between us soon passed. She told us she had seen Petie, that the result of his last misdemeanour had shocked him even more than she had expected. Apparently the judge had been absolutely scathing in his summing up, leaving Petie in no doubt that appearing before him as the result of any further misdemeanours was going to be a very bad idea.

'This may well be the final turning point,' she said, and she sounded very positive, adding, 'especially with Adam's job offer, which he accepted with alacrity, of course. Having him breathing down Petie's neck should keep him on the straight and narrow. He really likes Adam.'

So Jo and Adam's blossoming relationship would obviously have her son's blessing, I thought, and was trying hard to feel happy for them both, when Jo continued, 'Petie only thought there was something going on between me and Adam. Can you believe it? Where on earth would he get an idea like that? I told Petie straight, he's barking up the wrong tree, there, and that I'll never have time for a man in my life until I see the one I've already got permanently on the straight and narrow – namely him.'

I felt a huge surge of relief rush through me, and I really despised myself. Why couldn't I have just been happy for them if they *had* found mutual affection? It had been a dream of mine in the past, so what had changed? Surely I wasn't hoping that Lisbet would have a change of heart and come back to Adam, was I? If I was, I had to admit it seemed unlikely in the extreme, with Adam already setting the wheels of divorce in motion, and appearing grimly determined to put that particular chapter of his life behind him.

When Jason left, the atmosphere was noticeably lighter between Jo and me. She talked more about her hopes for Petie, and I told her about the half-formed plans I had come up with to try and get my mother and father to see what they were throwing away and, hopefully, reconsider.

'You sneaky thing,' she laughed, and then offered, 'Anything I can do to help?' before going on, 'Things seem to be going swimmingly for you and I'm really pleased.' I must have looked at her a bit oddly, because she continued, 'You know, Bobbi back at uni, Jason in a job. Why, with your mum and dad hopefully sorted, there'd only be you to get settled. How is it going with Sam? I have it on good authority that he really likes you.'

I stared at her, partly amused, and partly annoyed I would have to say. 'Now, where on earth would you have heard that?' I demanded with a touch of indignation in my tone.

'Aha,' she teased, 'When you go out with a public figure, you can't prevent a certain amount of chit-chat. You'll be in *Hello!* magazine before you know it.'

'I suppose so,' I said slowly, trying not to mind. I supposed I should be flattered if it was so obvious that Sam was making no secret of his feelings, it must mean he was fairly serious and not just playing games. He was quite a catch, after all, as my own daughter had been quick to point out.

I should have been flattered, delighted, instead I suddenly felt that it was all happening too fast for me. Here was another situation that I wasn't too happy about, there just seemed to be no pleasing me these days and I just couldn't for the life of me work out why.

CHAPTER 19

THERE JUST WASN'T ENOUGH WEEK left for me to fit everything into it that had to be done, comfortably. I seemed to spend the whole time chasing my tail and have to say I became increasingly irritated by the hundred and one minor problems that chose such an inconvenient time to land on my desk at work.

Jason and I managed between us to keep Bobbi calm by the means of constant telephone calls and endless patience with her very understandable fears and concerns. Jason also arranged to drive up to see her first thing on Saturday morning. He expected to stay overnight and had booked a place in a bed and breakfast establishment close to the university campus in readiness.

This fitted in rather well with the plans I was making regarding my parents, and a marital separation that looked increasingly like becoming permanent if I didn't do something to bring them back together – and quickly. I wasted no time before inviting my father to come for a meal on Saturday night, using the excuse that we hadn't had much chance to talk at the golf club, what with his 'friend' joining us at lunch.

My mother was advised that we'd be having a special meal on the same night. As far as she was concerned the sole purpose of the evening was to cheer Jo up, something she was obviously in need of given recent events in her life. I made no mention of my father's invitation. Elaine had no idea that Jason would be absent, or that neither Jo nor I had any intention of being there.

I'd dared Peggy to let slip that I would be spending the evening at a charity function with Sam, ignoring her evident disapproval at my interference with a, 'Trust me.' Showing a confidence in the successful outcome of my own meddling that I was actually very far from feeling.

Among all these hole-in-the-corner arrangements, I also had to find time to shop for food for the planned meal, and for an outfit that would be worthy of an occasion that promised to be at least modestly star-studded, for a local charity event. It was Adam who provided the easy answer to one problem by suggesting I simply order ready-prepared food in for the parental supper.

I was surprised to hear from him, though I couldn't have said why since he'd been a regular caller throughout the years of my marriage and even more so since Rob's death. He'd been a complete rock to me, keeping regular contact, offering practical advice or a shoulder to cry on when it was patently obvious he had troubles of his own to contend with. That knowledge made me feel incredibly guilty when the real reason for his call became apparent.

'Denise,' his tone gave away his concern, 'have I done something to upset you?

'Good Lord, no,' I answered immediately. 'Whatever makes you say that?'

'We've hardly seen each other lately,' he pointed out ruefully and all too truthfully. 'I know you have your family, and Jo says you've been seeing a bit of Sam recently. I'm pleased for you, I really am. It's just that I don't want to lose your friendship. It means a lot to me, Dee, and always has.'

'And yours to me,' I hurried to point out, feeling more dreadful by the minute. Especially knowing he was quite right, and that it was this ridiculous thing I'd had about him and Jo that led me to avoid him.

He continued as if I hadn't spoken. 'I don't want to sound self-pitying or selfish, Dee, but I've already lost enough friends through the break-up with Lisbet. Some appear to have taken her side, though why on earth folk can't remain neutral is beyond me, especially as she chose to leave and appears to be happy with that choice. Others just avoid me. You must know, of all people, that this often happens once you're no longer part of a couple.'

'Adam, I really am so sorry. It was unintentional. What can I do to put things right between us?'

I had to laugh when it became immediately apparent that he already had the answer to that off pat, and must have been prepared for me to ask.

'You could come out to lunch with me on Sunday? We might even make a day of it, if you can spare the time, maybe go somewhere a bit special. What do you say?'

'How can I refuse?' How could I, indeed, after shame-lessly neglecting someone who had been 'a friend indeed,' and all for the most pathetic of reasons, too? 'I'd love to,' I told him, and found that I really meant it.

We chatted a moment or two longer and that was when he came up with the idea of buying ready-prepared food or shelling out for caterers. The latter appealed the most, though the thought of the probable cost was a bit daunting.

That only left the matter of an outfit for the charity event. I knew there was nothing in my wardrobe that could be construed as remotely suitable, even after the undoubted boost given to the contents by recent shopping excursions. So, after waving Jason off early on Saturday morning, I made my way into town.

The journey brought back memories of that first fateful solo trip, and how things had changed since that day – not least my own personal view of things. I felt sure that I was a stronger person these days, that I had moved on with my life in a way I wouldn't have thought even possible a year before.

I recalled just how many times well-meaning folk had quoted the old favourite about 'time being a great healer', just when it was the very last thing I'd really wanted to hear. In those dark days when you've just lost the special someone who has been your whole life till then, you just cannot believe that the day will ever come when a heart so broken will indeed begin to mend.

It was still relatively early days, I understood that, but I could finally think of Rob with a smile instead of a tear. I could look back on all the good years we had shared, with the joy those memories deserved, and be glad for what we had and feel less sorrow for what would now never be for us.

I still had a life to live – and live it I would. I owed it to Rob and I owed it to myself. I had already taken huge strides forward, I felt, despite the problems I had encountered recently with my family – or perhaps it was even because of them. That was a strange thought, but other people's problems certainly had a way of taking your mind away from your own. I somehow doubted that anyone with a family could expect a completely trouble-free existence, but I knew I wouldn't want to be without mine, whatever difficulties they dropped into my lap.

Whether there would be another 'special someone' in my life in the future was as yet unknown. Sam was a lovely man, but was he the one for me, and vice-versa come to that? Time would tell, and time was still healing.

I wasted no time trawling round the shops that morning, I had none to spare in any case, but made my way immediately to my favourite boutique. The shop was the greatest discovery from that first trip into town alone and all thanks to the lady I'd shared the table with in the coffee shop. It was one recommendation I would always be grateful for.

The clothes, so tastefully arranged for ease of selection, were hardly of the cheap and cheerful variety, and certainly not mass-produced, but the higher cost was more than compensated for by the choice, the quality and by the fact you were highly unlikely to bump into anyone else wearing the same outfit.

I consoled myself that the extravagance was warranted if it made me feel good, made me look good, and gave me the much needed confidence to mix, unfazed, in Sam's elitist circles. I reminded myself that I hadn't splashed out as much as I had done recently, in many, many years.

I was greeted like an old friend by the proprietor, though I was still a relatively new customer. Leigh was tall and slender, always immaculately made up, with an olive skin and a mane of thick black hair swept back into her trademark silk scarf. It always matched her outfit of the day exactly. She was a perfect advertisement for the range of garments she offered to her appreciative customers.

She had the sort of honesty and integrity which was a rare commodity in the retail trade. I trusted Leigh to recognise what I had in mind for any given occasion, and knowing she wouldn't allow me to leave the shop with something that didn't do me justice was an added bonus. Risking a dissatisfied customer for the sake of a quick sale just wasn't her way and that was the sort of service you couldn't rely on getting in a chain store.

'I can guess why you're here,' Leigh said after the initial warm greeting. She was already making her way toward the rails of multi-coloured garments.

'You can?' I was taken aback, to say the least.

'Something to wear to the big charity event tonight, the one where everyone who's anyone is going to be.' Leigh smiled and touched the side of her nose knowingly, 'Sam Robbins' new mystery lady has already made the *Evening Echo*. The photo was a bit grainy, but if I hadn't recognised you, I'd have recognised the outfit as one of mine. The hair looks great by the way.'

Leigh flicked my shoulder-length bob with a careless hand, tipped, I couldn't help noticing, by nails lacquered in a shade of green to complement her outfit perfectly. Her attention to detail was faultless and made me wonder just how much time and energy went into achieving such perfection.

'Thanks,' I said, still disconcerted by the fact that my photo had been taken and placed in a newspaper without me even knowing. I wasn't sure if I liked the feeling of suddenly becoming public property. 'Was my name there – in the paper?'

'I don't think so, but it probably will be after tonight.' She looked at me closely. 'It doesn't worry you does it? He's quite a catch, is our Sam.'

'You know him, then?'

'Not intimately, you understand, but enough to nod in passing.' Leigh was selecting garments as she spoke, and bowing to her superior judgement, I simply followed her to the fitting-room. 'He's a nice guy,' she said, hanging dresses three at a time onto the available hooks.

Still being early for Saturday shoppers, I benefited from the whole of Leigh's expert attention and in no time a choice was made.

'You look gorgeous,' she said, and looking at my reflection in the full-length mirror, I almost believed her.

The dress was a shimmering sugar pink, the pastel colour and shoe-string straps flattering the quite believable tan I had managed to achieve with regular and careful applications from a bottle. The body of the dress was lace but not see-through, to my infinite relief, and from a mid-calf scalloped edge the skirt fell in a tasselled fringe to the floor.

As I moved the fringe parted to show tantalising glimpses of smoothly tanned leg, and I still couldn't believe the slender figure encased in the luxury lace garment belonged to me. I knew I had to have it, refusing to even look at the price label in case the cost made me have any second thoughts.

Leigh had some pink costume jewellery earrings that were no more than tiny feathers dangling from a fake gold stud, and she advised wearing shoes that were little more than straps in either a neutral pearly grey or beige colour. I was back home by mid-morning.

Feeling that caterers were an extravagance I couldn't really justify – and realising they'd probably be booked up at this late notice anyway – I set to with the items I'd purchased from Cheapsmart the night before.

A good paté for the first course presented absolutely no problem as the ready-made variety offered as wide a choice as you could possibly hope for. I'd settled on roast beef and Yorkshire pudding for the main course, knowing this to be one of my father's favourite meals, and livened this up with the addition of some of the less traditional vegetables.

In appreciation of my mother's and my father's sweet tooth, I'd purchased three separate puddings from the freezer section and I now placed these to thaw slowly in the fridge.

By the time my mother arrived home, everything was under control, and I was wearing a floor-length cotton housecoat over my dress. This was partly to prevent any splashes, but mainly to hide from Elaine the fact that I was rather overdressed for a family dinner party at home.

I couldn't believe it, when it all went like a dream. No sooner had Elaine gone up to shower and get ready, than my father arrived and I ushered him straight into the dining-room.

He wasn't surprised to find the table set for two, still under the impression that the evening was to give him and me the chance to talk, and soon busied himself with the wine.

'An excellent choice to go with paté,' he said, pouring a little into a glass and taking an appreciative sniff.

'I'll bring it in, then,' I said, listening for sounds that might indicate that my mother was about to come downstairs.

I had no sooner placed the plates and fresh toast on the table than my mother appeared in the doorway and stumbled to a halt at the sight of my father, in his best suit and tie, seated at the table. He stood up immediately and stared at her. I have to say I was never more pleased that my mother didn't need to be told twice to dress up for an occasion. She was a complete vision in peacock blue and every inch a lady.

'Now,' I said, ushering my dumbstruck mother into the room. 'I have a prior engagement elsewhere and no one else is coming. This evening is about giving you two the chance to talk – and I mean talk – about the things that really matter to you. If you then decide that you are better off apart, I will have to accept that decision. I love you both, enjoy your meal.'

I swept out of the house, discarding the house-coat, and picking up a clutch bag and light wrap I had placed ready on the way, to find Sam waiting round the corner as was previously arranged.

'How did it go?' he asked immediately, obviously understanding that meticulous timing had been crucial to the success of the whole plan.

'Well, Elaine didn't rush out shrieking, if that's what you mean.' I chewed my lip-glossed mouth worriedly. 'I just hope that I've done the right thing.'

'Well, it's really up to them, now, isn't it?'

He was right, of course, and I settled back against the leather seats of the sleek Jaguar, determined to put what was happening at home – and with Jason and Bobbi – out of my mind.

'Yes, it is,' I agreed, turning to look at Sam, 'Now, tell me who I can expect to see tonight, and what I might expect to happen.'

He described it as a celebrity event that was an annual occurrence, and I recognised a well-known footballer and his model wife the minute we pulled up in front of the hotel that was home to the affair. The couple greeted Sam by name, and with easy familiarity, as he came around to open the door and help me from the car. He returned the greeting briefly, but his attention was, flatteringly, all on me.

'You look stunning,' he said, his appreciative gaze warm with approval, and his arm round my waist was possessive as we walked into the glass-fronted foyer, to be greeted by the town of Brankstone's Mayor and Lady Mayoress, who were hosting the event. They also appeared to know Sam very well.

At first, the whole thing was great fun. Spotting celebrity faces and having the majority of them come and shake your hand had a certain novelty value – and I knew my own family, and Jo, would be kept enthralled by details of the people, the outfits, the food, and the plush surroundings for weeks to come.

I'm not quite sure when I realised, to my own astonishment, that I was becoming bored. Probably around the time that I found I was stifling my third yawn in swift succession, I suppose.

I couldn't fault Sam, he couldn't have been more attentive if he'd tried. I couldn't fault the food or my fellow guests who, well known or not, were absolutely charming, and at great pains not to leave me out of the conversation, but the evening seemed to go on for ever.

My mind kept wandering to my mother and father at home, and I wondered if the evening had been a success for them or an abysmal failure for me and my interference. I wondered if Bobbi and Jason had come to a decision about their own futures and that of their unborn child.

I wondered what Jo was doing and realised how much more I would have enjoyed myself had she been here to share the evening with. I even wondered about Adam, and realised I was looking forward to lunch with him much more than I was looking forward to the rest of this interminable evening.

'Are you all right, darling?' Sam touched my arm with caressing fingers and I almost jumped out of my skin. 'You're very quiet. Are you having a good time?'

I smiled a wide, false smile, insisting, 'I'm having the best time, really,' and I suddenly knew, without a doubt, that I was lying through my teeth.

A hectic social life, going to exotic places, eating exotic food and meeting exotic people was really not for me, not on a regular basis. I found, in the middle of all that glamour, that a night in front of the telly seemed totally appealing: that, or a family meal, with all the minor disagreements and the 'in-house' jokes that no one else outside the handful of people closest to you would understand.

I ached, I realised, for the life I had lost when Rob died, for the life that was 'me'. I knew, then, that this kind of living was not for me, and even Sam, as lovely as he was, could never be the man for me.

In the need to move on, to accept what I had lost, I had taken a step too far into an appealing world that was exciting, glamorous and unreal. In doing so I had begun to lose sight of the real me, the down-to-earth person who needed, always, to have her feet set firmly on the ground.

I looked down and almost laughed out loud. I wasn't this glamorous lady and would never live up to such an image indefinitely. I blessed Sam for believing that I might. He had obviously become fond of me in the short time we had known each other, there was no doubt about that, or that, to please him, I would have changed slowly into his sort of lady at the expense of the real me.

Eventually the bidding started, and in an instant my boredom was gone. This really was exciting. Huge amounts were offered, for holidays, balloon trips, pamper days, and pieces of jewellery and I laughed and clapped with everyone else. I stopped laughing when Sam began to bid for piece of jewellery and I realised with complete horror that the intended recipient was me.

'Please don't,' I leaned over, between bids and under cover of the laughter following a joke by the auctioneer. 'If it's for me, I won't – can't – accept it.'

'But ... ' he began, and I just looked at him and said again, much more firmly, 'Please don't,' and watched understanding dawn, and hope die in his eyes. I knew that he knew then – as I knew – that our short-lived romance was already over.

CHAPTER 20

THE HOUSE WAS DARK WHEN I LET MYSELF IN. I was conscious of Sam sitting in his blue Jaguar at the kerbside, but I didn't turn, didn't wave, there was no point.

Sam and I being together had been an impossible dream from the start, for both of us. I had been flattered by his attention and, yes, very attracted to him, and he had obviously seen something in me that he liked, perhaps just the very fact that I *was* different from the usual women he chose to date.

Opposites can attract, no doubt about that, but I wouldn't have wanted to live his sort of life every day, any more than he'd want to live mine. It was just as well at least one of us realised that, sooner rather than later, before it all went wrong and someone was seriously hurt.

I sighed deeply and wondered why life had to be so complicated, before tiptoeing to the dining-room and peeping in. Everything had been cleared away but the candles. They were out, but had burnt right down low in the holders. Was that a good or bad sign? The kitchen, when I looked in, had been similarly cleared.

'Mmm,' I mused, not quite sure what to make of the signs.

I walked quietly up the stairs and could see no sign of light showing under my mother's door. I placed my ear to the door, not quite sure what I expected to hear. The sound of sobbing, maybe – the sound of failure.

I took a deep breath. I had to know, one way or the other. I couldn't sleep without knowing *something*. There was nothing for it but to wake my mother up, so I tapped softly, and pushed the door open.

Elaine was sound asleep – they both were – heads side by side on the one pillow. They fit together like two spoons in a drawer, my mother held close in my father's arms.

I closed the door quietly, and smiled all the way to my own room. I was still smiling as I slipped between the sheets, and then I cried as if I was never going to stop. I was so happy for them – and yet I hadn't felt so lonely since the day my darling Rob had died.

*

I was all smiles again in the morning when my parents appeared in the kitchen together.

'You needn't look so pleased with yourself,' Elaine said, the affection in her tone belying the caustic words.

'Well,' my father said, coming to look over my shoulder and to give me a quick hug, 'I think you have every right to expect a pat on the back, and is that bacon you're cooking?'

'Harry,' my mother warned, 'think of the cholesterol, think of your heart.'

'Nothing wrong with my heart.' He patted his chest and added with a big smile, 'Not any more. I'll have a bit of everything you've got there, Denise, and then I shall help your mother pack her things and get her out from under your feet. I've told her, she can do all those things she wants to do with her life from her own home and, as always, she can do it with my blessing.'

They were upstairs packing when Jo phoned, and by the sounds of giggling, followed by murmuring, that wasn't all they were doing. I was, quite frankly, amazed at their stamina.

'How did it go?' Jo got straight to the point.

'Worked like a dream,' I told her, with a trace of smugness. 'They're upstairs packing my mother's things, right now, with plenty of kissing and canoodling going on, if I'm not mistaken.'

'Well, well,' she sounded almost as pleased as I was, 'and how was the charity bash and even more important how was Sam? Will I be seeing you both in *Hello!* magazine?'

'Hardly,' I said dryly, 'but perhaps the local freebie – just this once.'

'Oh?' There was a question in Jo's voice, but I think she already knew the answer.

'Sam's not really for me,' I told her, 'and I'm not the one for him. It was fun …'

'While it lasted,' she finished for me. 'Did you want to talk about it? I could come round.'

'That would have been nice,' I said honestly, grateful for the offer, 'but I have these two lovebirds to get off the premises, I'm expecting a call from Bobbi, and I'm meeting Adam for lunch.'

'Adam, eh?' she said, sounding inordinately pleased about something, but before I could ask her what, she continued, 'Talking of Adam that reminds me, I've got some

297

news of my own. He reckons if Petie's initial enthusiasm and the willingness to work hard continues he has the makings of an excellent tradesman.'

'Oh, Jo, that is good news.'

'We've both made it clear,' she said, sounding as if she really meant it this time, 'that this really is his very last chance. If he messes up Adam will have nothing more to do with him and I'll cut him out of my life, I really will.'

I didn't believe it, and in her heart, nor did Jo, but I had the feeling Petie may well have got the sharp shock he needed and, hopefully, finally learned his lesson. It was certainly time, but I was convinced he wasn't all bad. Possibly he'd just been in need of the stabilising male influence he would get in abundance from Adam. I sincerely hoped I was right.

The door had barely closed behind my parents when the telephone rang again and I hurried to answer it, wondering if I was ever going to be ready to meet Adam for a one o'clock lunch.

'Mum, is that you?'

I didn't even bother to joke about who Bobbi might think it was, if not me, answering my own phone in my own house. Confirming my identity, I went upstairs with the receiver to my ear, and began to pull items from the wardrobe to save time, while still managing to listen intently.

'I don't want to have an abortion, and Jason doesn't want that either,' she said, and feeling my shoulders sag with relief I realised I hadn't wanted that, not if I was honest.

Totally aware the decision had to be entirely their choice, I was also totally aware the baby – an inconvenience or not – was also my first grandchild.

'Okay,' I said carefully, 'have you formed any plans, or is it a bit early to be thinking ahead?'

'We've talked most of the night,' she explained, sounding incredibly mature, 'and this is what we've decided is the best thing for us all. You might think that it's not ideal, but …'

I felt as if all my nerves were jangling as I waited for Bobbi to tell me how any solution could rescue what was going to be a disastrous situation. Unplanned babies had a habit of turning lives upside down – as I knew only too well.

'I'll have to go and see my tutors again – and I don't expect they'll be too pleased – but I'm almost certain I can continue on my course until I go off on maternity leave.'

'You mean, you're staying up there?' I was so surprised at this turn of events that I stopped looking for outfits to give this conversation all of my attention. 'Is Jason going to come up there, too?'

I realised there were more surprises in store when Bobbi told me, 'Jason doesn't think that's a good idea. It will be distracting for me, he said, and he's also pretty sure he's on the verge of being offered a permanent post with the firm he's doing his agency work with, and doesn't want to blow it. So,' she went on, 'if you don't mind, he'll continue to lodge with you, for now, and I'll stay up here.' Taking the words out of my mouth, she then continued, 'We can decide exactly what to do next, after the baby is born, but as Jason said, if he gets a permanent job, he can eventually work for the same company anywhere in the country. He's going to see if there's a branch up this way, and I know there's a crèche on the campus, so I should still be able to finish my course up here.'

'Well,' I said, 'You've really thought it all out, haven't you? I'm impressed and I can't tell you how proud I am – of you both.'

'I do love Jason, especially the way he is now,' Bobbi said, her tone very grown up, 'and I know he loves me. He says being part of our family has taught him a lot about what love really means.'

'Tell him from me,' I said, and really meaning it, 'that this is his home for as long as he needs it. Oh, and Bobbi, Granny and Granddad have just gone home – together.'

Bobbi laughed, delighted, and told me, 'I wouldn't be a bit surprised if that didn't have something to do with you, Mum. You're magic,' she said, and then she was gone.

I finished getting ready with one eye on the clock. A very moist eye, I have to confess. Bobbi and Jason's life together wouldn't be plain sailing, but they were young and I was pretty sure they would handle whatever it threw at them from now on.

I'd just taken a final look at myself in the hall mirror when the doorbell rang, and I cursed softly under my breath. Now who on earth could that be? I asked myself, realising that at this rate I was going to be very late.

Perhaps Adam had taken it upon himself to call round for me, I thought suddenly, though we had arranged to meet at our favourite local hostelry in the end, and would decide what to do with the rest of the day later.

Just like him to save me the walk. I found myself smiling, and was still smiling when I opened the door and came face to face with Janice. The smile was gone in an instant as the memory of that last spiteful telephone call came clearly into my mind.

'Oh, Janice,' I managed to remain icily civil, though my first instinct was to order her off my premises. 'I was just going out.'

'To meet Sam Robbins,' she enquired in the most ingratiating tone of voice. 'I heard you were seeing him, from a friend of mine, and I just came to wish you all the best.'

'So, I have your permission to go out with him, how nice.'

Janice smiled – I didn't.

'As I said before,' I looked at her with dislike, realising just what a shallow person she must be, to be so obviously impressed by Sam's celebrity status, 'I was just on my way out. Do come back some other time, when,' I continued grittily, 'you can wish me well *whoever* I'm with. Until then, Janice, I really have nothing to say to you, and you have nothing to say that I especially want to hear. You may be Rob's sister, but you'll never be a patch on the person your brother was.'

With that I swept past her, slamming the door behind me, and walked off, leaving her standing, open-mouthed, on the step. I was sure I could hear Rob's deep, approving laughter in my ears as I walked along with my head held high, and suddenly I was laughing, too.

The sun was shining and I walked with a spring in my step. For the first time in months I felt really good about myself, good about my life and good about my family. After all, I reasoned, none of it was ever going to be perfect, but then it never had been – not perfect – but good, as good as it would be again, only in a different way.

I hurried, becoming conscious that I was going to be very late, but comfortable in the knowledge that Adam would still be waiting. He would know that if I said I would be there, I wouldn't let him down.

I rounded the next corner, and there he was, sitting outside in the sunshine and looking as if he didn't have a care in the world. I was so happy to see him and when he looked up I waved eagerly, willing him to see me, to be as obviously pleased to see me as I was to see him – and I wasn't disappointed as I watched his whole face light up.

He was standing as I reached him, and I greeted him in the way I had always used to do when Rob was alive, with a big hug and a kiss on the cheek. He held me close for a moment, and it felt so good, so nice and so comfortable that he seemed as reluctant as I was to separate.

We stepped back, looked at each other, laughing, and then he swept one arm in the direction of the pub's inviting doorway, and said, 'Lunch awaits you, madam.'

We were actually in no obvious hurry to eat, but chose a table near the window. I enjoyed a glass of Chardonnay and Adam sipped at a coke. We chatted easily about general things, the weather, his business, my job and the possibility of getting any holiday in before the summer was over.

'You were looking mighty pleased with yourself, when I first saw you?' There was a question in Adam's tone, and I told him about Janice and her about-face.

'Can you believe she accused me of breaking up your marriage?' I could hear the indignation in my voice. 'She indicated, in no uncertain terms that I had thrown myself at the first available bloke, and then,' I continued furiously, 'she turned up on my doorstep just now, obviously highly delighted that I was going out with a local celebrity, and had the almighty cheek to give me her blessing.'

'She always was easily impressed with status,' Adam pointed out wryly. 'She'll be the best friend you ever had now.'

'I don't think so. I sent her off with a flea in her ear.' I found myself laughing at the memory of her stunned face. 'Anyway,' I added, 'she'll soon go back to her old disapproving self when she realises I'm not seeing him any more.'

Adam went very still, and stared at me. 'You're not?' he said, and then, as if it was important, he asked, 'What happened? What went wrong?'

'I don't really know,' I told him honestly, perfectly willing to talk about it, if he wanted to listen. 'I just suddenly knew the whole thing didn't feel quite right. Sam might be a big fish in a small pond, and he is a lovely guy, but I suddenly felt like a fish out of water at that charity event.' I grimaced, 'I was bored, Adam, does that sound terrible?'

'Not to me,' he grinned, 'but I have a feeling that someone like Janice would find it hard to believe. Lisbet would think you had lost the plot, and ... ' he paused, 'talking of Lisbet, which I don't intend to do very much of in the future, we've agreed to set the wheels of a quickie divorce in motion. Irreconcilable differences is the legal terminology, I believe, for two people who should never have got married in the first place.

'This is what we both want and it's already in the hands of our solicitors. She can have most of what she wants – peace of mind is more important to me, and it's a chapter of my life I want closed.' The heartfelt sigh that accompanied this confession left me in little doubt of Adam's sincerity.

I touched his hand across the table. 'If it's what you want, Adam, then I'm pleased for you,' I said, and I meant it. 'A couple of free spirits, that's us,' I laughed, and thought how long it had taken us, and how far we had come on our different journeys to reach such a similar point.

'Let's eat,' Adam slapped his thighs, 'I'm starving, I don't know about you?'

'Starving,' I agreed, 'Let's have the "Big Combo Meal",' I went on, naming practically the biggest meal on the menu, with three kinds of meat, and not to mention fries, mushrooms, onion rings galore.

'The Combo it is,' Adam rose laughing to his feet. 'I do like a woman who enjoys her food and,' he went on sternly, 'you can put that money away. If I can't treat my best friend to a meal, who on earth can I?' With that he made his way to the food service area.

His best friend? I nodded, liking the feel of that. Yes, I supposed, with the loss of Rob it had been inevitable that I should inherit the title, and I hoped I was worthy of it. Adam was certainly the best friend I had ever had, bar none, and especially in a year that had been one of the most difficult of my whole life.

I looked at him, standing tall and totally relaxed, leaning forward a little to place his order. I found myself smiling and, turning, Adam smiled directly at me, his eyes crinkling in a way that was so familiar – and yet I felt my heart turn over in a way I had never experienced in all the years I had known him. It was almost like looking at a stranger, at someone I had never really seen.

Dragging my attention away from Adam for a minute, I took a long, hard, and very honest look at myself. I was an ordinary, uncomplicated person really, I acknowledged, suddenly seeing myself with new eyes.

Family was the most important thing to me, it always had been, and as long as they were all right I was happy. What I enjoyed most were the simple things in life – exotic just wasn't who I really was.

I had experienced the best kind of unselfish love in my life with Rob, and I knew suddenly I would never be able to settle for less than that in the future. To do so would be an insult to Rob and everything we had shared.

If I were ever to find love again, it would surely be with someone as uncomplicated as I thought I was. I watched Adam making his way towards me, and I knew what I wanted was a decent, ordinary man, perhaps even someone just like Adam.

I became very still, and the sounds of laughter, the buzz of conversation just faded into the background as the truth hit me so hard it left me totally stunned. What I wanted wasn't someone *like* Adam – looking into his face was like seeing him for the very first time – and I knew what I wanted was Adam, himself.

He stopped so suddenly that someone cannoned into the back of him, he didn't even notice, just stared at me. The stunned expression on his face was, I knew, mirrored on my own. I stood, held out my hands and as he walked into my life in a whole new way, I realised – as he obviously did – that happy endings may come when, and with whom, you least expect it.

CATAMARANS
FOR CRUISING

Catamarans for Cruising

JIM ANDREWS

Diagrams by the author

HOLLIS & CARTER

LONDON SYDNEY

TORONTO

Paperback edition I S B N 0 370 10294 0
Hard-cover edition I S B N 0 370 10339 4
Printed and bound in Great Britain for
Hollis & Carter
an associate company of
The Bodley Head Ltd
9 Bow Street, London WC2E 7AL
by Northumberland Press Limited
Gateshead
Set in Linotype Baskerville
*First published as a paperback and
simultaneously as a hard-cover edition 1974*
Reprinted 1977

TO D.M.D.

whose encouragement helped
me to become a writer